The *New York Times* bestselling author who brings "passion, spirit, and strength" (*Publishers Weekly*) to her unsurpassed Calder series and scores of other unforgettable novels,

# JANET DAILEY

is the #1 bestselling female author in North America!

Praise for the storytelling talents of

## JANET DAILEY

"[Dailey] moves her story ahead so purposefully and dramatically . . . readers will be glad they've gone along for the ride."

—*Chicago Sun-Times*

"Janet Dailey's name is synonymous with romance."

—*Tulsa World* (OK)

"Bittersweet. . . . Passion, vengeance, and an unexpected danger from the past add to the mix."

—*Library Journal*

"Enjoyable. . . . Dailey create[s] a kind of magic"

—*Booklist*

"A master storyteller of romantic tales, Dailey weaves all the 'musts' together to create the perfect love story."

—*Leisure* magazine

# JANET DAILEY

## SEPARATE CABINS

## THE SECOND TIME

**POCKET BOOKS**
New York London Toronto Sydney

POCKET BOOKS, a division of Simon & Schuster, Inc.
1230 Avenue of the Americas, New York, NY 10020

*Separate Cabins* copyright © 1983 by Janet Dailey
*The Second Time* copyright © 1982 by Janet Dailey

These stories were originally published individually by Silhouette Books

ISBN-13: 978-1-4165-2358-1
ISBN-10:    1-4165-2358-8

This Pocket Books paperback edition February 2007

10 9 8 7 6 5 4 3 2 1

POCKET and colophon are registered trademarks of Simon & Schuster, Inc.

Manufactured in the United States of America

These titles were previously published individually by Pocket Books.

For information regarding special discounts for bulk purchases, please contact Simon & Schuster Special Sales at 1-800-456-6798 or business@simonandschuster.com.

# SEPARATE CABINS

## ACKNOWLEDGMENTS

We wish to offer a special thanks to the Princess Cruise Lines for their cooperation and assistance during our research on their ship, the *Pacific Princess,* on its cruise to the Mexican Riviera. And a special acknowledgment, too, goes to Max Hall with the Princess Cruise Lines for his assistance. It was greatly appreciated. Lastly, we'd like to thank Captain John Young and the crew of the *Pacific Princess* for practically allowing us the run of the ship. We enjoyed his company immensely and especially his wonderful British wit.

BILL and JANET DAILEY

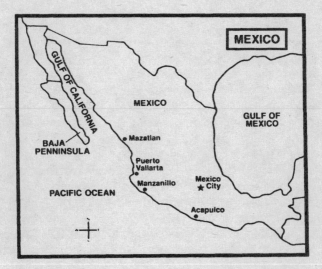

# Chapter One

"It will be approximately another twenty minutes before they'll begin boarding passengers. You'll be going through that door." The young woman, seated behind the table, pointed to the open doorway at the far end of the cavernous port terminal, then passed Rachel a long, narrow boarding card and two visitor passes. "Enjoy your cruise, Mrs. MacKinley."

"Thank you." Rachel stepped away from the table to make room for the next passenger in line, then paused to look around and locate the couple who had come to see her off.

The long table was one of several that had been set up to process the tickets and papers of arriving cruise passengers. Their location split the long half of the huge room nearly in the middle, separating the waiting area with seats from the baggage-handling section where passengers' luggage was loaded on a conveyer belt and carried out to the ship's hold. From there the luggage would be disbursed to the cabins indicated on their attached tags and be waiting in the passengers' assigned rooms when they came aboard.

The sitting area did not have enough seats to accommodate all of the hundreds of waiting passengers gathered in the terminal building of the port of Los Angeles. The size of the crowd was increased by the addition of friends or relatives who accompanied some of the passengers, like Rachel. The majority of the passengers and their guests were milling around the large open area near the entrance. Somewhere in that throng of people were Rachel's friends, Fan and John Kemper.

As Rachel moved toward the crowd her gray eyes made a slow, searching sweep of the faces, but it was the red-flowered silk of her friend's shirtwaist dress that caught her attention and guided Rachel to the waiting couple.

"Everything all set?" John Kemper inquired as Rachel rejoined them.

By profession he was an attorney, of medium height and blond hair thinning to show the start of a bald spot at the back of his head. On the weekends he avoided the conservative dress of his profession in favor of flashier garb, like the loud red slacks and plaid blazer he was wearing. Mac MacKinley had been a client of his. It was through that association and Rachel's long-time friendship with John's wife that she had met Mac, later marrying him.

"Everything is set," Rachel confirmed and handed him the two visitor cards. "Here are your passes. After all the passengers are on board, they'll let the visitors on the ship . . . which we won't board for another twenty minutes."

"If that's the case, let's wait outside," Fan suggested immediately. "It's so crowded and noisy in here that I can hardly hear myself think."

As Fan spoke Rachel was accidentally jostled by the person next to her, giving credence to her friend's suggestion. "Lead the way," she agreed.

John headed their exodus, threading a path through the press of milling people to the door. Single file, the two women followed after him with Rachel bringing up the rear. A faint smile touched the corners of her mouth at the way Fan kept glancing over her shoulder to be sure Rachel was behind them. It was a mother-hen trait that came naturally to Fan, accustomed to keeping track of her brood of four children, three boys and a much awaited girl.

The thought of the four towheaded youngsters brought a flicker of remorse, sobering the gray of her eyes. More than once in the last four years Rachel had wished she and Mac hadn't decided to wait awhile before starting a family. At the time it had seemed sensible, since their furniture business was expanding with branch stores. Mac had been such a big, strapping man, so full of life and ambition. No one could have foretold that a massive coronary would take his life before he turned thirty-five.

They passed out of the building's shade into the

slanting sunlight of a February afternoon. A drifting breeze picked up the scent of flowers from the bouquets for sale as bon voyage gifts just outside the terminal's entrance. Rachel made an effort to throw off those reflective thoughts of the past and look to the present and its surroundings.

A few other people shared their desire to escape the crowd inside the building and dawdled on the walk, watching the late arrivals as they drove up to the curb. A long row of buses was parked to one side, having already transported those passengers who had flown into the Los Angeles airport.

"We can sit over here on this ledge." Fan led them to a landscaped island of palms and shrubbery where there was room for them to sit on the concrete lip of the low wall.

Conscious of how quickly the skirt of her white suit showed the smallest trace of dust or dirt, Rachel brushed at the seat before she sat down. The femininely tailored suit was a flattering choice, showing the slimness of her long-legged figure. Its whiteness accented the ebony sheen of her black hair and the silvery lightness of her gray eyes, sooted in with dark, curling lashes. Her blouse was a jewel-bright shade of blue silk with a collar that tied into a wide bow. It was a striking outfit, made all the more stunning by the attractive beauty of the woman wearing it.

John remained standing, not taking a seat on the ledge beside them. "There's a catering truck parked down the way. Would you girls like something cold to drink?"

"I'll have a diet cola." Fan was quick to accept

her husband's offer, then glanced inquiringly at Rachel. "Rachel?"

"An orange drink, please."

"A diet cola and an orange drink coming right up," John repeated their orders, then sketched them a brief salute before moving away.

There was a thoughtful smile on Fan's face as she watched her husband leave. After a second she turned to Rachel and sighed, "I love it when he calls us 'girls.' It makes me feel as if I'm eighteen again." She laughed shortly, a merry sound full of fun at herself. "Half the time I think I still am. That is"—she qualified—"until those four little demons of mine come charging into our bedroom in the mornings. Then I'm forced to remember I passed the thirty mark two years ago."

"You look the same as you did the day we graduated from college," Rachel insisted, but made no comment about Fan's reference to her children. The mention of them came too quickly after her own thoughts of regret for her childless existence.

"Then how come the red dress I wore that day clings in all the wrong places when I try to wear it now?" Fan demanded with a mocking look. "I suppose after four children I should be grateful I can get into it at all."

"You look wonderful and you know it," Rachel assured her friend, because it was true.

There were minor changes in Fan's appearance. Her blonde hair no longer flowed silkenly to her waist; it was shorter and styled in a sophisticated French sweep. Her once pencil-thin figure was now well rounded but still slender. And Fan was the same person, actively involved in a half dozen projects at once and managing to successfully juggle them all. The quickest way to make an enemy of her was by still calling her Fanny instead of Fan, an appellation she hated.

"I look like exactly what I am—a country club mother of four children, wife of a successful attorney with a flourishing law practice, and committee member of a dozen charities. All the conventional things I vowed I would never be . . . until I met John. And I couldn't be happier and more fulfilled than I am now," she declared with a serenely contented smile.

"Sometimes I wonder where the years have gone." Rachel turned her wistful gray eyes to the pale blue sky and stared, lost in its infinity. "Graduation seems like only yesterday. I turn around, and here I am—thirty-two years old and—" She had been about to say "alone," but she stopped herself.

"And about to embark on a glorious seven-day cruise down the Mexican Riviera," Fan finished the sentence for her, deliberately steering it away from any potentially depressing thought.

Recognizing her friend's intention, Rachel swung her gaze around and smiled in silent gratitude of Fan's understanding. "I don't actually believe I'm going yet," she admitted with a touch of wryness. "I probably won't believe it until the ship leaves and I'm on it."

Her comment seemed to explain her lack of enthusiasm. She'd planned vacations before, but something had always come up at the last minute, forcing her to cancel. A small frown of concentration lay upon her features as Rachel mentally went over her checklist to see if she had overlooked any item that might now crop up.

"This time you're going," Fan stated. "John and I are personally going to make certain you are on the *Pacific Princess* when she leaves. After all I went through making the reservations and picking up your ticket last week, you're going."

Rachel smiled absently at the firm avowal. Something was nagging at her, holding any eager anticipation for the trip at bay. It darkened her gray eyes, giving them a vaguely troubled and faraway look.

"You could look a little more excited," her friend accused.

"Sorry." She flashed a glance at Fan, still slightly preoccupied. "I have this feeling I've forgotten something."

"I don't know what it could be." Now it was the blonde who frowned as she considered the possibilities. "Mrs. Pollock, next door, already has the key so she can water your houseplants. And you've arranged to have your mail held at the post office until you come back. You did check to make sure your passport hasn't expired, didn't you?"

"It's current," Rachel nodded. Even without it she had enough other identification with her to allow her to enter and leave Mexico.

"Everything else has been handled, and they've already taken your luggage aboard." Fan sighed and briefly shook her head. "I can't think of anything other than that."

"Other than what?" John returned with their cold drinks in time to catch the last part of his wife's

15

remark. His fingers were splayed to grip the three containers, slippery with the condensation coating their sides. Plastic straws were poking out of their tops.

"Rachel thinks she's forgotten something," Fan explained as she took two of the drinks from him before John dropped them, and passed the orange soda to Rachel.

"She has," he stated without hesitation and reached in the side pocket of his plaid blazer to offer them napkins.

"What?" Her gray eyes widened, surprised that he seemed to know something she didn't.

"The cares of the world," he pronounced, then let a knowing little smile curve his mouth. "Or more specifically, the care of the Country House, home of fine furniture. Which is the same thing since you've made it your whole world after you lost Mac."

"I wouldn't say it's my *whole* world." Rachel was obliged to protest his all-inclusive assessment, yet she realized it was true.

The furniture company had almost become the child she and Mac never had, the recipient of her time and attention. In the last four years since Mac's death she had lost touch with most of the friends who were outside her business sphere—with the exception of Fan. Even then, the close contact had been maintained mostly because John acted as both her business and personal attorney. Nearly everything in her life revolved around the company and its stores.

Fortunately she had worked in the company, both at the retail outlets and in the office, putting to practical use her college degree in business management, after she and Mac were married, so she'd had the knowledge and experience to run it herself when she had acquired sole ownership of it on his death. It hadn't been easy, but the challenge of putting the company on a more solid footing had been rewarding, both emotionally and monetarily. She'd had the satisfaction of taking something she and Mac had dreamed and making it come true.

"For all intents and purposes it might as well be," John countered, knowing her too well.

"Perhaps," Rachel conceded absently. His reference to the business had unrolled a new string of thoughts. She lifted back the cuff of her jacket sleeve and glanced at the thin gold watch around her wrist. "I should be able to catch Ben Atkins at the office. I have time before they begin boarding passengers, so I think I'd better phone him. That ad campaign is going to start running on television next and I need—"

"You are not going to call anybody." Fan laid a restraining hand on her arm, firmly asserting an authority born of friendship. "You are staying right here. I'm not going to let a last-minute phone call interfere with your vacation plans."

"This is not the most opportune time to be gone for two weeks." As soon as she said it Rachel recognized it was this knowledge that had been troubling her. She began to have doubts about the wisdom of leaving on the cruise just at the launch of a major ad campaign. Granted, the cruise only lasted seven days, but she had planned on staying in Acapulco a few days longer before flying back. Of course, she could always cut short that stay and return within a week.

"One of these days you're going to learn there isn't an opportune time to take a vacation when you own your own business," John calmly informed her. "Besides, you are the one who said Ben Atkins was capable of handling things while you're gone."

"He is." It was a rather grudging admission. "But I've worked hard to build the company to its present status. I'm not sure it's wise to leave now when we're launching a critical phase of new advertising. You were the one who advised against selling the company after Mac's death, and encouraged me to operate it myself. Now I'm going to be gone at a time when fast decisions need to be made."

"And if something important arises, Ben can contact the ship by radio. You aren't going to be completely out of touch," he reminded, countering her argument with calm logic.

"No, I suppose not," Rachel acknowledged and sipped thoughtfully through the straw, coral-red lipstick leaving its imprint on the clear plastic.

"When was the last time you took a vacation?" John changed his tactics, challenging her with the question.

"Five years ago," she admitted, "when Mac and I went fishing in British Columbia."

"You need this vacation," he asserted. "There was a time, shortly after Mac's death, when working long and hard had a therapeutic value, but you're over that stage now. You need to stop working so hard and start enjoying life again."

"I enjoy my life," Rachel insisted, but she knew

she was beginning to feel the strain of the constant pressure. It was a long time since she had truly relaxed and taken it easy. This cruise would provide her with a much needed respite from meetings and telephones and paperwork. By the same token she was daunted by the prospect of doing nothing for seven days. "I admit I need to get away and relax for a while, but I don't know what I'm going to do with myself for all that time. It isn't as if I know anybody on board. They're total strangers."

"Strangers are what you need right now," John said wisely. "If you were surrounded by friends, you'd start talking about the business. Instead of leaving it behind, you'd be bringing it with you. Getting to know new people will be good for you. Besides, after working so hard, it's time you were pampered. And a sea cruise is just the place for it. If you don't believe me, ask Fan."

"These cruise ships treat you like a queen." His wife was quick to back up his assertion. "I never had to lift a hand to do anything when John and I went on that trip through the Caribbean last fall. After taking care of four children and a husband, believe me, that was heaven!"

"I'm sure it's very nice." Rachel didn't question that.

"And the food aboard—it's an epicurean delight," Fan declared. "Of course, it isn't so delightful when you have to lose the five pounds you gained during the cruise."

"All your arguments are very sound," Rachel said, because the pair seemed to be ganging up on her. "But I just have some misgivings about this

19

trip. That doesn't mean I'm not going. I'm here and I have my ticket."

"Then stop saying things that make it sound like you're trying to back out at the last minute," Fan reproved her. "Especially after all I went through last week to make certain you had your ticket. Speaking of that"—a frown flickered across her expression as Fan was distracted by the run of her own thoughts—"I wonder what happened to the ticket they supposedly mailed to you. It's strange you never received it."

"It isn't so strange," John disagreed. "Considering how undependable the mail service is these days, it was probably lost."

"It was sent to the wrong address," Rachel said.

"How do you know that?" Fan looked at her with a frowning interest.

"I meant to tell you about it before, but with all the last-minute packing and preparations, I simply forgot to mention it." She began her answer with an explanation of why she hadn't cleared up the mystery before. "When the cruise line reissued the ticket, it was made out to Mrs. Gardner MacKinley all right, but the address they listed wasn't mine. Obviously the original one was mailed to that address, which is why I never received it."

"That explains it." John shrugged diffidently. "Sooner or later the missing ticket will be returned to the ship line."

"Do you suppose I should contact the Princess Cruises and tell them they have the wrong address listed for Rachel?" Fan asked, ever one to have things neatly in order.

"It's hardly necessary since I have my ticket and my pass to get on board." Rachel didn't see the need for it.

There was a lull in the conversation and Rachel sipped at her drink. A car pulled up to the curb to unload its occupants. Three young couples piled out, dragging with them a cooler and a large tray mounded with assorted sandwiches and cheeses —refreshments for their own private bon voyage party. As the luggage was unloaded from the trunk and given to a waiting baggage handler with a cart, it became apparent that only one couple in the group was going on the cruise. The other four had come along to see them off and tour the ship.

When the car had been emptied, the driver slipped behind the wheel to park it in the lot adjacent to the port terminal while the remaining five waited in front of the terminal entrance. A sleek black limousine swung quietly into the curbside spot the car had vacated and came to a halt. There was an immediate stirring of interest all around.

Fan leaned closer, murmuring to Rachel, "Who do you suppose is arriving?"

An answer wasn't expected for her question, but Rachel's curiosity was naturally aroused, like everyone else's. The limousine's smoked glass was designed to protect the privacy of the passenger, but it also heightened the interest of those wondering who might be inside.

The trunk latch was remotely released by a panel button. A second later a uniformed chauffeur was stepping out of the limousine and walking around the hood to open the rear passenger door. All eyes focused on the opening, including Rachel's.

A man emerged, unfolding his long length with loose-limbed ease. Tall, easily over six feet when he finally straightened to his full height, he was well built, wide shouldered, and slim hipped. A breeze immediately rumpled his hair as if it couldn't wait to run its fingers through the virile thickness and feel its vital texture. The slanting rays of an afternoon sun caught the desert-tan highlights that streaked his dark hair. His sun-browned features were strong and handsome, ingrained with a maturity tinged with wry cynicism.

As she studied him Rachel was reminded of a statue she'd seen once. Not because of his trimly muscled build or his male good looks. It was another quality that brought the memory to mind—a tempered hardness of form and character. Yet even that impression seemed belied by the laziness of his stance, so relaxed and at ease.

Rachel guessed he knew he was the cynosure of all eyes, but he appeared indifferent to the attention he attracted. His indifference did not appear to be arrogance, but as if he felt his presence was unimportant.

A slow smile pulled his lips apart, briefly showing a row of white, even teeth. He said something to the chauffeur, the words inaudible, but the soft timbre of his voice drifted to her, husky and warm. The uniformed driver immediately smiled back. Rachel had the feeling it was the natural response of anyone who was the recipient of that smile.

Her gaze traveled with the chauffeur as he moved

to the rear of the vehicle and began to unload the luggage from the carpet-lined trunk and pass it to the baggage handler. Then her glance swung back to the man in the tan sports jacket and brown slacks. In the brief interim he had squared around, providing her with a better view of his face.

Experience had hammered out any softness in his strongly handsome features and etched into them an understated virility that didn't rely on good looks for its attraction. A cigarette dangled from his mouth as he bent his head to the match flame cupped in his hand.

The unhurried action served as a misdirection while his partially lidded gaze made a slow sweep of the people on the walk outside. It paused to linger on Rachel with mild interest. There was a deliberateness about him, making no apologies for the good, long look he was taking. She had the sensation that his mind was absorbing her image, measuring her attributes against other women he'd known, but offering no judgment. She stiffened slightly, disturbed in some small way she couldn't define.

A pulsebeat later his gaze moved on as casually as it had paused. The match flame was shaken out while he exhaled the smoke he had dragged from the burning cigarette.

Fan's blonde head changed its angle, tipping a degree toward Rachel. "I don't know who he is," she murmured in an aside, "but he's one hunk of a man."

Silently Rachel agreed with that assessment of the man's potently attractive male looks. There seemed to be some magnetic pull that kept her gaze riveted to him even when she felt that her staring was bordering on rudeness.

Again that lazy smile spread across his face as he shook hands with the chauffeur, taking his leave of the man. A hint of it remained when he turned to the baggage handler and discreetly passed the man a folded bill with the ease of one accustomed to tipping. Then his easy-flowing stride was carrying him to the entrance of the terminal building. As Rachel followed him her gaze encountered John Kemper's frowning expression.

"His face is familiar," John said with a puzzled shake of his head. "But I can't think why I should know him."

"It's obvious he's going on the cruise," Fan said and slowly turned her head to look at Rachel. A light of scheming speculation gleamed in her eyes. "He's just the kind of man you need to meet."

"Fan, don't be silly," Rachel protested, her lips lying together in a patiently amused line.

"I'm serious," her friend insisted.

"Well, I'm not interested in getting involved with any man," Rachel asserted when she realized Fan wasn't teasing. "I'm going on this cruise to relax. I have no intention of being caught up in some shipboard affair."

"Who said anything about getting involved?" Fan lifted upturned palms in a blameless gesture. "But you are traveling on the *Love Boat*."

"Don't remind me." Rachel sighed with mild exasperation at the reference to the long-running television series, which had filmed its location shots aboard the *Pacific Princess*.

"Someone needs to remind you if you haven't thought about it." Fan's look was faintly skeptical.

"Let's just say that I haven't given it *much* thought," she replied. "And if I take any moonlight strolls around the deck, it will probably be alone. There's no percentage in becoming romantically entangled with a stranger for a week."

"I'm not suggesting romance," Fan corrected that impression.

"Then what are you suggesting?" Rachel demanded, becoming a little impatient with the subject.

Instead of immediately answering her, Fan threw a glance at her husband. "John, close your ears. A husband shouldn't hear the advice his wife gives to single women."

An indulgently amused smile twitched the corners of his mouth. "I'm as deaf as a mouse in a bell tower," he promised and looked in another direction, pretending an interest elsewhere.

Fan turned back to Rachel. "What I'm talking about is something a little more basic than romance," she said. "What you really need is a little sex; something to start the fires burning again. And that man looks like he's got what it takes to deliver the goods."

Advice like that had been offered before, but it was usually given by the man interested in becoming her sexual partner. If anyone else but her best friend had said that to her, Rachel would probably have thrown the orange drink in their face. Instead she set the container on the ledge and stiffly stood up, waiting as Fan rose also.

"My fires are burning nicely." At the moment most of the inner heat came from suppressed anger. She had never considered herself to be a prude. Lonely though she sometimes was, Rachel hadn't become so desperate for love that she resorted to casual sex.

Struggling against her rising agitation, she turned a cold shoulder to Fan. Her forward-facing gaze looked into the glass front of the terminal building. The shaded interior produced a mirrorlike backing for the glass, causing it to reflect a faint image of her own white-suited figure and obscuring the building's many occupants but not to the extent that she failed to recognize the tall, broad-shouldered man talking to one of the cruise staff.

The sight of him, posed so nonchalantly with one hand casually thrust in the side pocket of his slacks, seemed to add to the seething fury that heated her blood. Unquestionably he was sexy but not in any overt kind of way. It was much more subtle than that. Rachel recognized that and was impatient with herself because she did.

While she unwillingly watched him, he was taken over and introduced to another staff member, who greeted him familiarly. Then he was personally escorted past the roped-off boarding area around the open doorway. Her last glimpse of him was his tapering silhouette outlined briefly in the rectangular patch of light marking the doorway. While all the other passengers had to wait until the appointed boarding time, he was being escorted onto the ship. She supposed it meant he had friends in high places.

"I know I probably sounded crude," Fan continued, slightly defensive and apologetic. "But it seems to me that the longer you abstain from taking a lover, the more difficult it becomes. Rather like losing your virginity all over."

"Let's just forget it." Severely controlling her voice, Rachel was aware that her friend's advice was well intentioned. She was just personally uncomfortable with it.

There was a stirring of activity inside the terminal building. The crowd was beginning to bunch closer together and press forward against the ropes. It appeared that the boarding process would commence shortly.

Afraid that if she stayed Fan would continue on the same subject, Rachel decided that it would be better if she joined the other passengers inside before she lost her temper. She didn't want to start out on this vacation arguing with her best friend. And somewhere she seemed to have lost her sense of humor. She couldn't turn aside the conversation with a joke that would make light of it, even though she knew it was the best and the most diplomatic way to handle it.

"They've started boarding," she said. "They aren't admitting visitors until all the passengers are on the ship, so you two might as well wait here. I'll meet you later on the ship—by the gangway."

"We'll be there." John patted his breast pocket, where he had put their visitor passes.

With that agreement voiced, Rachel left them and walked briskly to the entrance, her white reflection in the glass following and merging as she passed through the open doors. It would be a slow process to board the hundreds of waiting passengers, but this was one time when Rachel didn't mind the long wait in line. It would give her a chance to simmer down. At the moment she was too tense, her nerves strung out like high-tension wires.

Voices ran together, creating a low din as Rachel reduced her pace and approached the pressing crowd of passengers. She found a place in the main flow and let it sweep her along to the gate that funneled them into a single line to the door.

# Chapter Two

Shining pristine white, the ship loomed beside the terminal building, tied to the pier only a few feet from the building's outside walls. Its massive size and sleek, pure lines demanded attention as Rachel followed the slow-moving string of passengers traveling along the raised walk to the gangway.

On the bow of the ship, high blue letters spelled out her name—*Pacific Princess*. The blue and green emblem of the cruise line, a maiden's head with long hair streaming out in waves, was painted on the black-ringed smokestack. Rows of portholes and deck railings marked off her many levels. Rachel was slightly awed by her size and stately majesty.

Ahead photographers were snapping pictures of passengers next to signboards welcoming them aboard the *Pacific Princess*. Usually they took photos of a couple; sometimes two couples wanted their picture taken together; sometimes it was a family shot.

But Rachel was traveling alone. It was the first time she'd gone on a pleasure trip without Mac or some member of her family or even a friend. The point was brought home to her as she stepped forward to take her turn in front of the camera. She thought she had become used to her solitary state, but she felt awkward and self-conscious. It was an unexpected reaction to something she thought she had accepted.

"How about a big smile?" the photographer coaxed with the camera to his face so his eye could frame her in the lens.

Rachel tried to oblige, but the forced movement was stiff and strained. The click of the camera captured it on film. Then the photographer was nodding to her that it was over, smiling at her with a hint in his glance of male appreciation for her striking looks.

An absent smile touched the corners of her mouth in return, but it faded quickly on an inner sigh as she stepped forward to make room for the couple behind her. She blamed her raw sensitivity on the strain of overwork and quickened her steps to close on the line of passengers progressing slowly up the gangway. After a couple of days rest she'd be her old self again.

Members of the ship's crew were on hand to receive the boarding passengers and direct them to their assigned staterooms. Rachel walked onto the rich blue carpet of the foyer and paused beside the white-uniformed officer, who inclined his head in greeting to her.

"Welcome aboard the *Pacific Princess*. Your cabin, madam?" His voice carried a British accent, reminding Rachel that the ship was of British registry.

"Mrs. MacKinley. Promenade 347." She had the number memorized after writing it so many times on her luggage tags.

He turned to a young, blond-haired man in a steward's uniform and motioned him forward. "Promenade 347," he repeated to the steward, then turned to Rachel, smiling warmly. "Hanson will guide you to your stateroom suite, Mrs. Mac-Kinley."

"Thank you." Her mouth curved in an automatic response, then Rachel moved past him to follow the young steward across the wide foyer to the stairwell flanked by elevators.

The decision to reserve a suite instead of a simple stateroom had been an impulsive one and admittedly extravagant, since she was traveling alone. Part of it had been prompted by Fan's urging that Rachel should do this vacation up right and travel in style, and part of it had been motivated by a desire to have uncramped quarters where she could lounge in comfortable privacy.

A landing divided the stairs halfway between each deck and split it into flanking arms that turned back on itself to rise to the next deck. The landings, the turns, the lookalike foyers on each deck, began to confuse Rachel as she followed the steward. Already cognizant of the size of the ship, she quickly realized that it would be easy to become turned around with so many decks and the maze of passageways.

Instead of relying solely on her guide, Rachel began to look for identifying signs so she would learn her route to the stateroom and not become lost when she had to find it again. The striding steward didn't give her much time to dawdle and still keep him in sight.

When they stopped climbing stairs, the steward crossed the foyer and started down a long passageway. The level was identified as the Promenade Deck. Rachel stopped for a second to read the small sign indicating the range of cabin numbers located in the direction of its pointing arrow.

Her gaze was still clinging to the sign when she hurriedly started forward to catch up with the steward before she lost track of him. She didn't see the person approaching from the opposite direction until the very last second. Rachel tried to stop abruptly and avoid the collision, but she had been hurrying too fast to completely succeed.

Her forward impetus almost carried her headlong into the man. She cringed slightly in anticipation of the impact, but a pair of hands caught her by the arms and reduced the collision to a mere bump. She'd been holding her breath and now released it in a rushed apology.

"I'm sorry." Her head came back to lift her gaze upward.

A half-formed smile of vague embarrassment froze on her face as Rachel recognized the man from the limousine. Only now his face was mere inches from hers. The detail of his solid features was before her—the sun wrinkles at the corners of his eyes, the angled plane of his jaw and chin, and the smooth, well-defined strength of his mouth.

Her pulse rate shot up as her glance flicked to his lazy brown eyes. A smiling knowledge seemed to perpetually lurk behind their dry brown surfaces. She felt it licking over her as his gaze absorbed her features from the tip of her nose to the curved bow of her lips and the midnight blackness of her hair, then finally to the silver brilliance of her widened gray eyes.

This flash of mutual recognition and close assessment lasted mere seconds. On the heels of it came the recollection of Fan's advice concerning this very man whose hands were steadying her. Rachel went hot at the memory, her glance falling before his as if she thought he might be able to read her thoughts. She began to feel very stiff and awkward.

His hands loosened their hold on her arms and came away. Belatedly Rachel noticed that he was holding his tan jacket, which he swung over his white-shirted shoulder, casually hooking it on a forefinger. His shirt collar was open, exposing the tanned column of his throat.

"I'm sorry," she said stiffly, repeating her apology for bumping into him, trying to distract her thoughts from the tingling sensation on her arms where his hands had been. "I'm afraid I wasn't looking where I was going."

There was a lazy glitter in his eyes as his mouth quirked. "That was my good fortune."

She didn't want him to come back with a remark

like that, not with echoes of Fan's advice ringing in her ears. It only added to her discomfort in the whole situation. Unable to respond to the casual advice, Rachel chose to ignore it.

"Excuse me." Her young guide had long since disappeared down the passageway. She brushed hurriedly past the man and started down the corridor in the direction the steward had taken.

It seemed crazy, but she could feel his gaze watching her go. She even knew the moment he turned and continued on his way. Only then did some of the stiffness leave her, the tension easing in her nerves. Slowing her steps slightly, Rachel drew in a deep, calming breath and felt her pulse settling down.

At the aft end of the passageway there was another foyer with its own stairwell and elevators. It was almost an exact duplicate of the one at the forward end of the Promenade Deck. She halted, looking around for some sign to point her in the right direction. Just then the steward appeared, having retraced his steps to look for her.

"Sorry, ma'am." There was a look of chagrin on his young face. "I thought you were right behind me."

"It's all right," she assured him. It didn't seem necessary to explain why she had been detained.

"Your suite is this way."

This time he made sure she stayed at his side as he led the way past the elevator and down a galleria-type corridor to the next section of staterooms. He stopped at the first door on Rachel's left, opened it, then stepped aside so she could enter.

"If there's anything you need, press the button on the telephone," he said. "That will summon your room steward. There's someone on duty twenty-four hours."

"Thank you," Rachel nodded.

"I hope you enjoy your cruise," he said and left her to explore the suite on her own.

Rachel closed the door and turned to survey the large sitting room. The drapes were open, letting in the afternoon light. The room was a blend of warm coral colors with brown upholstered chairs for accent. In addition there was a table and four chairs so she could eat in her room if she preferred. A wet bar stood against one wall, fully stocked with glasses.

The bedroom was tucked in an alcove off the sitting room. The twin beds were built-in and covered with a coral patterned spread. Floor-to-ceiling curtains could be drawn to shut off the bedroom from the sitting area. Rachel inspected the available storage, opening drawers and doors.

Her three pieces of luggage sat on the floor by the bed. For the time being she stowed them in a closet. There would be time enough to unpack later in the evening. At the moment she was only interested in getting it out of the way.

There was a private bath as well, with a huge tub and shower combination, and a well-lighted mirror at the sink vanity. Her quarters were very definitely more than comfortable.

When she returned to the sitting room Rachel spied a cabin key lying on the table and slipped it into her purse. There was a copy of the ship's daily activity paper, the *Princess Patter,* beside it. Rachel glanced through its information section and the schedule of the day's events. There was another small card on the table that gave her the number of her assigned table in the dining room. She noticed that she was in the "late-sitting" group.

With Fan and John Kemper due to come aboard anytime, Rachel didn't think she should linger any longer in her room. She double-checked to be sure she had the key before she left the cabin and retraced her route to the lobby at the gangway.

All too soon, it seemed, the last call requesting all visitors ashore had sounded and Rachel was leaning on the railing on the port side of the Promenade Deck and waving to her friends on the pier below. Passengers were lined up and down the railing on either side of her. Some, like herself, had friends or relatives in the crowd on the wharf while others merely wanted to watch the procedures of the ship leaving port.

A few colored paper streamers were prematurely unfurled and tossed to those ashore. The curling ribbons of paper drifted downward. Rachel had a half dozen of the coiled streamers in her hand, presented to her by Fan Kemper for the occasion.

"They're hauling in the lines," someone down the line remarked.

Within minutes the ship began to maneuver away from the pier. The water churned below as the midship engines pushed it away. There was a cheering of voices, and Rachel threw her streamers into

36

the air to join the cascade of bright paper ribbons onto the crowd waving a last good-bye.

As the ship sailed stately away from its port, Rachel lingered with the other passengers. The growing distance between the ship and the pier blurred the faces of the people ashore until Rachel could no longer distinguish her friends from the crowd. On either side of her people began to drift away from the railing. The sun was on the verge of setting, a gloaming settling over the sky.

An evening breeze swept off the water and whipped at her hair before racing on. Rachel lifted her hand and pushed the disturbed strands back into place. A faint sigh slipped from her as she turned from the railing to go back inside.

Her sliding gaze encountered a familiar figure standing at a distance. It was that man again, talking with one of the ship's officers. Irritation thinned the line of her mouth as her glance lingered an instant on the burnished gold lights the sun trapped in his chestnut-dark hair. Of the six hundred plus passengers on the ship it seemed incredible that she should be constantly running into this one person.

Before he had the opportunity to notice her, Rachel walked briskly to the double doors leading inside. Instead of going to her cabin, she descended the stairs to the Purser's Lobby on Fiesta Deck. There were some inquiries she wanted to make about the ship's services, including the procedure for making radio-telephone calls.

Judging by the line at the purser's desk, it seemed there were a lot of other passengers seeking information about one thing or another. There was another line on the mezzanine above her, passengers seeking table assignments or wishing to change the one they had been given. A small group of people were clustered around the board set up in the lobby with a list of all the passengers on board and their cabin numbers.

The congestion was further increased by passengers taking pictures of each other posing on the winding staircase that curved to the mezzanine on the deck above. Rachel decided against joining the line at the purser's counter and entered the duty-free gift shop to browse until some of the crowd cleared.

Half an hour later she realized there was little hope of that. There seemed to be just as many people now as before. Giving up until tomorrow, Rachel started for her stateroom by way of the aft staircase.

The Promenade Deck was three flights up. By the time she reached it, she felt slightly winded. Another couple were on their way down as she took the last step and released a tired breath. The pair looked at her and smiled in sympathetic understanding.

"I'm out of condition," Rachel admitted; she wasn't used to climbing stairs.

"You can always use the elevators," the man reminded her.

"I could, but I need the exercise," she replied.

"Don't we all." His wife laughed.

It was a friendly moment between strangers. When it was over and Rachel was walking down the passageway to her stateroom, there was a hint of a smile on her face. Being on the cruise gave everyone something they had in common and provided a meeting ground to exchange impressions and discoveries.

In this quiet and contemplative mood Rachel entered her stateroom and shut the door. She deposited her purse on the seat cushion of a chair near the door and slipped out of the white jacket, absently draping it over the same chair.

A footfall came from the bedroom. Rachel swung toward the sound, startled. Her mouth opened in shock when the man from the limousine came around the opened curtains. He was busy pushing up the knot of his tie and didn't see her until he lifted his chin to square the knot with his collar. There was an instant's pause that halted his action in mid-motion when he noticed her with a brief flare of recognition in his look.

He recovered with hardly a break in his stride. His glance left her and ran sideways to the wet bar, where a miniature bucket of ice now sat. A faintly bemused smile touched his mouth as he turned to it.

"I asked the room steward to bring me some ice." His lazy voice rolled out the statement. "But I didn't know I was going to be supplied with a companion as well." His sidelong glance traveled her length in an admiring fashion. "I must say I applaud his choice."

Rachel was stunned by the way he acted as if he belonged there. It was this sudden swell of indignation that brought back her voice.

"What are you doing here?" she demanded,

quivering with the beginnings of outrage. Her fingers curled into her palms, clenching into rigid fists at her sides.

Nonchalantly he dropped ice cubes into a glass and poured a measure of scotch over them. "I was about to ask you the same question." He added a splash of soda and swirled the glass to stir it.

"I'll have you know this is my cabin. And since I didn't invite you in here, I suggest you leave," Rachel ordered.

"I think you have things turned around." He faced her, a faint smile dimpling the corners of his mouth as he eyed her with a bemused light. "This is my cabin. I specifically requested it when I made my reservations."

"That's impossible!" she snapped. "This is my cabin." To prove it, Rachel turned and picked up her purse. She removed her cruise packet and opened it so he could see that she had been assigned to this stateroom.

He crossed the room to stand in front of her and paused to look at the ticket she held. His brown eyes narrowed slightly and flicked to her, a tiny puzzled light gleaming behind their sharply curious study.

"Is this some kind of a joke?" He motioned to the ticket with his drink. "Did Hank put you up to this?"

"A joke?" Rachel frowned impatiently. "I don't know what you're talking about."

"The name on that ticket," he replied and sipped at his drink, looking at her over the rim. There was a delving quality about his look that seemed to probe into sensitive areas.

Rachel felt a prickling along her defenses. She glanced at the ticket, then back to him. "It's my name—Mrs. Gardner MacKinley. I don't see anything funny about that," she retorted stiffly.

"Since I seem to be suffering from a memory blank, maybe you wouldn't mind telling me just when we were supposed to have been married," he challenged with a mocking slant to his mouth.

For a second she was too stunned to say anything. "I'm not married to you." She finally breathed out the shocked denial.

"At least we agree on that point." He lifted his glass in a mock salute and took another swallow from it.

"Whatever gave you the idea we were?" She stared at him, caught between anger and confusion.

He leaned a hand against the wall near her head, the action bringing him closer to her. There was a tightening of her throat muscles as she became conscious of his physical presence. There was a heightened awareness of her senses that noted the hard smoothness of his cheek and jaw and the crisply fragrant scent of after-shave lotion. The vein in her neck began to throb in agitation.

"The name and address on that ticket—" His glance slid to it again, then swung back to her face, closely watching each nuance in her expression. "If you leave off the Mrs. part, it's mine."

It took a second for the implication of his words to sink in. "Yours?" Rachel repeated. "Do you mean your name is—" She couldn't say it because it was too incredible to be believed.

"Gardner MacKinley," he confirmed with a slight nod of his head. "My friends call me Gard."

Rachel sagged against the wall, all the anger and outrage at finding him in her cabin suddenly rushing out of her. It seemed impossible and totally improbable, yet—her thoughts raced wildly, searching for a plausible explanation. Her glance fell on the ticket.

"The address—it's yours?" She lifted her gaze to his face, seeking confirmation of the claim he'd made earlier.

"Yes." He watched her, as if absorbed by the changing emotions flitting across her face.

"That must be how it happened," Rachel murmured absently.

"How what happened?" Gard MacKinley queried, tipping his head to the side.

"Last week my friend went to the offices of the cruise line to find out why I hadn't received my ticket. They assured her it had been mailed, but I'd never gotten it. They reissued this one," she explained as the pieces of the puzzle began to fall into place. "I noticed the address was wrong, but I just thought that was why I hadn't received the first one. But it was sent to you," she realized.

"Evidently that's the way it happened," he agreed and finished the rest of his drink.

"It sounds so incredible." Rachel still found it hard to believe that something like this could happen.

"Let's just say it's highly coincidental," Gard suggested. "After all, telephone directories are full of people with the same names. Imagine what it would be like if your surname were Smith, Jones, or Johnson?"

"I suppose that's true," she admitted because he made it seem more plausible.

For a moment he studied the ice cubes melting in his glass, then glanced at her. "Where's your husband?"

Even after all this time the words didn't come easily to her. "I'm a widow," Rachel informed him, all her defenses going up again as she eyed him with a degree of wariness against the expected advance.

But there was no change in his expression, no sudden darkening of sexual interest. There remained that hint of warmth shining through the brown surfaces of his eyes.

"You must have a name other than Mrs. Gardner MacKinley, or is your first name Gardner?" There was a suggestion of a smile about his mouth.

"No, it's Rachel," she told him, oddly disturbed by him even though there had been no overt change in his attitude toward her. When he straightened and walked away from her to the wet bar, she was surprised.

"The foul-up must have happened when our two reservations were punched into the computer." He swung the conversation away from the personal line it had taken and brought it back to its original course. "No one told it differently so it linked the two of us together." His dark gaze ran back to her, alive with humor as his mouth slanted dryly. "What the computer has joined together, let no man put asunder."

His paraphrase of a portion of the marriage ceremony seemed to charge the air with a sudden, intimate tension. There was a knotting in the pit of her stomach, a tightness that came from some hidden source. The suggestion that this inadvertent union was in any way permanent sent her pulse to racing. It was a ludicrous thought, but that certainly didn't explain this sudden stimulation of all her senses.

# Chapter Three

Rachel straightened from the wall she had so recently leaned against and broke eye contact with him, but that didn't stop the nervous churnings inside. Moving briskly, she returned the ticket packet to her purse, a certain stiltedness in her actions.

"That's very amusing, Mr. MacKinley." But there was no humor in her voice. Just saying his name and knowing it was the same as her own seemed to add to this crazy turmoil.

"Gard," he insisted, irritating her further with his easy smile because it had a certain directness to it.

She ignored his invitation to address him more familiarly. "We were both assigned to the same cabin by mistake, but it's a mistake that can be remedied," she informed him with a trace of curtness, her gray eyes flashing. "The simplest thing for you to do would be to simply move to another cabin."

"Now, I disagree." There was a negative tip of his head. "The simplest thing would be to let the present arrangement stand. This suite comes with two *separate* beds, and there's more than enough room for both of us." The corners of his mouth deepened in the suggestion of a dryly amused smile.

All sorts of images flashed through her mind—the prospect of lying in one twin bed knowing he was in the other, bathing with him in the next room, wakening in the morning as he was dressing. Rachel was disturbed by the direction of her own imagination.

It made her rejection that much stronger. "I think not."

"Why?" Behind the calmness of his question she could see that he was amused by her curt dismissal of the idea. "It could be interesting."

"I don't think that is the word I would use to describe it," she replied stiffly. "But it hardly matters, since I have no intention of sharing my cabin with you."

"Somehow I knew that would be your answer," Gard murmured dryly and set his empty glass down to walk to the telephone. She watched him pick up the receiver and dial a number. "This is MacKinley in 347 on the Promenade Deck," he said into the mouthpiece, sliding a glance at Rachel. "We have a rather awkward situation here. You'd better have the purser come up." The response must have been an affirmative one because a moment later he was ringing off. "Until it's decided whose cabin this will be, may I offer you a drink?" Gard gestured toward the wet bar, offering her its selection.

"No, thank you." The urge was strong to pace the room. The purser couldn't arrive soon enough and rectify this whole mess as far as Rachel was concerned, but she tried to control her impatience.

Gard took a pack of cigarettes out of his pocket, then hesitated. "Cigarette?" He shook one partway out of the pack and offered it to her.

"No, I don't smoke but go right ahead." She motioned for him to smoke if he wished.

He gave her a look of mock reproval. "You don't drink. You don't smoke. You don't share your cabin with strange men. You must lead a very pure . . . and dull life." A wickedly teasing light danced in his eyes.

"So others have informed me," Rachel acknowledged and wondered where her sense of humor had gone. Half the reason Gard MacKinley was making these baiting remarks was because she kept snapping at them. She was handling the situation poorly, and she wasn't too pleased about it.

A silence followed, broken only by the strike of a match and a long breath expelling smoke into the air. The quiet was nearly as unnerving to Rachel as the conversation had been.

Gard seemed to take pity on her and asked a casual question. "Is this your first cruise?"

"Yes." Rachel tried to think of something to add to the answer, but her mind was blank.

"Are you traveling alone or do you have friends aboard?" He filled in the gap she'd left with another question.

"No, I'm alone," she admitted. "I don't know a soul."

"You know me," Gard reminded her.

"Yes, I do—now." She was uncomfortable, but how could she be natural with him when they had met so unnaturally?

The knock at the door startled Rachel even though she'd been listening for it. She pressed a hand to her stomach as if to check its sudden lurch. Before she could move to answer it, Gard was swinging across the room to open the door.

"Hello, Gard. It's damned fine to see you again, boy." The officer greeted him with a hearty welcome, clasping his arm as he shook his hand. "Hank told me you were aboard this trip."

"Come in, Jake." Gard escorted the officer into the sitting room.

He was a short, rounded man with full cheeks and a jovial, beaming smile. When he noticed Rachel in the room, his blue eyes brightened with interest and he removed his hat, tucking it under his arm.

"What seems to be the problem?" he asked, looking from one to the other.

"Both Mr. MacKinley and I have been given this cabin," Rachel explained in an even voice. "But we aren't married."

"Even though the British pride themselves on running a taut ship, I doubt if Jake would be either shocked or surprised by such an announcement," Gard informed her dryly, then glanced at the officer. "I'm sorry, Jake. I didn't introduce you. Meet Mrs. Gardner MacKinley."

"Mrs. MacKinley?" he repeated and frowned as if he were sure he hadn't heard right. "But she just said you weren't married." He pointed a finger at Rachel. "Are you divorced? I don't even recall Hank telling me that you'd ever been married."

"I haven't." Gard assured him on that score. "Rachel and I merely share the same name. Unfortunately she doesn't wish to share the same cabin with me." His amused glance danced over to her.

She reddened slightly but managed to keep her poise. "Evidently Mr. MacKinley and I made our separate reservations at approximately the same time, and someone must have assumed that we were man and wife."

"I see how it could happen, all right." The officer nodded and raised his eyebrows. "Well, this is a bit awkward."

"What other staterooms do you have available?" Gard asked.

"That's the problem," he admitted reluctantly. "There aren't any comparable accommodations available. All the suites are taken, and the deluxe outside rooms. The only thing I have empty are some inside staterooms on Fiesta Deck."

"Is that all?" An eyebrow was lifted on a faintly grim expression.

"That's about it." A light flashed in the man's eyes, a thought occurring to him. "Maybe not." He took back his answer and moved to the telephone. "Let me check something," he said as he dialed a number.

Feeling the tension in the air, Rachel strained to

hear his conversation, but his voice was pitched too low for her to pick out the words. With his back turned to them, she couldn't even watch his lips. When the officer hung up the phone and turned around, he was smiling.

"The owner's suite is empty this cruise," he informed them. "It's on the Bridge Deck where the officers are quartered. Under the circumstances I can't offer it to Mrs. MacKinley, since it might not look right to have an attractive and unattached woman staying in their area, but you're welcome to it, Gard."

"I accept. And I'm sure Mrs. MacKinley appreciates your concern for her good reputation," he added with a mocking glance in her direction.

He was making her feel like a prude, which she certainly wasn't. The gray of her eyes became shot with a silvery fire of anger, but Rachel didn't retaliate with any sort of denial. It would only add to his considerable store of ammunition.

"I'll arrange for the room steward to bring your luggage topside to the owner's suite," Jake offered. "In the meantime I'll show you to your quarters."

"It's a good thing I didn't get around to unpacking. My suitcases are sitting in the bedroom." Gard turned and faced her. "It was a pleasure sharing the cabin with you—for however short a period of time. Maybe we can try it again sometime."

"I'm sure you'd like that." Her smile was tinged with a wide-eyed sweetness. At last she'd found her quick tongue, which could answer back his deliberately teasing remarks.

"I'm sure I would," Gard murmured, a new

appreciation of her flashing across his expression along with a hint of curiosity.

With his departure the room suddenly seemed very empty and very large. The sharp tang of his after-shave lotion lingered in the air, tantalizing her nose with its decidedly masculine scent. After his stimulating presence there was a decidedly let-down feeling. Rachel picked up the glass he'd drunk from and carried it into the bathroom, where she dumped the watery ice cubes into the sink and rinsed out the glass.

The piped-in music on the radio speakers was interrupted by a ship announcement. "Dinner is now being served in the Coral Dining Room for late-sitting guests." The words were slowly and carefully enunciated by a man with a heavy Italian accent. *"Buon appetito."* The bell-sweet notes of a chime played out a short melody that accompanied the end of the announcement.

But Rachel had no intention of going to dinner until the steward came for Gard's luggage. She didn't want any of her suitcases being accidentally taken to his cabin and have that mix-up on top of the duplicate cabin assignment.

A few minutes later the steward knocked at the door. Curiosity was in his look, but he never asked anything. As soon as Rachel had supervised the removal of Gard's luggage, she freshened her make-up, brushed her waving black hair, and put the white jacket on.

When she arrived at the dining room on the Coral Deck, the majority of the passengers had already been seated. Tonight they weren't expected to sit at their assigned table. Since she was arriving late, Rachel requested one of the single tables.

After she'd given the dark-eyed Italian waiter her order, her gaze searched the large dining room, unconsciously looking for Gard. Only when she failed to see a familiar face did she realize she'd been looking for him. She immediately ended the search and concentrated on enjoying the superb meal she was served.

Upon entering the cabin on her return from the dining room, Rachel discovered that the steward had been in the room during her absence. The drapes at the window were pulled against the rising of a morning sun and one of the beds was turned down. There was a copy of the next day's *Princess Patter* on the table with its schedule of events.

Briefly she glanced through it, then walked to the closet to take out her suitcases and begin the tedious business of unpacking. It was late when she finally crawled into bed, much later than she had anticipated retiring on her first night at sea. There was little motion of the ship, the waters smooth and calm.

In the darkness of the cabin her gaze strayed to the twin bed opposite from the one she lay in. Its coral spread was smoothed flatly and precisely over the mattress and pillows. Its emptiness seemed to taunt her. She shut her eyes.

The February sky was blushed with the color of the late-rising sun as Rachel opened the drapes to let the outside light spill into her cabin. According to her watch, it was a few minutes after seven. It seemed that the habit of rising early was not easy to break even when she could sleep late.

She paused a moment at the window to gaze at the gold reflection of the sunlight on the sea's serene surface, then walked to the closet and began to go over her choices of clothes. Her breakfast sitting wouldn't be until half past eight, but coffee was available on the Sun Deck. Although it would probably be warm later in the day, it would likely be cool outside at this early hour of the morning. Rachel tried to select what to wear with that in mind.

A gentle knock came at her door, just loud enough to be heard and quiet enough not to disturb her if she was still sleeping. Rachel tightened the sash of her ivory silk nightrobe as she went to answer the door. A few minutes earlier she had heard the room steward in the passageway outside her stateroom. She expected to see him when she opened the door.

She certainly didn't expect to see Gard MacKinley lounging indolently in her doorway, a forearm braced nonchalantly against its frame. He was dressed in jogging shorts and shoes, a loose-fitting sweatshirt covering his muscled shoulders and chest. Rachel wasn't prepared for the sight of him—or the sight of his long legs, all hard flesh and corded muscle.

The upward-pulled corners of his mouth hinted at a smile while the warm light in his brown eyes wandered over her. Rachel was immediately conscious of her less than presentable appearance. The static cling of her robe's silk material shaped itself to her body and outlined every curve. Her face had been scrubbed clean of all makeup the night before, and she hadn't even brushed her sleep-rumpled hair, its tousled thickness curling in disorder against her face and neck.

Before she could check the impulse, she lifted a hand and smoothed a part of the tangle, then kept her hand there to grip the back of her neck. The suggestion of a smile on his mouth deepened at her action, a light dancing in his look.

"I wouldn't worry about it," Gard advised her with a lazy intonation of his voice. "You look beautiful."

With that, he straightened, drawing his arm away from the frame and moving forward. Her instinctive response was to move out of his way and maintain a distance between herself and his blatantly male form. Too late, Rachel realized that she should have attempted to close the door to her cabin instead of stepping back to admit him. By then his smooth strides had already carried him past her into the sitting room. It was this lapse on her part that made her face him so stiffly.

"What do you want?" she demanded.

There was an interested and measuring flicker of light in his eyes as he idly scanned her face. He seemed to stand back a little, in that silent way he had of observing people and their reactions.

"I made a mistake yesterday evening when I said I hadn't unpacked," Gard replied evenly. "I'd forgotten that I'd taken out my shaving kit so I could clean up before going to dinner. I didn't discover it until late last night. Somehow"—a hint of a mocking twinkle entered his eyes—"I had the feeling you'd get the wrong idea if I had come knocking on your door around midnight."

"You're mistaken about the shaving kit." Rachel ignored his comments and dealt directly with the issue. "You didn't leave it here. I unpacked all my things last night and I didn't find anything of yours while I was putting mine away."

"You must not have looked everywhere because I left it in the bathroom." He was unconvinced by her denial that it wasn't in the cabin.

"Well, you didn't—" But Rachel didn't have a chance to continue her assertion because Gard was already walking to the bathroom door. She hurried after him, irritated that he should take it upon himself to search for it. "You have no right to go in there."

"I know you won't be shocked if I tell you that I've probably seen the full range of feminine toiletries in my time," he murmured dryly and paid no attention to her protests, walking right into the bathroom.

Rachel stopped outside the door, her fingers gripping the edge of the frame, and looked in. The bathroom was comfortably spacious, but she still didn't intend to find herself in such close quarters with him.

"You look for yourself," she challenged, since he intended to do just that anyway. "You'll see it's not here."

He cast her a smiling look, then reached down and pulled open a drawer by the sink. It was a drawer she hadn't opened because she hadn't needed the space. When she looked inside, there was a man's brown shaving kit.

"Here it is—just where I left it," he announced, dark brows arching over his amused glance.

"So it is." Rachel was forced to admit it, a resentful gray look in her eyes. "I guess I never looked in that drawer."

"I guess you didn't," Gard agreed smoothly—so smoothly it was almost mocking.

He half turned and leaned a hip against the sink, shifting his weight to one foot. A quiver of vague alarm went through Rachel as she realized that he showed no signs of leaving either her cabin or her bathroom. There was a slow, assessing travel of his gaze over her.

"How long will it take you to dress and fix your hair?" he asked.

"Why?"

"So I'll know what time to meet you topside for some morning coffee."

"It won't make any difference how long it takes for me to get dressed, since I won't be meeting you for coffee," Rachel replied, stung that he was so positive she would agree.

"Why?" he asked in a reasonable tone.

"It hardly matters." She swung impatiently away from the bathroom door, the silken material of her long robe swishing faintly as she moved to the center of the sitting room. When she heard him following her, Rachel whirled around, the robe swinging to hug her long legs. "Hasn't anyone ever turned down an invitation from you?"

"It's happened," Gard conceded. "But usually they gave a reason if only to be polite. And I just wondered what yours is?"

Her features hardened with iron control. Only her eyes blazed to show the anger within. "Perhaps I'm tired of men assuming that I'm so lonely I'll accept the most casual invitation. Every man I meet immediately assumes that because I'm a widow I'm desperate for male companionship." Her scathing glance raked him, putting him in the same category. "They're positive I'll jump at the chance to share a bed with them—or a cabin—just because they can fill out a pair of pants. According to them, I'm supposed to be frustrated sexually."

It didn't soothe her temper to have him stand there and listen to her tirade so calmly. "Are you?" Gard inquired blandly.

For an instant Rachel was too incensed to speak. The question wasn't worthy of an answer, so she hurled an accusation at him instead. "You're no better than the others! It may come as a shock to you, but I'd like to know something about a man besides the size of his shorts before I'm invited into his bed!"

She was trembling from the force of her anger and the sudden release of so much bitterness that had been bottled up inside. She turned away from him to hide her shaking, not wanting him to mistake it as a sign of weakness.

"What does meeting for coffee have to do with going to bed together?" he wondered. "Or has your experience with men since your husband died been such that you don't accept any invitations?" There was a slight pause before he asked, "Do you want to be alone for the rest of your life?"

The quiet wording of his question seemed to pierce through the barriers she had erected and exposed the need she'd kept behind it. She wanted to love someone again and share her life with him. She didn't want to keep her feelings locked up inside, never giving them to anyone.

When she swung her gaze to look at him, her gray eyes were stark with longing. She had lived in loneliness for so long that she hadn't noticed when it had stopped being grief. His dark gaze narrowed suddenly, recognizing the emotion in her expression. Rachel turned away before she showed him too much of the ache she was feeling.

"No, I don't want to be alone forever," she admitted in a low voice.

"Then why don't you stop being so sensitive?" Gard suggested.

"I'm not," Rachel flared.

"Yes, you are," he nodded. "Right now you're angry with me. Why? Because I think you are a very attractive woman and I've tried to show you that I'm attracted to you."

"You came for your shaving kit," she reminded him, not liking this personal conversation now that she was becoming the subject of it. "You have it, so why don't you leave?"

She tried to brush past him and walk over to open the door and hurry him out, but he caught at her forearm and stopped her. His firm grip applied enough pressure to turn her toward him.

"I'm not going to apologize because I find you attractive and say things that let you know I'm interested," Gard informed her. "And I'm not going to apologize because I have the normal urge to take you in my arms and kiss you."

She looked at him but said nothing. She could feel the vein throbbing in her neck, its hammering beat betraying how his seductive voice disturbed her. She was conscious of his closeness, the hand that came to rest on the curve of her waist, and the steadiness of his gaze.

"And if the kiss lived up to my expectations, I would probably be tempted to press it further," he admitted calmly. "It's natural. After all, what's wrong with a man wanting to take a woman into his arms and kiss her? For that matter, what's wrong with a woman wanting to kiss a man?"

For the life of her Rachel couldn't think of a thing, especially when she felt his hand sliding smoothly to the back of her waist and drawing her closer. As his head slowly bent toward her, her eyelids became heavy, closing as his face moved nearer.

His mouth was warm on the coolness of her lips, moving curiously over them. Her hands and arms remained at her side, neither coming up to hold or resist. The pressure of his nuzzling mouth was stimulating. Rachel could feel the sensitive skin of her lips clinging to the faint moistness of his mobile mouth.

Behind her outward indifference her senses were tingling to life. Her body had swayed partially against him, letting the solidness of his body provide some of her support. There was a faint flavor of tobacco and nicotine on his lips, and the clean scent of soap drifted from his tanned skin.

There was a roaming pressure along her spine as his hand followed its supple line. It created a pleasant sensation and Rachel leaned more of her weight against him, feeling the outline of his hips and thighs through the thin, clinging material of her robe. The nature of his kiss became more intimate, consuming her lips with a trace of hunger. Within seconds a raw warmth was spreading through her system, stirring up impulses that Rachel preferred to stay dormant.

She lowered her head, breaking away from the sensual kiss and fighting the attack of breathlessness. The minute his arms loosened their hold on her, she stepped away, avoiding his gaze.

It would have been so easy to let his experienced skill carry her away. It was so ironic, Rachel nearly laughed aloud. A little sex was what her friend had recommended. There wasn't any doubt in Rachel's mind that Gard could arouse her physical desire, but she wanted more than that.

"You didn't slap my face," Gard remarked after

the silence had stretched for several seconds. "Should I be encouraged by that?"

"Think what you like. You probably will anyway," Rachel replied and finally turned around to look at him, recovering some of her calm. "If you don't mind, I'll ask you to leave now. I'd like to get dressed."

"How about coffee on the Sun Deck?" He repeated the invitation that had started the whole thing.

Her wandering steps had brought her to the table where the telephone sat. Rachel pushed the call button to summon the steward, aware that his gaze sharpened as he observed her action.

"Let's do it some other time, Mr. MacKinley," she suggested, knowing that the indefiniteness of her answer was equal to polite refusal.

"Suit yourself." He shrugged but his narrowed interest never left her.

There was a warning knock before the door was opened by the room steward. Curiosity flared when he saw Gard in the cabin, but he turned respectfully to Rachel. "Did you want something, Mrs. MacKinley?"

"Mr. MacKinley had left his shaving kit here. I thought you might have seen it," she lied about the reason she had called him. "But we found it just this minute. Thank you for coming, though."

"No problem," he assured her. "Is there something else I can do? Perhaps I can bring the two of you coffee?"

"No thanks," Rachel refused and looked pointedly at Gard. "Mr. MacKinley was just leaving."

Lazy understanding was in his looks at the way she had maneuvered him into leaving under the escort of the steward. He inclined his head toward her and moved leisurely to the door the steward was holding open.

# Chapter Four

There was some morning coolness in the breeze blowing through the opened windows at The Lido on the Sun Deck, but her lavender sweater jacket with its cowled hood provided Rachel with just enough protection that she didn't feel any chill. There were a lot of early risers sitting at the tables and taking advantage of the coffee and continental breakfast being served.

On the Observation Deck above, joggers were tramping around the balcony of the sun dome, pushed open to provide sunshine and fresh air to The Lido. As Rachel waited in the buffet line for her coffee she looked to see if Gard happened to be among the joggers. Not all of them had made a full circle before the people in line ahead of her moved and she followed.

She bypassed the fruit tray of freshly cut pineapples, melon, and papaya and the warming tray of sweet rolls, made fresh daily at the ship's bakery. It all looked tempting, but she intended to breakfast in the dining room, so she kept to her decision to have only coffee.

There was an older couple directly in front of her. When she noticed that they were having difficulty trying to balance their plates and each carry a glass of juice and a cup of coffee as well, Rachel volunteered to carry some of it for them. She was instantly overwhelmed by their rush of gratitude.

"Isn't that thoughtful of her, Poppa," the woman kept exclaiming to her husband as she carefully followed her mate to a table on the sheltered deck by the swimming pool.

"You are a good woman to do this," he insisted to Rachel. "Momma and I don't get around so good—but we still get around. Sometimes it's nice to have help, though."

"Please sit with us," his wife urged as Rachel set their glasses of juice on the table for them. "We appreciate so much how you helped us. If you hadn't, I would have spilled something for sure, then Poppa would have been upset and—" She waved a wrinkled hand in a gesture that indicated she could have gone on about the troubles that might have occurred. "How can we thank you?" she asked instead.

"It was nothing, honestly," Rachel insisted, a little embarrassed at the fuss they were making over her. Both hands were holding her coffee cup as she backed away from the table. "Enjoy your breakfast."

"Thank you. You are so kind." The elderly man beamed gratefully at her.

As Rachel turned to seek a quiet place to sit and drink her coffee, she spied Gard just coming off the ladder to the Observation Deck. His sweatshirt was clinging damply to him, a triangular patch of wetness at the chest, and his skin glistened with perspiration. He was walking directly toward her. Rachel stood her ground, determined not to spend her entire cruise trying to avoid him. Even though he looked physically tired, there was a vital, fresh air about him, as if all the fast-running blood in his veins had pumped the cobwebs out of his system. She envied that tired but very alive look.

He slowed to a stop when he reached her, his hands moving up to rest on his hips. "Good morning, Mrs. MacKinley." Amusement laced his warm greeting as he smiled down at her, his eyes skimming over her ebony hair framed by the lavender hood.

"Good morning, Mr. MacKinley," she returned the greeting.

His gaze drifted to her lips, as if seeking traces of the imprint his mouth had made on them. There was something almost physical about his look. Rachel imagined that she could feel the pressure of his kiss again.

"I see you have your morning coffee," Gard observed.

"Yes, I do." She braced herself for his next remark, expecting it to be some reference to his invitation.

"I'll see you later." He started forward, changing

his angle slightly to walk by her. "I have to shower and change before breakfast."

For a stunned second she turned to watch him leave. Behind her she heard the elderly couple at the table speaking about them.

"Did you hear that, Poppa?" the woman was saying. "They call each other Mister and Missus."

"The way we used to, eh, Momma."

"He called her Mrs. MacKinley," the woman said again.

"And she called him Mr. MacKinley," the man inserted.

"That's so nice and old-fashioned, isn't it?" the woman prompted.

Suppressing the impulse to walk to their table, Rachel moved in the opposite direction. It hardly mattered that they had the mistaken impression she was married to him. Correcting it might involve a long, detailed explanation and she didn't want to go into it. Besides, what they had overheard had brought back some fond memories of their early married life. They were happy, so why should she spoil it with a lot of explanations that didn't really matter to them.

Shortly after late-sitting breakfast was announced, Rachel entered the dining room and was shown to her assigned table. It was located in a far corner of the room, quiet and away from the flow of traffic to the kitchen and the waiter service areas. Two couples were already sitting at the table for eight when Rachel arrived.

An exchange of good mornings was followed by

introductions. She was immediately confused as to which woman was Helen and which one was Nanette, and their husbands were named something like John or Frank. Rachel didn't even make an attempt to remember their last names. Since they would be sharing every meal together from now on, she knew she would eventually get the right names with the right faces.

While the waiter poured a cup of coffee for her, Rachel glanced over the breakfast menu. A third couple arrived, a young pair in their twenties, compared to what Rachel judged to be the average age of forty for the other four. After they were seated, there was only one vacant chair—the one beside Rachel.

"I'm Jenny and this is my husband, Don," the girl said. There was a bright-eyed, playful quality about her that seemed to immediately lighten the atmosphere at the table.

Her introduction started the roll call around the table again, ending with Rachel. "I'm Rachel MacKinley." Although the others hadn't, she tacked on her surname. She supposed it was probably a business habit.

The waiter hovered by her chair to take her order. "Orange juice, please," she began. "Some papaya, two basted eggs, and Canadian bacon."

When she partially turned in her chair to pass the menu to the waiter, Rachel saw Gard approaching their table. All the ones close to them were filled, so his destination could be none other than the empty chair next to her.

Something should have forewarned her. Until

this moment she hadn't given a thought to where he might be seated. But it was obvious they would be seated at the same table. They had been assigned to the same cabin, so naturally as man and wife, supposedly, they would be assigned to the same table.

That moment of shocked realization flashed in her eyes, and Gard saw the flicker of surprise in their gray depths. A smile played at the edges of his mouth. Rachel faced the table again and reached for her coffee cup, trying to keep the grim resignation out of her expression.

"Sorry I'm late," Gard said to the table in general as he pulled out the vacant chair beside Rachel and sat down. "It took longer to shower and change than I thought. Has everyone ordered?"

"We just got here, too," said Jenny, of the young married couple, assuring him quickly that he wasn't the only late arrival. "I'm Jenny, and this is my husband, Don."

The round-robin of names started again, but Rachel stayed out, not needing to introduce herself to him. "I'm Gard MacKinley," he finished the circle and unfolded the napkin to lay it on his lap. "Is this your first cruise, Jenny?"

"Yes. It's kind of a second honeymoon for Don and me," she explained. So far, Rachel couldn't recall Jenny's young husband saying a word. "Actually I guess it is our first honeymoon since we didn't go anywhere after our wedding. Both of us had to work, so we kept putting it off. Then the baby came—"

"You have a baby?" The balding man looked at

her in surprise. Helen's husband—or was it Nanette's? As many times as their names had been said, Rachel would have thought she'd have them straight, but with Gard sitting beside her, she wasn't thinking too clearly.

There was a crisp darkness to his hair, still damp from the shower, and the familiar scent of his after-shave lotion drifted to her. No matter how she tried not to notice, he seemed to fill her side vision.

"You don't look old enough to be a mother," the balding, forty-year-old man insisted as he eyed the young girl.

"Timmy is six years old, so I've been a mother for a while." Jenny laughed. "I'm twenty-five."

"Where's your little boy?" Helen or Nanette asked.

"Grandma and Grandpa are keeping him so Don and I could take this cruise. It was a chance of a lifetime, and we couldn't pass it up. The company Don works for awarded him this all-expense-paid cruise for being the top salesman in his entire region." It was plain to see how proud she was of his achievement. "It's really great, even if I do miss Timmy already."

"Nanette and I have three children," the man said, providing Rachel with the name of his wife.

"We have four." Which meant that woman was Helen. Helen with the henna-hair—Rachel tried for a word association and discovered the woman had turned her glance to her. "How many children do you have?"

"None," she replied, knowing how much she regretted that now. The waiter came and set the orange juice and papaya before her, thus relieving the need to add anything more to her answer.

"You're leaving it a little late, aren't you . . . Gard?" Helen's husband hesitated before coming up with his name.

"I suppose I am," he murmured dryly and slid a bemused glance at Rachel.

The elderly couple was one thing, but Rachel didn't intend to let this misconception continue. Her cheeks were warm when she looked away from him to face the rest of their companions at the table.

"Excuse me, but we aren't married, even though we do have the same surname." Her assertion attracted startled and curious looks to both of them. "I know it's all very confusing."

"I'm sure you can all appreciate that it's a long and complicated story." Gard quietly followed up on her statement. "So we won't bore you with the details. But she's right. We aren't married to each other."

There was an awkward silence after their announcement. Rachel had the feeling that henna-haired Helen would love to have been "bored with the details." There were a lot of questions in their eyes, but Gard's phrasing had indicated they wouldn't be welcomed. For the time being, their curiosity was being forced to the side.

A minute later everyone was trying to talk at once and cover up that awkward moment. The waiter took the last three breakfast orders while his assistant served the meals of the first ones. With food to be eaten, there wasn't as much need for conversation.

"What kind of work do you do?" Rachel heard someone at the table ask of Gard. It probably seemed a safe inquiry. She slid him a curious, side-long glance, realizing again how little she knew about this man.

"I'm an attorney in Los Angeles," Gard replied.

Rachel had never prided herself on being able to fit people to occupations by sight, yet she wouldn't have guessed he was in the law profession either. There was no resemblance at all between Gard and John Kemper. Thinking of her friend's husband, she was reminded that John thought he had recognized Gard. Since they were in the same profession in the same city, it was probable he had.

"Is this your first cruise?" Jenny put to him the same question he had asked her.

"No." There was a brief show of a smile. "I've sailed on the *Pacific Princess* many times. The engineer happens to be a personal friend of mine. This is about the only way to spend any time with him, since he's out to sea more than he's in port."

Which explained to Rachel why it had appeared he'd been given preferential treatment when he'd been allowed onto the ship prior to the normal boarding time—and why the purser had known him.

The table conversation digressed into a discussion of the crew, the advantages of working aboard ships, and speculation about the length of time they were away from home at any one stretch. Rachel mostly listened while she ate her breakfast.

She stayed at the table long enough to have a last cup of coffee after the meal. When Nanette and her husband pushed back their chairs to leave, she elected to follow them. Gard still had a freshly poured cup of coffee to drink—not that she really thought he would make a point of leaving when she did, or even wished to avoid it. But when she left the dining room, she was alone.

The ship was huge, virtually a floating city with a population of almost a thousand. It was amazing to Rachel how many times she saw Gard that first day at sea, given the size of the ship and the number of people aboard. Some of it was to be expected, since he was assigned to the same station when they had emergency drills that morning. Naturally she saw him at lunch—and again in the afternoon when she went sunning on the Observation Deck.

Soon she would be meeting him again at dinner. It was nearly time for the late-sitting guests to be permitted into the dining room. In anticipation of that moment a crowd had begun to gather, filling the small foyer outside the dining room and overflowing onto the flight of steps. Rachel waited in the stair overflow, standing close to the bannister.

With the suggested dress that evening calling for formal wear, there was a rainbow of colors in the foyer. The style of women's dress seemed to range over everything from simple cocktail dresses to long evening gowns, while the men wore dark suits and ties or tuxedos.

Her own choice of dress was a long flowing gown in a simple chemise style, but the black tissue faille was a match with her jet-black hair. A flash of silver boucle beadings and cording was created by the splintered lightning design across the bodice, a compliment to her pewter-gray eyes. Rachel had brushed her black hair away from her face, the curling ends barely touching her shoulder tops. Her only jewelry was a pair of earrings, dazzling chunks of crystal. The result was a striking contrast between the understatement of the gown's design, with its demure capped sleeves and boat neckline, and the sleek, sexy elegance of black hair and fabric.

Near the base of the stairs Rachel spotted the henna-haired Helen and her husband, Jack, standing next to Nanette and her husband, whose name Rachel still hadn't gotten straight. She considered joining them, since they shared the same table, but it would have meant squeezing a place for herself in the already crowded foyer, so Rachel decided against it.

Her attention lingered on the couples. Helen looked quite resplendent in a red and gold evening dress that alleviated some of the brassiness of her copper-dyed hair. When she turned to say something to Nanette, her voice carried to Rachel.

"I don't care what you say," she was insisting. "No one will be able to convince me those two are brother and sister—or even cousins."

Nanette's reply was lost to Rachel, but she tensed at Helen's remark. Although Helen hadn't identified the people by name, Rachel had an uneasy suspicion she was one of them. A second later it was obliquely confirmed.

"You heard both of them say they weren't married, but they are still sharing the same cabin. I know," Helen stated with a smug little glance. "I was looking at the roster of passengers this afternoon to find out what cabin the Madisons were in so I could call them and change our bridge date. It was right there in black and white—both of their names with the same cabin number. Just what does that suggest to you?"

There was a sinking feeling in the pit of Rachel's stomach. It was obvious that Helen had construed that she and Gard were lovers. It was one thing to have people believe they were married, and another thing entirely to have them suspect they were conducting an illicit affair.

With the way Helen's mind was running now, Rachel doubted that she would ever believe the true story. The coincidence was so improbable that she would think it was a poor attempt to cover up their affair. Trying to explain what had actually happened would be futile now. More subtle tactics were required.

The dining room opened and the waiting guests poured in. Rachel let herself be swept along with the inward flow while her mind continued to search for a way to divert the mounting suspicions. The two couples were already seated when she approached the table.

"That's a stunning gown you're wearing, Rachel," Helen complimented as Rachel sat in the chair the waiter held for her. "Especially with your black hair."

"Thank you." Rachel smiled with poise, not

revealing in her expression that she had any knowledge of the conversation she'd overheard. "It was a favorite of my late husband's," she lied, since she had purchased it the year after Mac's death to wear to a social function she had been obliged to attend.

"You're a widow?" Nanette inquired.

"Yes." Rachel didn't have an opportunity to add more than that, the exchange interrupted by Gard's arrival. On its own, it did nothing to dispel suspicion.

Her glance went to him as he pulled out the chair beside her. His black formal suit enhanced the long, lean look of him, adding to that worldly, virile air. The hand-tailored lines of the jacket were smoothly formed to the breadth of his shoulders and his flatly muscled chest. The sight of him made a definite impact on her senses, alerting her to the powerful male attraction that he held.

"Good evening." It was a general greeting in a masculinely husky voice as Gard sat down and brought his chair up to the table. Then he turned a lazy and probing glance to her. She felt the touch of his gaze move admiringly over her smoothly sophisticated attire. "I didn't see you at the captain's cocktail party in the Pacific Lounge."

"I didn't go," she replied evenly, but she had difficulty preventing her breath from shallowing out under his steady regard.

"So I gathered," he murmured dryly, as if mocking her for stating the obvious.

Out of the corner of her eye Rachel was conscious that Helen was interestedly observing their quiet exchange. She increased the volume of her voice slightly, enough to allow Helen to hear what she was saying.

"You never did mention how you liked the owner's suite," she said to Gard. "Is it satisfactory?"

A smile lurked in his dry brown eyes, knowledge showing that he had caught the change in her voice while he attempted to discern the purpose. Rachel tried to make it appear that her inquiry was merely a passing interest, with no ulterior purpose.

"I could hardly find fault with the owner's suite." Gard spoke louder, too. Covertly Rachel stole a look at the red-haired woman and observed the flicker of confusion as it became apparent that they weren't sharing a cabin. "Why don't you come up after dinner and I'll give you a tour of it?" Gard invited smoothly. Rachel shifted her glance back to him.

Any distance she had managed to put between them in Helen's mind, had been wiped out by his few words, which could be read with such heavy suggestion. Irritation glittered as she met his dry glance.

"I hardly think that would look proper, would you?" she refused with mock demureness.

"And we must be proper at all times, mustn't we?" he chided in a drolly amused tone.

His response was even more damning. Seething, Rachel gave up the conversation and reached stiffly for her menu. By innuendo Gard had implied that they were having an affair and trying to cover it up in front of others. At this point an outright denial would add fuel to the growing suspicions, and Rachel didn't intend to feed anything but herself.

The waiter paused beside her chair, pen and pad in hand. Rachel made a quick choice from the menu selection. "Prosciutto ham and melon for an appetizer," she began. "The cold cream of avocado soup and the rainbow trout almondine."

There was a lull in the table talk as the others perused the menu and made their decisions. When the young couple joined them, Rachel deliberately turned away from Gard and engaged the talkative Jenny in conversation.

# Chapter Five

There was a languid warmth to the night air as the ship's course entered the fringes of the tropics. The breeze was no more than a warm breath against her bare arms as Rachel stood at the railing and looked into the night. A wrap was not necessary in this mild air.

Beyond the ship's lights the sea became an inky black carpet, broken now and then by a foamy whitecap. Far in the distance lights winked on the horizon, indicating land, but there was no visible delineation between where the sea stopped and the land began, and the midnight sky faded into the distant land mass.

The stars were out, a diamond shimmer of varying brilliance, and the roundness of a silver moon dissolved into a misty circle. In the quiet there was only the muted sound of the ship's engines and the subdued rush of water passing the ship's cleaving hull.

She had the port side of the Promenade Deck to herself. The passengers who hadn't retired for the night were either attending one of the lounge shows or gambling at one of the casinos on board. After dinner Rachel had sampled each of the ship's entertainment offerings until a restlessness had taken her outside into the somnolent warmth of the tropical night.

Her mind seemed blank of any thoughts save the gathering of impressions of the night's surroundings. The opening of a door onto the outer deck signaled the intrusion of someone into her solitude. Rachel sighed in a resigned acceptance of the fact. It was too much to expect that it could have stayed this way for long, not with the number of passengers aboard.

With idle interest she glanced back to see her fellow sojourner of the night. Her fingers tensed on the polished wood railing as she saw Gard's dark figure against the lighted backdrop of the ship's white bulkhead. His head was bent, the reflected glow of a cupped match flame throwing its light on the angular planes of his handsome features.

When he straightened and shook out the match, there was no indication that he'd seen her. The blackness of her long gown and hair helped to lose her form in the darkness of the night. Rachel held herself still, yet she was disturbed by the certain knowledge that it was inevitable that he would eventually notice her standing there, off to one side.

She waited and watched while he turned his gaze

seaward. As the moment of discovery was prolonged, the anticipation of it began to work on her nerves. Her pulse was jumping when his gaze made an idle drift toward the stern. There was the slightest hesitation before he changed his angle and wandered over to her. Rachel made a determined effort to appear indifferent to his approach, casually turning her gaze away from him to the distant land lights.

"I thought you'd be safely tucked in your bed by now," Gard said, casually voicing his surprise at finding her there.

When he stopped, it was only inches from her—much too close for her strained composure to handle. Rachel turned at right angles to face him, thus increasing the intervening space. She felt the stirring of her senses in direct reaction to his presence.

"It's such a beautiful night that I came out for some fresh air before turning in." It was a defensive answer, as if she needed to justify her reason for being there. She was disturbed by the effect he was having on her.

"Don't let my coming chase you inside," Gard murmured, seeming to know it was in her mind to leave now that he was here.

"I won't," she replied in denial of her true desire.

"It's a calm night," he observed, briefly releasing her from the steadiness of his dark gaze to cast an eye out to sea. "You're lucky to have such smooth seas on your first cruise."

"It's been perfect," Rachel agreed.

His gaze came back to drift over her smoothly composed features. "It isn't always like this when you sail on the 'bosom of the deep.' At times you're forcibly reminded that bosoms have been known to heave and swell."

The downward slide of his gaze lingered on the bodice of her gown, subtly letting her know that he was aware of the agitated movement of her breasts, which betrayed her altered breathing rhythm. The caressing quality of his look seemed to add to the excitement of her senses. Irritated that he had noticed her disturbance and, worse, that he had drawn attention to it, Rachel could barely suppress her resentment.

"And I'm sure you are an expert on bosoms, aren't you, Mr. MacKinley?" There was veiled sarcasm in her accusing observation.

"I'm not without a limited experience on the subject," Gard admitted with a heavy undertone of amusement in his voice.

"I believe that," she said stiffly.

"I knew you would," he murmured and dragged deeply on the cigarette. Smoke clouded the air between them, obscuring Rachel's view of him. "I don't believe I mentioned how becoming that gown is to you."

"Thank you." Rachel didn't want a compliment from him.

"I suppose it's fitting. Black, for a not-so-merry widow." He seemed to taunt her for the apparent absence of a sense of humor.

"It's hardly widow's weeds." She defended her

choice of dress. "No well-dressed woman would be without a basic black in her wardrobe."

"I'm glad to hear it. If you aren't regarding that gown as widow's black, you must have begun accepting social invitations," Gard concluded. "I'm having a small cocktail party in my suite tomorrow evening and I'd like you to come."

"A small party . . . of one?" Rachel was skeptical of the invitation. A jet-black brow arched in challenge. "Am I supposed to accept, then find out when I arrive that nobody else was invited?"

"That's a bit conceited, don't you think?" The glowing red tip of his cigarette was pointed upward for his idle contemplation of the building ash before his glance flicked to her.

"Conceited?" His response threw her.

"You inferred my invitation was a ruse to get you alone in my cabin. That is presuming that I *want* to get you alone in my cabin. Don't you think you're jumping to premature conclusions?"

"I . . ." Rachel was too flustered to answer, suddenly caught by the thought that she might have misjudged him. An inner heat stained her cheeks with a high color.

An ashtray was attached to the railing post and Gard snubbed out the cigarette and dropped the dead butt into it. When he looked at Rachel, she was still struggling for an answer.

"I admit the idea is not without a definite appeal, but it isn't behind the reason I invited you to my suite," he assured her. "I am having a few of my friends on board in for cocktails—Hank and the purser among others. I thought you might like to join us—especially since you expressed an interest in the suite at dinner this evening."

"That was for Helen's benefit." Rachel admitted the reason behind her inquiry.

"Why?" he asked with a quizzical look.

"Because she found our names on the passenger list posted in the Purser's Lobby, with the same cabin number." She paused to lend emphasis to the last phrase. "She remembered I had said we weren't married. She put two and two together and came up with a wanton answer. So I tried to make it clear to her that we weren't sharing a cabin."

A low chuckle came from his throat, not improving the situation at all. Her brief spate of embarrassment fled, chased by a sudden rush of anger.

"I don't think it's funny," Rachel said thinly.

"It's obvious you don't." Gard controlled his laughter, but it continued to lace through his voice. "It wouldn't be the first time an unmarried couple shared the same cabin on a ship. Why do you care what that woman thinks? You know it isn't true and that should be good enough."

"I knew I shouldn't have expected you to understand." It was a muttered accusal as Rachel made to walk past him rather than waste any more of her time trying to make him see her side of it.

A black-sleeved arm shot out in front of her and blocked the way, catching her by the arm and swinging her back to face him. Both hands held her when she would have twisted away. A slate-colored turbulence darkened her eyes as Rachel glared up at him.

"Why should it upset you so much because a

bunch of strangers might think we're having an affair?" There was a narrowed curiosity in his probing look. "I'm beginning to think the lady protests too much," Gard suggested lazily.

"Don't be ridiculous." But Rachel strongly suspected that she had become too sensitive about any involvement with him, thanks to Fan's advice. It had put her thoughts toward him on a sexual basis right from the start.

The grip of his hands was burning into her flesh, spreading the sensation of his touch through her body. In defense of being brought any closer to him, her hands had lifted and braced themselves against the flatness of his hard stomach.

"What is it you're fighting, Rachel?" he asked with a quizzical look. "It isn't me. So it must be yourself."

"I simply find it awkward being alone with you when so many people have made the mistake of thinking we're married," she insisted, her pulse flaring at this contact with him. "It's bound to put ideas in your head."

"And yours?" Gard suggested knowingly.

There was a split-second hesitation before Rachel slowly nodded. "Yes, and mine, too."

"And these ideas," he continued in a conversational tone while his hands began absently rubbing her arms and edging closer to her shoulder blades in back, slowly enclosing the circle, "you don't want anything to come of them."

"Nothing would," she insisted because the cruise only lasted seven days. And at the end of it they would also part. That was always the way of it.

These sensations she was feeling now would leave, too, when the freshness of them faded.

"How can you be so sure?" Gard questioned her certainty.

"I'm not a starry-eyed girl anymore." She was a mature woman with certain adult needs that were beginning to be brought home to her as she started to feel the warmth of his body heat through the thin fabric of her gown. "I know all things have a beginning and an end."

"But it's what's in between that counts," he told her and lowered his head to fasten his mouth onto her lips.

The searching intimacy of his kiss unleashed all the restless yearnings to sweep through her veins and heat her with their rawness. Her hands slid inside the warmth of his jacket and around the black satin cummerbund to spread across the corded muscles of his back, glorying in the feel of the hard, vital flesh beneath her fingers.

There was sensual expertise in his easy parting of her lips and the devastating mingling of their mouths. Her senses were aswim with the stimulating scent of him, male and musky. The beat of her heart was a roar in her ears, deafening her to any lingering note of caution. His shaping hands moved at random over her spine and hips, pressing her to his driving length.

A raw shudder went through her as his mouth grazed across her cheek to nibble at her ear, his breath fanning the sensitive opening and sending quivers of excitement over her skin. Rachel turned her head to the side when he continued his intimate trail down the cord in her neck and nuzzled at the point where it joined her shoulder. She could hear the roughened edge of his breathing. There was a measure of satisfaction in knowing she wasn't the only one aroused.

Then he was drawing back slightly to rest his hard cheekbone against her temple, his lips barely brushing the silken texture of her black hair. While his hands were curved to the hollow of her back, Rachel slipped her arms from around him so she could glide them around his neck.

"I told you it's what's in between that counts," Gard said with a rough edge to his voice that left her in no doubt of his desires. "And you can't deny there's something between us."

"No." The way she was trembling inside, Rachel couldn't possibly deny it. Neither could she tell whether it was purely sexual or if there was an emotional fire there as well. Liking a person was often a spontaneous thing; so was physical attraction. But love took a little longer.

"I thought I'd get an argument out of you on that one," he murmured, absently surprised at her easy agreement, but only she knew the qualification she had attached to it.

When his mouth turned toward her, she welcomed its possession. Her fingers curled into the mahogany thickness of his hair to pull his head down and deepen the kiss. She arched her body more tightly against the vital force of his, her breasts making round impressions on his solid chest. There was a completeness to the moment, the iron feel of a man's arms about her and the passion of a hungry kiss breathing life into her desires.

Locked together in the heat of their embrace, it was several seconds before either of them became aware of the suppressed titters behind them and the whispered voices. Their lips broke apart as they both turned their heads to see the elderly couple tiptoeing past them. Rachel recognized them as the pair that had been so grateful for her help that morning when she had carried juice to the table for them.

They had seemed a romantic pair despite their advanced age. She didn't really mind that they had been the ones who had seen her kissing Gard. Still, this was a fairly public place to indulge in such private necking. She lowered her arms to his chest and gently pushed away.

"I think I'd better go to my cabin before I become drunk on all this fresh air," Rachel murmured.

"It wasn't the air I found intoxicating," Gard countered with lazy warmth and let her move out of the circle of his arms.

"I'll bet you've used that line more than once." The lighthearted feeling prompted her to tease him.

"As an attorney, I'd do well to plead the Fifth Amendment rather than respond to that remark," he retorted and held out a hand to her. "I'll walk you to your cabin."

"No." Rachel put her hands behind her back, in a little girl gesture, to hide them from his outstretched palm. "I'll tell you good night here."

There was a hesitation before he surrendered to

her wishes. "I'll see you at breakfast in the morning
. . . Mrs. MacKinley."

Something in the way he said her name made it
different, like it was his name she possessed. Her
heart tumbled at the thought, her pulse racing. She
schooled her expression to give none of this away to
him and smiled instead.

"I'll see you in the morning." She avoided speaking his name and swung away to walk to the steps
leading to the door.

After she had pulled it open, she paused and
turned to look aft. He was standing at the railing
where they had been, lighting another cigarette, all
male elegance in his black formal suit. The urge was
strong to go back to his side, and Rachel lifted her
long skirt to step over the raised threshold and
walked inside before that urge could override her
sense of caution.

At breakfast the next morning Gard extended
invitations to his private cocktail party to the three
couples at their table. After they had accepted, his
roguish glance ran sideways to Rachel.

"Will you come now?" His question mocked her
with the proof that she wasn't the only one invited,
as she had once accused.

"Yes, thank you." She kept her answer simple,
knowing how the red-haired woman was hanging on
her every word and partly not caring. She'd run into
gossips before who simply had to mind everybody's
business but their own.

After last night there was no point in denying her

attraction to Gard any longer—and certainly not to herself. She had begun to think that if a relationship developed on the cruise, it wouldn't necessarily have to end when the ship reached its destination in Acapulco. Both of them lived in Los Angeles. They could continue to see each other after this was over. Part of her worried that it might be dangerous thinking. But Rachel knew she was nearly ready to take the chance.

After she had finished her morning meal, she stopped in the Purser's Lobby on her way topside to the Sun Deck. For a change no one was waiting at the counter for information. When Rachel asked to speak to the purser, an assistant directed her to his private office.

When she entered, his short, round body bounced off the chair and came around the desk to greet her. "Good morning, Mrs. MacKinley." His recognition of her was instant, accompanied by a jovial smile. "No more mix-ups, I trust."

"Only one," she said, admitting the reason for wanting to see him. "The passenger list posted outside—"

"That oversight has already been corrected," he interrupted her to explain. "I saw Gard early this morning and he mentioned that he was still listed as being in the cabin assigned to you. I changed that straightaway."

"Oh." She hadn't expected that. "I'm sorry. It seems I've taken your time for nothing."

"I wouldn't worry about that," he insisted and walked with her as she turned to leave. "Will I be seeing you at the cocktail party Gard is having tonight?"

"Yes, I'm coming," she nodded.

"We've been giving him a bad time about having a wife on board," he told her with a broad wink. "His friends have had a good laugh over the mix-up, although I know it was probably awkward for you."

"It was, at the time," Rachel admitted, but her attitude had changed since then, probably because her wariness of Gard was not so strong.

"If I can help you again anytime, come see me." When they reached his office door, he stopped. "I'll see you tonight."

"Yes." She smiled and moved away into the lobby.

As Rachel headed for the gracefully curved staircase rising to the mezzanine of Aloha Deck, her course took her past the board with the passenger list. She paused long enough to see for herself that the cabin number beside Gard's name had been changed. It was no longer the same as hers.

It was late in the afternoon when the ship's course brought it close to a land mass. Rachel stood at the railing with the crowd of other passengers and watched as they approached the tip of the Baja Peninsula, Cabo San Lucas.

The cranberry-colored jump-short suit she wore was sleeveless with a stand-up collar veeing to a zippered front. It showed the long, shapely length of her legs and the belted slimness of her waist. Even though her skin was slow to burn in the sun, Rachel had limited her amount of exposure to this hot, tropical sun. As a result her arms and legs had a soft, golden cast.

A brisk breeze was taking some of the heat out of the afternoon. It whipped at her black hair and tugged a few wisps from the constraining ponytail band, blowing them across her face. With an absent brush of her hand she pushed them aside and watched while the ship began its swing around the point of Cabo San Lucas.

Around her the passengers with cameras were snapping pictures of the stunning rock formations. Centuries of erosion by the sea and weather had carved the white rocks, creating towering stacks and spectacular arches to guard the cape. At this point of land, the Sea of Cortez met the waters of the Pacific Ocean.

As the *Pacific Princess* maneuvered into the bay, giving the passengers a closer look at the sprawling fishing village of San Lucas, Rachel was absently conscious of the person on her left shifting position to make room for someone else. Those with cameras were constantly jockeying for a better position at the rail, and the non-photographers among the passengers generously made room for them. So she thought nothing of this movement until she felt a hand move familiarly onto the back of her waist.

Her body tensed, her head turning swiftly. The iciness melted from her gray eyes when she saw Gard edge sideways to the railing beside her. She felt the sudden sweep of warm contentment through her limbs and relaxed back into her leaning position on the rail.

"It's quite a sight, isn't it?" Rachel said, letting her gaze return to the white cliffs and the small village tumbling down the hillside to the bay. Then she remembered that Gard was a veteran of this cruise. "Although you've probably seen it many times before."

"It's still impressive." The soft, husky pitch of his voice seemed to vibrate through her, warm and caressing. "You didn't come down to lunch."

"No," she admitted, conscious of the solid weight of his arm hooked so casually around her waist. "I realized I couldn't keep eating all these wonderful meals. I have to watch my figure," she declared lightly, using the trite phrasing.

When she turned her head to look at him again, her pulse quickened at the way his inspecting gaze slowly traveled down the length of her body as if looking for the evidence of an extra pound or two. Her breasts lifted on an indrawn breath that she suddenly couldn't release. The soft material of her jump-shorts was stretched by the action and pulled tautly over her maturely rounded breasts.

Her stomach muscles tightened as his gaze continued its downward inspection and wandered over the bareness of her thighs. It was more than the mere intimacy latent in his action. He seemed to be taking possession of her, body and soul. Rachel was shaken by the impression. The impact wasn't lessened when his gaze came back to her face and she saw the faintly possessive gleam in the brown depths of his eyes.

"I don't see anything wrong with your figure," he

murmured, understating the approval that was so obvious in his look.

Rachel curled her fingers around the railing and tried to keep a hold on reality. "There would be if I started eating three full meals a day." She stuck to the original subject, not letting him sidetrack her into a more intimate discussion.

"You could always come jogging with me in the mornings and run off that extra meal," Gard suggested.

"No thanks," Rachel refused with a faint laugh. "I came on this cruise to rest and relax. I don't plan to do anything more strenuous than—"

"Making love?" he interrupted to finish the sentence with his suggestion.

Everything jammed up in her throat, blocking her voice and her breath and her pulse. Rachel couldn't speak; she couldn't even think. The seductive phrase kept repeating itself in her mind until a resentment finally wedged through her paralyzed silence because he was setting too fast a pace.

"Don't be putting words in my mouth." Rachel faced the village, her features wiped clear of any expression.

"Why not?" He continued to study her profile with lazy keenness. "Last night you admitted you had ideas in your head. What's wrong with saying the words to go along with them?"

The hand on her waist moved in a rubbing caress, its warm pressure seeming to go right through the material to her skin. Rachel felt the curling sensation of desire beginning low in her stomach. A hardened glint came into her gray eyes as she swung her gaze to him.

"Because some ideas are stupid, and I'd rather not turn out to be a fool." It was too soon for her to know whether she could handle a more intimate relationship with him, and she refused to be rushed into a decision.

His faintly narrowed gaze measured her, then a slow smile spread across his face. "I guess I can't argue with that." Gard straightened and let his hand slide from her waist. "Don't forget cocktails at seven thirty in my suite."

There was an instant when Rachel had an impulse to change her mind and not go, even though she wanted to attend the party. It was something she couldn't explain.

"I'll be there." She nodded.

"Good." He glanced at the watch on his wrist, then back to her. "I'll see you in a couple of hours then. In the meantime, I'd better go shower and dress—and make sure there's plenty of mix and snacks on hand."

"Okay." Rachel didn't suggest that he leave the party preparations until later and stay with her a little longer.

His gaze lingered on her, as if waiting for her to say there was plenty of time. Then he was leaving her and walking away from the railing.

Soberly she watched him striding away, her gaze wandering over the broad set of his shoulders beneath the form-fitting knit shirt. Somehow Rachel had the feeling that Gard was skilled at playing the waiting game. She began to wonder whether he wasn't patiently wearing down her resistance—and an affair was a foregone conclusion.

Troubled by the thought, her eyes darkened somberly as she swung back to the rail. A wrinkled hand patted the forearm she rested on the smooth wood, drawing Rachel's startled glance to the elderly woman beside her. There was no sign of her husband, but Rachel recognized the woman instantly as half of the couple she'd helped the day before.

"Don't be too hard on your husband, Mrs. Mac-Kinley." Her look was filled with sympathetic understanding. "I'm certain he truly cares for you. If you try hard enough, I know you will find a way to work out your problems. You make such a lovely couple."

"I—" Rachel was dumbfounded and lost for words.

But the woman didn't expect her to say anything. "Poppa and I have had our share of arguments over the years. Sometimes he has made me so angry that I didn't want to see him again, but it passes," she assured Rachel. "No marriage is wonderful all the time. In fact, often it is only some of the time." A tiny smile touched her mouth as she confided her experience.

"I'm sure that's true." Rachel's expression softened. There were always highs and lows, but most of the time marriages were on a level plateau.

"One thing I do know," the woman insisted with a scolding shake of her finger. "You will solve nothing by sleeping in one cabin while your husband sleeps in another."

At last Rachel understood what this was all

about. The woman had obviously seen the corrected passenger list and noticed that Gard was in a different cabin. She tried very hard not to smile.

"I'm sure everything will work out for the best. Thank you for caring," she murmured.

"Just remember what I said," the woman reminded her and toddled off.

# Chapter Six

Punctuality had always been important to Rachel. At half past seven on the dot she walked into the passageway running lengthwise of the Bridge Deck and stopped at the first door on her right. It stood open, the sound of voices coming from inside the suite, signaling the arrival of other guests ahead of her.

Uncertain whether to knock or just walk in, Rachel hesitated, then opted for the latter and walked into the suite unannounced. Four ship's officers in white uniforms were standing with Gard in the large sitting room, drinks in hand while they munched on the assorted cheeses and hors d'oeuvres arranged on trays on a round dining table.

When Gard turned and saw her, a smile touched the corners of his eyes. He separated himself from the group and crossed the room to greet her. Although Rachel was used to being the lone woman in business meetings, the feeling was different in a social situation.

"You did say seven thirty," she said to Gard, conscious of the smiling stares of the, so far, all-male guests.

"I did." He nodded as his gaze swept over her dress, patterned in an updated version of a turn-of-the-century style out of a raspberry-ice crepe.

The high-buttoned collar rose above a deeply veed yoke created by tiny rows of pleated tucks and outlined with a ruffle. The tucks and ruffles were repeated again in the cuffs of the long sleeves. A narrow sash, tied in a bow at her waist, let the soft material flow to a knee-length skirt. In keeping with the dress's style, Rachel had loosely piled her ebony-dark hair onto her head in an upsweep. A muted shade of raspberry eye shadow on her lids brought a hint of amethyst into the soft gray of her eyes.

"You look lovely," Gard said with a quirking smile that matched the dryly amused gleam in his eyes. "But I can't help wondering if that touch-me-not dress you're wearing is supposed to give me a message."

His remark made Rachel wonder if she hadn't subconsciously chosen this particular dress, which covered practically every inch of her body, for that very reason. But that would indicate that she felt sexually threatened by her own inner desires, which she was trying to keep locked in.

"Hardly," she replied. "You'd probably see it as a challenge."

"You could be right there," he conceded, then took her by the arm to lead her over to his other guests. "I have some friends I'd like you to meet."

He introduced her to the four officers, including the purser, Jake Franklin, whom she'd already met. But it was Gard's close friend, Hank Scarborough, who put a quick end to polite formalities and meaningless phrases of acknowledged introductions.

"Ever since I heard about you, Mrs. MacKinley, I've been anxious to meet you." Hank Scarborough was Gard's age, in his middle to late thirties, not quite as tall and more compactly built, with sandy-fair hair and an engaging smile. There was a gleam of deviltry in his eye that seemed to hint that he was fond of a good story. "You more than live up to your reputation."

"Thank you," Rachel said, not sure whether she should take that as a compliment.

"I admit I was curious about a woman who would first pass herself off as Gard's wife, then boot him out of his own cabin with not so much as a 'by your leave.'" He grinned to let her see that he knew the whole story and the unusual circumstances. His mocking glance slid to Gard. "You should have kept her for your wife."

"Give me time, Hank," he advised.

A sliver of excitement pierced Rachel's calm at Gard's easy and confident reply. She had to remind herself that he was just going along with the razzing.

It did not necessarily mean that he was developing a serious interest in her. When his dark gaze swung to her, she was able to meet it smoothly.

"What would you like to drink?" Gard asked and let his gaze skim her nearly Victorian dress. "Sherry, perhaps?" he mocked.

"I'll have a gin and tonic," she ordered.

There was a subdued cheer from the officers. "A good British drink." They applauded her choice. "You'll fit right in with the rest of us chaps."

By the time Gard had mixed her drink, other guests had begun to arrive for the private cocktail party. It wasn't long before the large sitting room was crowded wall-to-wall with people. The captain stopped in for a few minutes, entertaining Rachel and some of the other guests with his dry British wit.

It seemed the party had barely started when it was interrupted with the announcement that dinner was being served in the Coral Dining Room. There was an unhurried drifting of guests out of the suite. Rachel would have joined the general exodus, but she had been cornered by Hank Scarborough and found herself listening to a long, detailed account of his life at sea.

The last guest had left before Gard came to her rescue. "You've monopolized her long enough, Hank," he said and casually curved an arm around her waist to draw her away. "I'm taking the lady to dinner."

"I suppose you must," Hank declared with a mock sigh of regret. "I'll have the steward come in and clean up this mess. The two of you run along."

Rachel became suspicious of the glance they exchanged. As Gard walked her out to the elevators she eyed him with a speculating look.

"You arranged it with Hank to keep me detained so you could take me down to dinner, didn't you?" she accused with a knowing look.

His mouth was pulled in a mockingly grim line. "I'll have to have a talk with Hank. He wasn't supposed to be so obvious about it," Gard replied, virtually admitting that had been his ploy.

She laughed softly, not really minding that it had all been set up. The elevator doors opened noiselessly and Rachel stepped into the cubicle ahead of Gard.

Dinner was followed by a Parisian show at the Carousel Lounge and, later, dancing. All of which Rachel enjoyed in Gard's company. A midnight buffet snack was being served in the aft portion of the Riviera Deck. Gard tried to tempt her into sampling some of the cakes and sweets, but she resisted.

"No." She avoided the buffet table and kept an unswerving course to the stairs. "It's time to call it a night," she insisted, tired yet feeling a pleasant glow that accompanied a most enjoyable evening.

"Would you like to take a stroll around the deck before turning in?" Gard asked as they climbed the stairs, stopping at the Promenade Deck, where her cabin was located.

"No, not tonight," Rachel refused with visions of last night's embrace on the outer deck dancing in her head.

When they reached the door to her cabin, Rachel

turned and leaned a shoulder against it to bid him good night. Gard leaned a forearm against the door by her head, bending slightly toward her and closing the distance between them. She tipped her head back in quiet languor and let it rest against the solid door while she gazed at him. There was a pleasant tingle of sensation as his glance drifted to her lips.

"You could always invite me in and ring the steward for some coffee," he murmured the suggestion.

"I could." Her reply was pitched in an equally soft voice as she began to study the smooth line of his mouth, so strong and warm. Rachel knew the wayward direction her thoughts were taking, but she had no desire to check them from their forbidden path.

"Well?" Gard prompted lazily.

Regardless of what she was thinking, she said, "I could, but I'm not going to ask you to come inside."

His rueful smile seemed to indicate that her decision was not at all unexpected. "Maybe you're right. That single bed would be awfully tight quarters."

A little shiver of excitement raced over her skin at such an open admission of his intention. When his head began a downward movement, blood surged into her heart, swelling it until it seemed to fill her whole chest. Her lips lifted to eliminate the last inch that separated her from his mouth.

The hard, male length of him was against her, pinning her body to the door with his pressing weight. His hand lay familiarly on her hip bone while his kiss probed the dark recesses of her mouth with evocative skill. Beneath her hands she could feel the warmth of his skin through the silk dress shirt. Some sensitive inner radar picked up the increased rate of his breathing.

The tangling intimacy of the deep kiss aroused an insistent hunger that made her ache inside. Rachel strained to satisfy this trembling need by responding more fiercely to his kiss. But a much more intimate union was required before the aching throb of her flesh could know gratification.

She sensed his shared frustration as Gard abandoned his ravishment of her lips and trained his rough kisses on the hollow behind her ear and the ultrasensitive cord in her neck. She gritted her teeth to hold silent the moan that rose in her throat. It came out in a shuddering sigh.

His hand moved up her waist and cupped the underswell of her breast in the span of his thumb and fingers. The thrilling touch seemed to fill her with an explosive desire. The deep breath she took merely caused her breasts to lift and press more fully into his caress.

There was a labored edge to his breathing when his mouth halted near her ear. "Are you sure you don't want to change your mind about that coffee?" Gard asked on a groaning underbreath.

Inside she was trembling badly—wanting just that. But she was afraid she wanted it too badly. It was the desires of the flesh that were threatening to rule her. She'd sooner listen to her heart or her head than something so base.

"No," Rachel answered with a little gulp of air and finally let her closed lashes open. "No coffee." Her hands exerted a slight pressure to end the embrace.

There was an instant when Gard stiffened to keep her pinned to the door. His dark eyes smoldered with sensual promise while he warred with his indecision—whether to believe her words or the unmistakable signals he received from her body. Rachel watched him; slowly he eased himself away, his jawline hardening with grim reluctance.

"You make things hard for a man," he muttered in faint accusation.

"I know," she admitted guiltily. "I—"

He put his fingers to her mouth, silencing her next words. "For God's sake, don't say you're sorry." His fingers traced over the softness of her lips, then moved off at a corner and came under her chin, rubbing the point of it with his knuckles.

"All right, I won't," Rachel agreed softly because she wasn't truly sorry about the open way she had responded to him.

"Good night, Rachel." There was a split-second's hesitation before he caught the point of her chin between his thumb and finger, holding it still while his mouth swooped down and brushed across her lips in a fleeting kiss.

"Good night," she managed to reply after he was standing well clear of her.

Under his watchful eye she turned and shakily removed the key from her evening purse to insert it in the lock. Before she entered the cabin, Rachel glanced over her shoulder once and smiled faintly at him, then stepped inside.

For a long moment she leaned against the closed door and held on to the lingering after-sensations, trying to separate emotional from physical pleasure. They were too deeply merged for her introspective study to divide.

Slowly Rachel moved away from the door into the center of the room. All the preparations for her retirement had already been made by the night steward—the bed was turned down and the drapes were closed. The next day's issue of the *Princess Patter* was on the table.

Rachel slipped off her silver-gilt shoes and set them on a chair cushion with the matching evening purse. She reached behind her neck and began to unfasten the tiny eyehooks of the dress's high collar. The first one slipped free easily, but the second was more stubborn.

"Damn," she swore softly in frustration, unable to see what she was doing and obliged to rely on feel alone.

"Need some help?" Gard's lazy voice sounded behind her.

Startled, she swiveled around, her fingers still at the back of her collar. He stood silently inside her cabin door and calmly pushed it shut. Wide-eyed, she watched him, certain the door had been locked and the key replaced in her purse.

"How did you get in here?" She finally managed to overcome her surprise and shock and ask him the question.

"I had a key to this cabin to start out with—remember?" There was a glint in his eye as he crossed the room to where she stood. "For some reason I . . . haven't remembered to turn it in." He held it up between his thumb and forefinger to show her. "I decided it was time I removed temptation from my pocket."

It hadn't occurred to Rachel that Gard still might have a key to the cabin they had shared so briefly. When he offered it to her, she extended an up-turned palm to receive it. The metal key felt warm against her skin when Gard laid it in the center of her palm. Her hand closed around it as her silently questioning gaze searched his face.

"You could just as easily have knocked," Rachel said.

"I could have," he admitted as his glance went to the hand still clutching the back neckline of her dress. No apology was offered for the fact that he had let himself in. "I guess I didn't want to have the door shut on me again."

Her eyes ran over him, taking in the masculinity of his form and finding pleasure in the presence of a man in her room . . . in her life.

"I think you'd better leave now." Her suggestion was completely at odds with what she was feeling.

"Not yet." His mouth quirked. "First I'll help you with those hooks. Turn around."

Rachel hesitated, then slowly turned her back to him and tipped her head down. Her stomach churned with nervous excitement at the firm touch of his fingers on the nape of her neck.

"If nothing else," Gard murmured dryly, "I'll

have the satisfaction of doing this . . . even if it means the cold comfort of a shower afterward."

The material around her throat was loosened as he unfastened the three remaining hooks that held the high collar. An aroused tension swept through her system when she felt his fingers on the zipper. He slowly ran it down to the bottom, the sensation of his touch trailing the length of her spine. With a hand crossed diagonally, Rachel held the front of her raspberry dress to her body.

His hands rested lightly on each shoulder bone. She felt the stirring warmth of his breath against the bared skin of her neck an instant before his warm mouth investigated the nape of her neck, finding the pleasure point where all sensation was heightened to a rawly exciting pitch. Her mouth went dry as a weakness attacked her knees. Somehow she managed to hold herself upright without sagging against him.

"I think you'd better leave, Gard." Rachel didn't dare turn around, because she knew if she did, she'd go right into his arms.

Disappointment welled in her throat when he moved away from her and walked to the door. But he paused there, waiting for her to look at him. When she did, Rachel was glad of the distance that made the longing in her eyes less naked.

"I never did get around to giving you a tour of the owner's suite," Gard said. "It has a double bed."

"Does it?" Her voice was shaking a little.

"Next time I'll invite you to my place . . . for coffee," he added on an intimate note and opened the door.

When it had closed behind him, Rachel discovered she was gripping the extra key in her hand. She looked at it for a long moment, almost wishing he had it back. A degree of sanity returned and she slipped the key into her purse with its mate.

Rachel stood at the bow in front of the wheelhouse as the ship steamed into the inlet of the bustling Mazatlan Harbor. High on a hill, the massive lighthouse of El Faro kept a watchful eye on the ship while shrimp boats passed by on their way out to sea.

"Are you going ashore when we dock?" Gard asked, coming up behind her.

She really wasn't surprised to see him. In fact, she'd been expecting him. "Yes, I am." She cast a glance at him, the vividness of last night's interlude still claiming her senses.

In denims and a pale blue shirt, he looked bronzed and rugged. Those hard, smooth features were irresistibly handsome. Rachel wondered if she didn't need her head examined for taking it so slow.

"Did you sign up for one of the tours?"

"No." She shook her head briefly and tucked her hair behind an ear, almost a defensive gesture to ward off the intensity of his gaze. "I thought I'd explore on my own."

"Would you like a private guide?" Gard asked. "I know where you can hire one—cheap."

"Does he speak English?" She guessed he was offering his services, but she went along with his gambit, albeit tongue-in-cheek.

*"Sí, señorita,"* he replied in an exaggerated Mexican dialect. "And *español,* too."

"How expensive?" Rachel challenged.

"Let's just say—no more than you're willing to pay," Gard suggested.

"That sounds fair." She nodded and felt the run of breathless excitement through her system.

"We'll go ashore after breakfast," he said. "Be sure and wear your swimsuit under your clothes. We'll do our touring in the morning and spend the afternoon on the beach."

"Sounds wonderful."

When they went ashore, Gard rented a three-wheeled cart, open on all sides, to take them to town. As he explained to Rachel, it was called a *pulmonia,* which meant "pneumonia" because of its openness to the air.

Their tour through town took them past the town square with its statue of a deer. Mazatlan was an Indian name meaning "place of the deer." Gard directed their driver to take them past the Temple of San Jose, the church constructed by the Spanish during their reign in Mexico. Afterward he had the driver let them off at El Mercado.

They spent the balance of the morning wandering through the maze of stalls and buildings. The range of items for sale was endless. There were butcher shops with sides of beef and scrawny plucked chickens dangling from hooks, and fruit stands and vegetable stands. And there was an endless array of crafts shops, souvenir stores, and clothing items.

For lunch Gard took her to one of the restaurants along the beach. When Rachel discovered their seafood had been caught fresh that morning, she feasted on shrimp, the most succulent and flavorful she'd ever tasted.

Later, sitting on a beach towel with an arm hooked around a raised knee, Rachel watched the gentle surf breaking on shore. After the morning tour and the delicious lunch, she didn't have the energy to do more than laze on the beach. Gard was stretched out on another beach towel beside her, a hand over his eyes to block out the sun. It had been a long time since he'd said anything. Rachel wondered if he was sleeping.

Off to her left an old, bowlegged Mexican vendor shuffled into view. Dressed in the typical loose shirt and baggy trousers with leather huaraches, he ambled toward Rachel and held up a glass jar half-filled with water. Fire opals gleamed on the bottom.

*"Señora?"* He offered them to her for inspection.

"No, thank you." She shook her head to reinforce her denial.

"Very cheap," he insisted, but she shook her head again. He leaned closer and reached into his back pocket. "I have a paper—you buy."

Gard said something in Spanish. The old man shrugged and put the folded paper back in his pocket, then shuffled on down the beach. Rachel cast a curious glance at Gard.

"What was he selling?" she asked.

"A treasure map." He propped himself up on an elbow. "This harbor was a favorite haunt of pirates.

Supposedly there're caches of buried treasure all over this area. You'd be surprised how many 'carefully aged' maps have been supposedly found just last week in some old chest in the attic." There was a dryly cynical gleam of amusement in his eyes.

"And they're for sale—cheap—to anyone foolish enough to buy them." Rachel understood the rest of the game.

Turning the upper half of her body, she reached into the beach bag sitting on the grainy sand behind her and took out the bottle of sun oil lying atop their folded clothes. She uncapped the bottle and began to smooth the oil on her legs and arms.

There was a shift of movement beside her as Gard again stretched out flat and crooked an arm under his head for a pillow. His eyes were closed against the glare of the high afternoon sun. With absent movements Rachel continued to spread the oil over her exposed flesh while her gaze wandered over the bronze sheen of his longly muscled body, clad in white-trimmed navy swimming trunks.

The urge, ever since he'd stripped down, had been to touch him and have that sensation of hard, vital flesh beneath her hands. It was unnerving and stimulating to look at him.

"Enjoying yourself?" His low taunt startled Rachel.

Her gaze darted from his leanly muscled thighs to his face, but his eyes were still closed, so he couldn't know she had been staring at him. His question was obviously referring to something else.

"Of course." She attempted to inject a brightness

111

in her voice. "It's a gorgeous day and the beach is quiet and uncrowded."

"That isn't what I meant, and you know it." The amused mockery in his voice had a faint sting to it. "I could feel the way you were staring at me, and I wondered if you liked what you saw."

Rachel was a little uncomfortable at being caught admiring his male body. She concentrated all her attention on rubbing the oil over an arm.

"Yes." She kept her answer simple, but some other comment was required. "I suppose you're used to women staring at you." It was a light remark, meant to tease him for seeking a compliment from her.

"Why? Because I could feel your eyes on me?" Gard shifted his dark head on the pillow of his arm to look at her. "Can't you feel it when I look at you?"

The rush of heat over her skin had nothing to do with the hot sun overhead. It was a purely sexual sensation caused by the boldness of his gaze. It was a look that did not just strip her bathing suit away. His eyes were making love to her, touching and caressing every hidden point and hollow of her body. It left her feeling too shaken and vulnerable.

"Don't." The low word vibrated from her and asked him to stop, protesting the way it was destroying her.

The contact was abruptly broken. "Hand me my cigarettes," Gard said with a degree of terseness. "They're in my shirt pocket."

Rachel wiped the excess oil from her hand on a

towel and tried to stop her hand from shaking as she reached inside the beach bag, then handed him the pack of cigarettes and a lighter. She leaned back on her hands and stared at the wave rolling into shore. The silence stretched, broken only by the rustle of the cigarette pack and the click of the lighter.

"Tell me about your husband," Gard said.

"Mac?" Rachel swung a startled glance at him, noting the grim set of his mouth and his absorption with the smoke curling from his cigarette.

"Is that what you called him?" His hooded gaze flicked in her direction.

"Yes," she nodded.

"There's consolation in that, I suppose." His mouth crooked in a dry, humorless line. "At least I'll have the satisfaction of knowing that when you say my name, you aren't thinking of someone else."

Rachel's gray eyes grew thoughtful as she tried to discern whether it was jealousy she heard or injured pride that came from being mistaken for someone else.

"What was he like?" Gard repeated his initial question, then arched her another glance. "Or would you prefer not to talk about him?"

"I don't mind," she replied, although she wasn't sure where to begin.

When she looked out to sea, Rachel was looking beyond the farthest point. The edges blurred when she tried to conjure up Mac's image in her mind. It wasn't something recent. It had been happening gradually over the last couple of years. Her memory of him always pictured him as being more handsome than photographs showed. But it was natural for the mind to overlook the flaws in favor of the better qualities.

"Mac was a dynamic, aggressive man," Rachel finally began to describe him, even though she knew her picture of him was no longer accurate. "Even when he was sitting still—which was seldom—he seemed to be all coiled energy. I guess he grabbed at life," she mused, "because he knew he wouldn't be around long." Sighing, she threw a glance at Gard. "It's difficult to describe Mac to someone who didn't know him."

"You loved him?"

"Everyone loved Mac," she declared with a faint smile. "He was hearty and warm. Yes, I loved him."

"Are you still married to him?" Gard asked flatly. Rachel frowned at him blankly, finding his question strange. A sardonic light flashed in his dark eyes before he swung his gaze away from her to inhale on his cigarette. "Even after their husbands die, some women stay married to their ghosts."

The profundity of his remark made Rachel stop and think. Although she had wondered many times if she would ever feel so strongly for another man again, she hadn't locked out the possibility. She wrapped her arms around her legs and hugged them to her chest, resting her chin on her knees.

"No," she said after a moment. "I'm not married to Mac's ghost." Her glance ran sideways to him. "Why did you ask?"

"I wondered if that was the reason you didn't want me in your cabin last night." Gard released a short breath, rife with impatient disgust. "I wonder if you realize how hard it was for me to leave last night."

"You shouldn't have come in." Rachel refused to let him put the onus of his difficulty on her.

"I'm not pointing any fingers." Gard sat up, bringing his gaze eye-level with hers. She was uncomfortable with his hard and probing look. "I'm just trying to figure you out."

There was something in the way he said it that ruffled her fur. "Don't strain yourself," she flashed tightly.

Amusement flickered lazily in his eyes. "You've been a strain on me from the beginning."

In her opinion the conversation was going nowhere. "I think I'll go in the water for a swim," Rachel announced and rolled to her feet.

"That's always your solution, isn't it?" Gard taunted, and Rachel paused to look back at him, wary and vaguely upset. "When a situation gets too hot and uncomfortable for you, you walk away. You know I want to make love to you." He said it as casually as if he were talking about the weather.

There was a haughty arch of one eyebrow as her eyes turned iron-gray and cool. "You aren't the first." She saw the flare of anger, but she turned and walked to the sea, wading in, then diving into the curl of an oncoming wave. There was a definite sense of anger at the idea that simply because he had expressed a desire for her, she was supposed to fall into his arms. If anything, his remark had driven her away from him.

Rachel swam with energy, going against the surf the same way she went against her own natural inclination. Eventually she tired and let the tide float her back to shore where Gard waited. But the tense scene that had passed before had created a strain between them that wasn't easily relieved.

# Chapter Seven

Alone, Rachel strolled along a street in downtown Puerto Vallarta, the second port of call of the *Pacific Princess.* As it had yesterday, the ship had berthed early in the morning. This time Rachel settled for the continental breakfast served on the Sun Deck and disembarked as soon as the formalities with the Mexican port authorities were observed and permission was given to let passengers go ashore.

To herself she claimed it was a desire to explore the picturesque city on her own. It was merely a side benefit that she hadn't seen Gard before she'd left the ship. Common sense told her the coolness that had come between them yesterday was a good thing. She needed time to step back and look at the relationship to see whether she'd been swept along by a strong emotional current or if she'd been caught in a maelstrom of physical desire.

Few of the shops were open before nine, so Rachel idled away the time looking in windows and eyeing the architecture of the buildings. At intersections she had views of the surrounding hills where the city had sprawled high onto their sides, creating streets that were San Francisco steep.

Something shimmered golden and bright against the skyline. When Rachel looked to see what it was, a breath was indrawn in awed appreciation. The morning sunlight was reflecting off the gold crown of a steeple and making it glow as if with its own golden light.

With this landmark in sight Rachel steered a course toward it for a closer look. Two blocks farther she reached the source. It was the cathedral of Our Lady of Guadalupe. The doors of the church stood invitingly open at the top of concrete steps, but it continued to be the crown that drew Rachel's gaze as she stood near the church's base with her head tipped back to stare admiringly at it.

"It's a replica of the crown worn by the Virgin in the Basilica at Mexico City."

At the sound of Gard's voice, Rachel jerked her gaze downward and found him, leaning casually against a concrete side of the church steps and smoking a cigarette. She felt the sudden rush of her pulse under the lazy and knowing inspection of his dark eyes. The cigarette was dropped beneath his heel and crushed out as he pushed away and came toward her. A quiver of awareness ran through her senses at his malely lean physique clad in butternut-brown slacks and a cream-yellow shirt.

"I've been waiting for you to turn up," Gard said calmly.

The certainty in his tone implied that he had known she would. It broke her silence. "How could you possibly know I would come here?" Rachel demanded with a rush of anger. "I didn't even know it."

"It was a calculated risk," he replied, looking at her eyes and appearing to be amused by the silver sparks shooting through their grayness. "Puerto Vallarta basically doesn't have much in the way of historical or cultural attractions. It's too early for most of the shops to be open, so you had to be wandering around, looking at the sights. Which meant, sooner or later, you'd find your way here."

It didn't help her irritation to find that his assumption was based on well thought out logic. "Always presuming I had come ashore." There was a challenging lift to her voice.

"Don't forget"—a slow, easy smile deepened the grooves running parenthetically at the corners of his mouth—"I know most of the officers and crew from the bridge, including the man on duty at the gangway. He told me you were one of the first to go ashore this morning. I have spies everywhere."

His remark was offered in jest, but Rachel wasn't amused. "So it would seem," she said curtly, reacting to the threading tension that was turning her nerves raw. His sudden appearance had thrown her off balance.

"Would you like to see the inside of the cathedral?" Gard inquired, smoothly ignoring her shortness and acting as if there hadn't been any cool constraint between them.

"No." She swung away from the church steps and began to walk along the narrow sidewalk in the direction of the shopping district.

"I rented a car for the day." He fell in step with her, letting his gaze slide over her profile.

"Good for you." Rachel continued to look straight ahead. She felt slightly short of breath and knew it wasn't caused by the leisurely pace of her steps.

"I thought we could drive around and see the sights." There was a heavy run of amusement in his voice.

She tossed a glance in his direction that didn't quite meet his sidelong study of her. Some of her poise was returning, taking the abrasive edge out of her voice. But it didn't lessen her resentment at the way Gard was taking it for granted that she would want to spend the day with him—just as yesterday when he had taken it for granted that because he had expressed a desire to make love to her, she should have been wildly impressed.

"I thought you just said there weren't any sights to see in Puerto Vallarta," she reminded him coolly.

"I said there weren't any major cultural attractions," Gard corrected her. "But there's plenty of scenery. I thought we could drive around town, maybe stop to see some friends of mine—they have a place in Gringo Gulch where a lot of Americans

120

have vacation homes—then drive out in the country."

"It's a shame you went to so much trouble planning out the day's activities for *us* without consulting me," Rachel informed him with honeyed sweetness. "I could have told you that I'd already made plans and you wouldn't have wasted your time."

"Oh?" His glance was mildly interested, a touch of skepticism in his look. "What kind of plans have you made?"

Rachel had to think quickly, because her plans were haphazard at best. "I planned to do some shopping this morning. There're several good sportswear lines that are made here, and I want to pick up some small gifts for friends back home."

"And the afternoon?" Gard prompted.

The beach bag she carried made that answer rather obvious. "I'm going to the beach."

"Any particular beach?"

"No." Her gaze remained fixed to the front, but she wasn't seeing much. All her senses were tuned to the man strolling casually at her side.

"I know a quiet, out-of-the-way spot. We'll go there this afternoon after you've finished your shopping."

"Look." Rachel stopped abruptly in the middle of the sidewalk to confront him. Gard was slower to halt, then came halfway around to partially face her. His handsomely hewn features showed a mild, questioning surprise at this sudden stop. "I'm not going with you this afternoon."

"Why?" He seemed untroubled by her announcement.

There was frustration in knowing that she didn't have an adequate reason. Even more damnably frustrating was the knowledge that she wouldn't mind being persuaded to alter her plans. She became all the more determined to resist such temptation.

"Because I've made other plans." Rachel chose a terse non-answer and began to walk again.

"Then I'll go along with you." With a diffident shrug of his shoulders, Gard fell in with her plans.

She flicked him an impatient glance. "Are you in the habit of inviting yourself when you're not asked?"

"On occasion," he admitted with a hint of a complacent smile.

More shops were beginning to unlock their doors to open for business. Out of sheer perversity Rachel attempted to bore him by wandering in and out of every store, not caring whether it was a silversmith or a boutique, whether it sold copper and brassware or colorful Mexican pottery.

Yet she never detected any trace of impatience as he lounged inside a store's entrance while she browsed through its merchandise. She did make a few small purchases: a hand-crafted lace mantilla for her secretary, a hand-embroidered blouse for Mrs. Pollock next door, and two ceramic figurines of Joseph with Mary riding a donkey for Fan's collection of Christmas decorations. Gard offered to carry them for her, but she stubbornly tucked them inside her beach bag.

In the next boutique she entered, Rachel found a two-piece beach cover-up patterned in exactly the same shade of lavender as her swimsuit. The sales clerk showed her the many ways the wraparound skirt could be worn, either long with its midriff-short blouse or tied sarong fashion. After haggling good-naturedly over the price for better than half an hour, Rachel bought the outfit.

"You drive a hard bargain," Gard observed dryly as he followed her out of the store.

Bargaining over the price was an accepted practice in most of Mexico, especially when a particular item wasn't marked with a price, so Rachel was a little puzzled why he was commenting on her negotiation for a lower price.

"It's business," she countered.

"I agree," he conceded. "But you practiced it like you were an old hand at negotiating for a better price."

"I suppose I am." She smiled absently, because she was often involved in negotiating better prices for bulk-order purchases of furniture or related goods for her company. "It's part of my work."

"I didn't realize you worked." Gard looked at her with frowning interest.

Rachel laughed shortly. "You surely didn't think my only occupation was that of a widow?"

"I suppose I did." He shrugged and continued to study her. "I didn't really give it much thought. What do you do?"

"I own a small chain of retail furniture stores." Her chin lifted slightly in a faint show of pride.

"If they're managed properly, they can be a

sound investment." The comment was idly made.
"Who have you hired to handle the management of
them for you?"

"No one." Rachel challenged him with her
glance. "I manage them myself."

"I see." His expression became closed, withdraw-
ing any reaction to her announcement. That, in
itself, was an indication of his skepticism toward her
ability to do the job well.

"I suppose you think a woman can't run a business," she murmured, fuming silently.

"I didn't say that."

"You didn't have to!" she flared.

"You took me by surprise, Rachel." Gard attempted to placate her flash of temper with calm
reasoning. "Over the years I've met a few successful
female executives. You just don't look the type."

"And what is the type?" Hot ice crystallized in
her voice as she threw him a scathing look. "Ambi-
tious and cold and wearing jackets with padded
shoulders?" She didn't wait for him to answer as her
lips came thinly together in disgust. "That is the
most sexist idea I've ever heard!"

"That isn't what I meant at all, but the point is
well taken," he conceded with a bemused light in
his dusty brown eyes. "I deserved that for generaliz-
ing."

She was too angry to care that Gard admitted
he'd been wrong. She turned on him. "Why don't
you go back to the ship . . . or go drive around in
your rented car? Go do whatever it is that you want
to do and leave me alone! I'm tired of you following
me!"

"I was wrong and I apologize," Gard repeated with a smooth and deliberately engaging smile. "Let's find a restaurant and have some lunch."

"You simply don't listen, do you?" she declared in taut anger and looked rawly around the immediate vicinity.

A uniformed police officer was standing on the corner only a few yards away. Rachel acted on impulse, without pausing to think through the idea. In a running walk she swept past Gard and hurried toward the policeman.

"Officer?" she called to attract his attention.

He turned, his alert, dark eyes immediately going to her. He was of medium height with a stocky, muscular build. His broad features had a no-nonsense look, reinforced by a full black mustache. He walked to meet Rachel as she approached him, his gaze darting behind her to Gard.

"Officer, this man is annoying me." Rachel turned her accusing glance on Gard as he leisurely came up to stand behind her.

His expression continued to exhibit patience, but there was a hard glint in his eyes, too, at her new tactic. When she looked back at the policeman, Rachel wasn't sure he had understood her.

"This man has been following me." She gestured toward Gard. "I want him to stop it and leave me alone."

"The *señor* makes trouble for you?" the officer repeated in a thick accent to be certain he had understood.

"Yes," Rachel nodded, then added for further clarification, *"Sí."*

The policeman turned a cold and narrowed look on Gard while Rachel watched with cool satisfaction. He started to address Gard, but Gard broke in, speaking in an unhesitating Spanish. The policeman's expression underwent a rapid change, going from a stern to a faintly amused look.

"What did you say to him?" Rachel demanded from Gard.

"I merely explained that we'd had a small argument." The hard challenge continued to show behind his smiling look. "I was tired of shopping and wanted some lunch. And you—my wife—insisted on going through more stores first."

Her mouth opened on a breath of anger, but she didn't waste it on Gard. Instead she swung to the officer. "That isn't true," she denied. "I am not his wife. I've never seen him before in my life."

An obviously puzzled officer looked once more to Gard. *"Señor?"*

There was another explanation in Spanish that Rachel couldn't understand, but it was followed by Gard reaching into his pocket and producing identification. The edge was taken off her anger with the dawning realization of how she was being trapped.

"Would you care to show him your passport or driver's license, Mrs. MacKinley?" Gard taunted softly.

*"Señora,* your papers?" the officer requested.

Dully she removed her passport from the zippered compartment in her purse and showed it to him. A grimly resigned look showed her acceptance of defeat for the way Gard had outmaneuvered her.

With the difficulties of the language barrier, she couldn't hope to convincingly explain that even though their surnames were the same, they weren't related.

When the policeman returned the passport, he observed her subdued expression. It was plain that he considered this a domestic matter, not requiring his intervention. He made some comment to Gard and grinned before touching a hand to his hat in a salute and moving to the side.

"What did he say?" Rachel demanded.

Before she could tighten her hold on the beach bag, filled to the top now with her morning's purchases, Gard was taking it from her and gripping her arm just above the elbow to propel her down the sidewalk. Rachel resisted, but with no success.

"He was recommending a restaurant where we could have lunch," he replied tautly, ignoring her attempts to pull free of his grasp.

"I'm not hungry," she muttered.

"I seem to have lost my appetite, too." His fingers tightened, digging into her flesh as he steered her around a corner.

The line of his jaw was rigid, hard flesh stretched tautly across it. Her own mouth was clamped firmly shut, refusing to make angry feminine pleas to be released. She stopped actively struggling against his grip and instead held herself stiff, not yielding to his physical force.

Halfway down the narrow cross street he pulled her to a stop beside a parked car and opened the door. "Get in," he ordered.

Rachel flashed him another angry glance, but he didn't let go of her arm until she was sitting in the passenger seat. Then he closed the door and walked around to the driver's side. She toyed with the idea of jumping out of the car, but it sounded childish even to her. Her beach bag was tossed into the back seat as Gard slid behind the wheel and inserted the key into the ignition switch.

Holding her tight-lipped silence, she said nothing as he turned into the busy traffic on the Malecon, the main thoroughfare in Puerto Vallarta, which curved along the waterfront of Banderas Bay. At the bridge over the Cuale River the traffic became heavier as cabs, trucks, burros, and bicycles all vied to cross.

The river was also the local laundromat. Rachel had a glimpse of natives washing their clothes and their children in the river below when Gard took his turn crossing the bridge. Under other circumstances she would have been fascinated by this bit of local atmosphere, but as it was, she saw it and forgot it.

Her sense of direction had always been excellent. Without being told, she knew they were going in the exactly opposite direction of the pier where the ship was tied. It was on the north side of town and they were traveling south. The road began to climb and twist up the mountainside that butted the sea, past houses and sparkling white condominiums clinging to precarious perches on the steep bluffs. When the resorts and residences began to thin out, Gard still didn't slow down.

Rachel couldn't stand the oppressive silence any longer. "Am I being abducted?"

"You might call it that," was Gard's clipped answer.

Not once since he'd climbed behind the wheel had his gaze strayed from the road. His profile seemed to be chiseled out of teak, carved in unrelenting lines. She looked at the sure grip of his hands on the steering wheel. Her arm felt bruised from the steely force of his fingers, but she refused to mention the lingering soreness.

As they rounded the mountain the road began a downward curve to a sheltered bay with a large sandy beach and a scattering of buildings and resorts. Recalling his earlier invitation to spend the afternoon in some quiet beach area, Rachel wondered if this was it.

"Is that where we're going?" The tension stayed in her voice, giving it an edge.

"No." His gaze flashed over the bay and returned to the road, the uncompromising set of his features never changing. "That's where they filmed the movie *The Night of the Iguana.*" His voice was flat and hard.

"You can let me off there," Rachel stated and stared straight ahead. "I should be able to hire a taxi to take me back to town."

There was a sudden braking of the car. Rachel braced a hand against the dashboard to keep from being catapulted forward as Gard swerved the car off the road and onto a layby next to some building ruins overlooking the bay.

While Rachel was still trying to figure out what was happening, the motor was switched off and the emergency brake was pulled on. When Gard swung

around to face her, an arm stretching along the
seatback behind her head, she grabbed for the door
handle.

"Oh, no, you don't," he growled as his snaring
hand caught her wrist before she could pull the door
handle.

"Damn you, let me go!" Rachel tried to pry loose
from his grip with her free hand, but he caught it,
too, and jerked her toward him.

"I'm not letting you go until we get a few things
straight," Gard stated through his teeth.

"Go to hell." She was blazing mad.

So was Gard. That lazy, easygoing manner she
was so accustomed to seeing imprinted on his
features was nowhere to be seen. He was all hard
and angry, his dark eyes glittering with a kind of
violence. He had stopped turning the other cheek.
Recognizing this, Rachel turned wary—no longer
hitting out at him now that she discovered he was
capable of retaliating. But it was too late.

"If I'm going to hell, you're coming with me," he
muttered thickly.

He yanked her closer, a muscled arm going
around her and trapping her arms between them as
he crushed her to his chest. His fingers roughly
twisted into her hair, tugging at the tender roots
until her head was forced back.

When the bruising force of his mouth descended
on her lips, Rachel pressed them tightly shut and
strained against the imprisoning hand that wouldn't
permit her to turn away. The punishment of his kiss
seemed to go on forever. She stopped resisting him
so she could struggle to breathe under his smother-

ing onslaught. Her heart was pounding in her chest
with the effort.

As her body began to go limp with exhaustion the
pressure of his mouth changed. A hunger became
mixed with his anger and ruthlessly devoured her
lips. She was senseless and weak when he finally
dragged his mouth from hers. Her skin felt fevered
from the soul-destroying fire of the angry kisses.
The heaviness of his breathing swept over her
upturned face as she forced her eyes to open and
look at him.

The fires continued to smolder in his eyes, now
tempered with desirous heat. He studied her swollen lips with a grimness thinning his own mouth.
The fingers in her hair loosened their tangling grip
that had forced her head backward.

"Woman, you drive me to distraction." The rawly
muttered words expressed the same angry desire
she saw in his solid features. "Sometimes I wonder
if you have any idea just how damned distracting
you are!"

Her hands were folded against his muscled chest,
burned by the heat of his skin through the thin
cotton shirt. She could feel the hard thudding of his
heart, so dangerously in tune with the disturbed
rhythm of her own pulse. She watched his face,
feeling the run of emotions within herself.

"I know that I made you angry yesterday," Gard
admitted while his gaze slid to the sun-browned
hand on her shoulder. "When I watched you rubbing that lotion over your body, I wanted to do it for
you."

As if in recollection, his hand began to glide

smoothly over the bareness of her arm. His gaze became fixed on the action while images whirled behind his smoldering dark eyes. Rachel didn't have to see them. She knew what he was imagining because she could visualize the scene, too, and the sensation of his hands moving over her whole body, not just her arm. A churning started in the pit of her stomach and swirled outward.

"But I knew if I touched you"—his gaze flicked to her eyes and looked deeply inside their black orifices—"I wouldn't be able to stop. Instead I had to lie there and pretend it didn't faze me to watch you spread oil all over your skin."

She dropped her gaze, unwilling to comment. It was disturbing to look back on the scene yesterday on the beach and know what he was thinking and feeling at the time.

"And I've made you angry this morning," Gard continued on a firmer note. "I never claimed to be without flaws, but damnit, I want to spend the day with you. Do you want to spend the day with me? And answer me honestly."

When she met his gaze, she had the feeling she was a hostile witness being cross-examined by a ruthless attorney and sworn to an oath of truth. Discounting all her petty resentments, Rachel knew what her answer was.

"Yes." She reluctantly forced it out. "Do you always ask such leading questions?"

Some of the hardness went out of his features with the easing of an inner tension. There was even the glint of a smile around his eyes.

"A good lawyer will always lead the conversation

in the direction he wants it to go, whether in contract negotiations or court testimony," he admitted. "Unfortunately you objected to the way I was leading."

"But my objection was eventually overruled," Rachel murmured, relenting now that the outcome was known and she had a clearer understanding of why it had happened.

"And you aren't going to appeal the decision?" His mouth quirked.

"Would you listen?" Her voice was falling to a whisper. She wasn't even sure if she knew what they were talking about as his mouth came closer and closer.

It brushed over her tender lips, gently at first, then with increasing warmth until he was sensually absorbing them. His tongue traced their swollen outline and licked away the soreness. Rachel twisted in the seat and arched closer to him, sliding her hands around his neck and spreading her fingers into his hair.

The quarters of the car were too restricting, forcing positions that were too awkward. Breathing heavily, Gard pulled away from her to sit back in the seat. He sent her a dryly amused look.

"It's impossible but every time I get into this with you, the surroundings go from bad to worse," he declared. "Last time it was the dubious comfort of a single bed. Now it's a car seat."

Her laughter was soft; the fire he had ignited was still glowing warm inside her. As he started the car's motor she settled into her own seat.

"You never did tell me where we're going," she

reminded him after he had pulled onto the road again.

"Believe it or not"—he turned his head to slide her a look—"I'm taking you to paradise."

"Promises, promises," Rachel teased with a mock sigh.

"You'll see," Gard murmured complacently.

When she looked out the window, she was amazed to notice how clear and bright the sky was. The steep mountains were verdantly green and lush. Below, the ocean rolled against them in blue waves capped with white foam. Afterward her gaze was drawn back to a silent study of Gard. There were flaws, but none that really mattered.

# Chapter Eight

They followed the paved road for several more twisting miles before Gard turned onto a short dirt road that led to a parking lot. Rachel read the sign, proclaiming the place as Chico's Paradise.

"I told you I was taking you to paradise," he reminded her as he braked the car to a stop alongside another.

"What is it?" Rachel climbed out of the parked car. The ground seemed to fall away in front of it, but she could see the roof of a building below . . . several buildings loosely connected, as it turned out. "A restaurant?"

"Among other things," Gard said, being deliberately close-mouthed when he joined her.

Absently Rachel noticed that he was carrying her beach bag, but since they were high in the moun-

135

tains and some distance from the ocean, she presumed he had brought it rather than leave it in the car where it might possibly be stolen. The lush foliage grew densely around the entrance path, leading down to the buildings. It was barely wide enough for two people to walk abreast.

Gard took her hand and led the way. The first adobe building they passed housed a gift and souvenir shop. Then the path widened into a small courtyard with a fountain and a statue of a naked boy. To the right a woman was making flour tortillas in an open shed area.

It appeared to Rachel that the path dead-ended into an open-air restaurant, but Gard led her through it to a series of stone steps that went down. There was a tangling riot of red bushes that looked to be some relation to the poinciana.

A second later she caught the sound of tumbling, rushing water. She looked in the direction of it. Through the flame-red leaves she saw the cascading waterfall tumbling over stone beds and creating varying levels of rock pools. When she turned her widened eyes to Gard, he was smiling.

"I told you I was taking you to paradise," he murmured softly and offered her the beach bag. "The changing rooms are down here if you want to slip into your swimsuit."

A second invitation wasn't required as she took the beach bag from him and skimmed the top of the steps as she hurried to the small adobe building. When she returned, wearing her lavender swimsuit, Gard had already stripped down to his swimming trunks. He used her beach bag to store his clothes.

Rushing water had worn the huge gray boulders smooth and gouged out holes to make placid pools while the musical cascade of water continued on its way down to the sea. A dozen people were already enjoying the idyllic setting, most of them sunbathing on the warm stone.

"Watch your step," Gard warned when the crudely fashioned steps ended and they had to traverse the massive boulders.

Luckily Rachel had put on her deck shoes. The ridged soles gave her traction to travel over the uneven contours of the huge stones, part of the mountain's core that had been exposed by centuries of carving water. Once they were at the rushing stream's level, Gard turned upstream.

There was no formal path, no easy way to walk along the water's course. Moving singly, they edged around a two-story boulder, flattened against its sheer face with a narrow lip offering toeholds. They passed the main waterfall, where the stream spilled twenty feet into a large, deep pool, and continued upstream. It seemed to require the agility of a mountain goat, climbing and jumping from one stone to another. Sometimes they were forced to leave the stream to circle a standing rock.

No one else had ventured as far as they did, settling for the easy access of the rock pool at the base of the waterfall and the lower-level pools that weren't so difficult to reach. Rachel paused to catch her breath and looked back to see how far they'd come.

The open-air restaurant with its roof of thatched palm leaves sat on the bluff overlooking the main waterfall. Tropical plants crowded around it. At this distance the brilliant scarlet color predominated, looking like clusters of thousands of red flowers.

Almost an equal distance ahead of Rachel she could see a narrow rope bridge crossing the stream. On the other side of the stream there was a knoll where a long adobe house sat in the shade of spreading trees. A large tan dog slept on a patch of cool earth, and from somewhere close by a donkey brayed. But always in the background was the quiet tumble of water on its downward rush to the sea.

"Tired?" Gard's low voice touched her.

"No." Rachel turned, an inner glow lighting her eyes as she met his gaze. "Fascinated."

He passed her a look of understanding and swung back around to lead the way again. "I found a place." The words came over his shoulder as Rachel fell in behind him.

Between two boulders there was a narrow opening and the glistening surface of a mirror-smooth pool just beyond it. Gard squeezed through the opening and disappeared behind one of the boulders. Rachel ventured forward cautiously. From what little she could see of the rock pool, it was walled in by high, sheer stones.

But there was a narrow ledge to the right of the opening that skirted the pool for about four feet. At that point it curved onto another boulder lying on its side, forming a natural deck for the swimming hole. It was secluded and private, guarded by the high rocks surrounding it. Gard stood on the long, relatively flat stones and waited for her to join him.

"Well? Was it worth the walk?" There was a

knowing glitter in his eyes when she traversed the last few feet to stand beside him.

"I don't know if I'd call it a 'walk.'" Rachel said, questioning his description of their short trek. "But it was worth it."

His finger hooked under her chin and tipped her head up so he could drop a light kiss on her lips. His lidded gaze continued to study them with disturbing interest, causing a little leap of excitement within Rachel.

"Get your shoes off and let's go for a swim." His low suggestion was at odds with the body signals he was giving, but it seemed wiser to listen to his voice.

"Okay," she breathed out.

While he kicked off his canvas loafers, Rachel sat down on the sun-warmed stone to untie her shoe-laces. When both shoes were removed, his hand was there to pull Rachel to her feet. Gard held onto the boulder as he led her down its gentle slope to the pool's edge.

"Is it deep?" She didn't want to dive in without knowing and tentatively stuck a toe in the water to test the temperature. She jerked it back. "The water's cold."

"No," Gard corrected. "The sun is hot, and the water is only warm." His hand tightened its grip on hers and urged her forward. "Come on. Let's jump in."

"Hmm." The negative sound came from her throat as she resisted the pressure of his hand. "You jump in," she said and started to sit down to ease herself slowly into the cool water. "I prefer the gradual shock."

"Oh, no." With a pull of his hand he forced her upright, then scooped her wiggling and protesting body into his arms.

The instant Rachel realized that there was no hope of struggling free, she wrapped her arms around his neck and hung on. "Gard, don't." Her words were halfway between a plea and an empty threat.

There was a complacent gleam in his dark eyes as he looked down at her, cradled in his arms. An awareness curled through her for the sensation of her body curved against the solidity of his naked chest and the hard strength of his flexed arm muscles imprinted on her back and the underside of her legs. It tightened her stomach muscles and closed a hand on her lungs.

Gard sensed the change in her reaction to the moment. A look of intimacy stole into his eyes, too, as his gaze roamed possessively over her face. His body heat seemed to radiate over her skin, warming her flesh the way his look was igniting her desire.

"I'm not going to let you back away this time." His low voice vibrated huskily over her, the comment an obvious reference to the way she had backed away from making love to him. "Sooner or later you're going to have to take the plunge."

"I know," Rachel whispered, because she felt the inevitability of it. At some time or another it had stopped being a question of whether it was what she wanted and become instead when she wanted it to happen.

A smile edged the corners of his mouth. "Damn you for knowing"—his look was alive, gleaming with a mixture of desire and wickedness—"and still putting me through this."

Rachel started to smile, but it froze into place as he suddenly heaved her away from his body. Her hands lost their hold on his neck. For a second there was the sensation of being suspended in air, followed by the shock of cool water encapsulating her body.

Something else hit the water close by her as Rachel kicked for the surface where light glittered. She emerged with a sputtering gasp for air and pushed the black screen of wet hair away from her face and eyes. There was no sign of Gard on the stone bank.

Treading water, Rachel pivoted in a circle to locate him, realizing that he must have dived into the pool after he'd thrown her in. He was behind her, only a couple of yards away. Laughter glinted in his expression.

"It wasn't so traumatic, was it?" mocked Gard.

"A little warning would have been nice," she retorted. "Maybe then I wouldn't have swallowed half the pool."

Now that she'd gotten over the shock, the water seemed pleasantly warm and refreshing. Striking out together, they explored the boundaries of their quiet pool, discovering a small cave hollowed into five feet of solid stone. Its floor was underwater, and the ceiling was too low to allow them to stand inside it.

They stayed in the rock pool for more than an hour, swimming, sometimes floating and talking, sometimes diving to explore the clear depths. Gard climbed out first and helped Rachel onto the stone slab, made slick by the water dripping from their bodies.

Although there were towels in her beach bag, neither made use of them. Instead they sprawled contentedly on the sun-warmed rock and let the afternoon air dry them naturally. Her body felt loose and relaxed as she sat and combed her fingers through the wet tangle of her black hair. She felt tired and exhilarated all at the same time. When she leaned back and braced herself with her hands, she gave a little toss of her head to shake away the wet strands clinging to her neck. It scattered a shower of water droplets onto Gard.

"Hey!" he protested mildly. "You're getting me all wet."

"Look who's complaining about a little water," Rachel mocked him playfully. "You're the same man who threw me into that pool an hour ago."

"That's different." He smiled lazily and raised up on an elbow alongside her.

"That's what I thought." She shifted into a reclining position supported by her elbows. "You can dish it out, but you can't take it."

"It depends on what's being served," Gard corrected and sent an intimating look over her curving figure, outlined by her wet and clinging bathing suit. She felt a response flaring within at his caressing look, but it was wiped from his expression when his gaze returned to her face, a dark brow lifting. "Which reminds me—we never did get around to having lunch."

"That's true. I'd forgotten." Food had been the farthest thing from her mind.

"Are you hungry?"

Rachel had to think about it. "No," she finally decided. "But considering how much I've eaten since I've been on the cruise, I don't think my stomach knows it didn't have lunch today." And she had tried to make a practice of skipping lunch so she wouldn't find herself overeating, but it seemed only fair to put the question to him. "How about you? Are you hungry?"

Her lavender swimsuit was held in place by straps tied around her neck. One wet end was lying on the ridge of her shoulder. Taking his time to answer her question, Gard reached over and picked up the strap, studying it idly as he held it between his fingers.

"Don't you know by now, Rachel"—his voice was lowered to a husky pitch, then his darkening gaze swung slowly to her face—"that I'm starving. I don't know about you, but it's been one helluva long time between meals for me."

When he leaned toward her, Rachel began to sink back onto the stone to lie flat, her hands free to take him into her arms as he came to her. His mouth settled onto her lips with hungry need, the weight of his body moving onto her.

She slid her hands around his broad shoulders, melting under the consuming fire of his kiss. The hard skin of his ropey shoulders was warm and wet to the touch, sensual in its male strength and alive in its silken heat. There was a stir and a rush of blood through her veins; the beat of her heart lifted.

His fingers hadn't lost their hold on the end of her bathing suit strap. In an abstract way Rachel felt the slow, steady pull that untied the wet bow and relieved the pressure behind her neck. But it was the taste of him, driving full into her mouth, that dominated her senses and pushed all other sensation into secondary interest. It was the hot wetness of his mouth, the tang of tobacco on his tongue, and the salty texture of his skin that she savored.

Her hand curled its fingers into the damp, satin strands of his russet hair and pressed at the back of his head to deepen the kiss so she could absorb more of him. Soon it ceased to matter as his mouth grazed roughly over her features, murmuring her name and mixing it in with love words. There followed near delirious moments when Rachel strained to return the rain of kisses, her lips and the tip of her tongue rushing over the hard angles of his cheekbone and jaw.

Then Gard was burying his face in the curve of her neck, nuzzling her skin and taking little love bites out of the sensitive ridge of her shoulder. His tugging fingers pulled down the front of her bathing suit, freeing her breasts from the confining, elasticized material of her suit. Behind her closed eyes Rachel could see the golden fire of the sun, but when his hand caressed the ripe fullness of a breast, that radiant heat seemed to blaze within her. She was hot all over, atremble with the desires shuddering through her.

She dug her fingers into the hard flesh of his shoulders as his mouth took a slow, wandering route to the erotically erect nipple. He circled it with the tormenting tip of his tongue. Rachel arched her body in raw need, driving her shoulders onto the unyielding rock slab and feeling none of the pain, only the soaring pleasure of his devouring mouth. A building pressure throbbed within her, an ache in her loins that couldn't be satisfied by the roaming excitement of his skillful hand.

Sounds came from somewhere, striking a wrong chord in the rhapsody of the moment, only beginning to build to its crescendo. Rachel tried to isolate it from the beating of her heart and the sibilant whispers of her sawing breath.

The discordant sounds were voices—high-pitched, laughing voices. She moaned in angry protest and heard Gard swear under his breath. The weight of his body pressed more heavily onto her as if to deny the intrusion while each tried to will it away. But the voices were becoming clearer, signaling the approach of someone.

When Gard rolled from her, he caught her hands and pulled her up to sit in front of him. His broad chest and shoulders acted as a shield to conceal her seminudity in case anyone had come close enough to see them. He struggled to control the roughness of his breathing while the unbanked fires in his eyes were drawn to the swollen ripeness of her breasts and their state of high arousal.

"It sounds like we have a bunch of adventurous teenagers exploring the cascade," he said as Rachel fumbled with the straps of her suit and pulled the bodice into place.

In her passion-drugged state she lacked coordination. There was a languid weakness in her limbs and

a heaviness in her eyelids. None of the inner
throbbings had been satisfied, and the ache of
wanting was still with her.

Gard looked in no better shape when she finally
met his eyes. One side of his mouth lifted in a dryly
commiserating smile. She found herself smiling
back with a hint of bemusement.

"So much for the appetizer course, hmm?" he
murmured and pushed to his feet. "Since our little
paradise is being invaded, do you want to head
back?"

"We might as well," Rachel agreed and reached
for her shoes.

On the way back they passed a family with four
adolescents determined to travel as far upstream as
they could go. When they reached the adobe buildings on the bluff, Rachel didn't bother to change out
of her swimming suit into her clothes. It had long
since dried. She simply put on the lavender print
cover-up she'd purchased instead.

"The ship isn't scheduled to sail from Puerto
Vallarta until late this evening, and we still have a
couple of hours of afternoon left," Gard said as the
car accelerated out of the parking lot onto the paved
road. "Is there anyplace you'd like to go?"

"No, I don't think so." Rachel settled back into
the seat, that unsatisfied inner tension not allowing
her to completely relax. "Besides, I'd rather not go
anywhere when I look such a mess."

She'd had a glimpse of herself in the mirror. Her
ebony hair was a black snarl of waving curls, damply
defying any style, and most of her makeup had been
washed off during the swim.

"You look good to me," he insisted with a sliding glance that was warm with approval.

"I'm told if you're hungry enough, anything looks good," she retorted dryly, a teasing glow in her smoky eyes.

A low chuckle came from his throat but he made no reponse.

There was an easy silence in the car during the long ride back to town on the twisting, coastal road, each of them privately occupied with their own thoughts. When they reached the port terminal, Gard left the car in a lot and together they walked to the ship's gangway.

"Found her, did you?" The officer on duty smiled when he recognized Gard with Rachel.

"I certainly did." There was a lightly possessive hand on her waist as he guided her onto the gangway.

After the glare and the heat of the Mexican sun, the ship seemed cool and dark when Rachel entered it, until her eyes adjusted to the change of light. Instead of taking the stairs, Gard pushed the elevator button.

"We've done enough walking and climbing for one day," he explained while they waited for it to descend to their deck. "Why don't you come to my cabin? We'll have a drink, and maybe have the steward bring us a snack."

"I'd like that," Rachel agreed. "But why don't I meet you there in half an hour? That will give me time to freshen up and change into something decent."

"Okay. It will probably take me that long to turn

the car into the rental agency." The elevator doors swished open and Gard stepped to the side, allowing Rachel to enter first. "But when you change, I'd rather you put on something 'indecent,'" he added with an engaging half-grin.

It was a little more than half an hour before Rachel knocked at the door of his cabin. With the magic of a blow-dryer and a styling brush, she had fixed her midnight-black hair into a loose and becoming style. Her simple cotton shift was grape colored, trimmed with white ribbing, and cinched at the waist with a wide white belt. Her nerves were leaping and jumping like wildfire when the door opened.

Gard's features were composed in almost stern lines, a flicker of raw impatience in the dry brown look that swept her. Before she could offer a word of greeting, he was reaching for her hand and pulling her inside to close the door.

Rachel was taken by surprise when his mouth rolled onto her lips in a hot and moist kiss. She swayed into him, feeling his hands grip her shoulders with caressing force. When he lifted his head, he had taken her breath as well as the kiss.

"What kept you?" The demand was in his eyes, but Gard tried to inject a careless note into his voice. "I was beginning to think you were going to stand me up."

"It took me longer to get ready than I thought." When his eyes ran over her and darkened with approval, Rachel was glad about the extra time she'd spent.

With the tip of his finger he located the metal pull

of the hidden zipper down the front and drew it down another four inches, so the neckline gaped to show her full cleavage. The sensation licked through her veins like heat lightning. A pleased satisfaction lay dark and disturbing in his half-closed eyes.

"Now it's closer to being indecent," he murmured in soft mockery, then swung away from her to walk to the drink cabinet in the corner. "I promised you a drink. What will you have? Gin and tonic?"

"Yes." She was absurdly pleased that he remembered what she usually ordered.

While Gard fixed a drink for each of them, Rachel took the opportunity to study him unobserved. The backlight of the bar made the hard, smooth contours of his handsome features stand out in sharp relief. During that brief but exhilarating kiss she had caught the spicy scent of fresh aftershave on his skin. The cleanness of his jaw and cheek seemed to verify that he'd taken time to shave before she'd arrived. Her gaze openly admired his male body, so trimly built yet so muscular. Just looking at him was a heady stimulation all its own.

When he turned with the drinks, Rachel pretended an interest in the large sitting room, not quite ready to let him see what was in her mind. "The room seems much larger without so many people in it," she remarked idly, recalling how small and crowded it had seemed at the cocktail party he'd given.

"It does," he agreed and handed her the glass of

gin and tonic water. He raised his glass in a semblance of a silent toast and carried it to his mouth, sipping at it and looking at her over the rim, quietly assessing and measuring. "It seems we've done this before—only last time you didn't accept the drink I offered," he said, tipping his head down as he watched the glass he lowered, then flicking a look at her through the screen of his lashes.

"Yes, the night I discovered you in my cabin," she recalled, aware of the suddenly thready run of her pulse.

"At that point it was *our* cabin." A glint of amusement shimmered in his eyes, then faded. Again some inner impatience turned him away from her. "I'll call the steward and find out what he can offer us in the way of a snack. Is there anything special you'd like?" Gard took a step toward the phone.

"I can't think of anything." She held the glass in both hands, the ice cubes transmitting some coolness to her moist palms.

That impatience became more pronounced as he stopped abruptly and swung around to face her. "It's no good, Rachel. I'm not interested in eating anything—unless it's you." The probing intensity of his dark gaze searched her face, hotly disturbing her. "You know why I asked you to my cabin. Now I want to know why you came."

The weighty silence didn't last long, but when Rachel finally spoke, her voice throbbed on a husky pitch, too emotionally charged to sound calm.

"For the same reason you asked me—because I wanted to pick up where we left off at the rock pool." But something went wrong with her certainty when she saw the unmasked flare of dark desire in his expression. As Gard took a step toward her a rush of anxiety made her half-turn away from him.

He immediately came to a halt. "What's wrong, Rachel?" It was a low, insistent demand.

Her throat worked convulsively, trying to give voice to her fears. She turned her head to look at him and forced out a nervous laugh. "I'm afraid," she admitted while trying to make light of it.

"Afraid of what?" His forehead became creased with a puzzled frown while his narrowed gaze continued to search out her face.

"I guess I'm afraid that it won't be as wonderful as I think it will," Rachel explained with a wry smile.

"Of all the—!" His stunned reaction was blatant evidence that he had expected some other explanation. The tension went out of him like an uncoiling spring. "My God, I thought it was something serious," he muttered under an expelling breath.

"I know it sounds silly—" she began.

"No, it isn't silly." In two long strides Gard was at her side, taking the glass out of her hands and setting it on a table. Then he lifted Rachel off her feet and cradled her against his chest. "It's beautiful," he said huskily as he looked down at her.

When he carried her to the bedroom door, he was so much the image of the conquering male that Rachel couldn't help smiling a little. Yet the thought was soon lost in the thrilling rush of anticipation sweeping through her veins.

Once inside the room Gard let her feet settle onto

the floor, his gaze never leaving her face, locking
with her eyes in a disturbing fashion. Conscious of
the tripping rhythm of her pulse, she slowly dragged
her gaze from his face to glance at the double bed
that occupied the room.

"As soon as I saw that," Gard murmured, following her glance, "I knew I'd much rather share this
cabin with you than the one we were both assigned
to originally."

A comment wasn't required. Any thought of one
flew away at the touch of his fingers on the front
zipper of her dress. While he opened it, Rachel
unfastened the belt around her waist and let it fall
somewhere to the side. Gard undressed her slowly,
taking her in with his eyes.

Moments later they were lying naked on the soft
comfort of the double bed, facing each other. His
hand made a leisurely trace of the soft, flowing lines
of her breast, stomach, and hips while her fingertips
made their own intimate search of his hard male
contours as they loved with their eyes.

As his hand shifted to the small of her back, he
applied slight pressure to gently arch her toward
him. With a beginning point on her shoulder he
trailed a rough pattern of nibbling kisses to the base
of her throat. Rachel quivered with the wondrous
sensations dancing over her skin.

"It doesn't bother me, Rachel, that I'm not the
first man to love you," Gard murmured thickly into
the curve of her neck. "But I'm damned well going
to be the last."

Her heart seemed to leap into her throat, releasing the admission that she'd been telling him in

everything but words. "I love you, Gard," she whispered achingly and turned her head to meet the lips seeking hers.

In a relatively short period of time it became apparent to Rachel that she had not underestimated how wonderful it would be in his arms. His hands and his mouth searched out every pleasure point on her body, discovering everything that excited her.

The union of their flesh came after they had become intimately familiar with each other. Nothing existed but pleasing the other, moving in rhythmic harmony, the tempo gradually increasing. It was a glorious spiraling ascent that exploded in a golden shower of sensation, unequaled in its blazing brilliance.

# Chapter Nine

With her head pillowed comfortably in the hollow of Gard's shoulder, Rachel dreamily watched the lazy trail of smoke rising from his cigarette. The bedsheet was drawn up around their hips, cool against their skin. The contentment she felt was almost a feline purring. She had no desire to move for a thousand years.

"Well?" His voice rumbled under her ear. "No comment?"

Reluctant to move, she finally tipped her head back to send him a vaguely confused glance. "About what?"

His hooded eyes looked down at her. "Did you worry for nothing?"

A sudden smile touched the corners of her mouth as Rachel realized what he was talking about. She had long ago abandoned the conern that her expectations were too high. Her head came down again.

"You know I enjoyed it," she murmured, being deliberately casual.

"Enjoyed it?" Gard taunted her mockingly. "You only *enjoyed* it? I must be losing my touch."

Her laughter was a soft sound. "Was I supposed to say I was devastated?"

"Something like that," he agreed, this time with the humor obvious in his voice, teasing her.

There was a small lull during which Gard took a last drag on his cigarette and ground out the butt in the ashtray on the stand by the bed. In that short interim Rachel's thoughts had taken her down a serious and thoughtful path.

"You know that I loved Mac," she mused aloud, sharing her thoughts with Gard. "A part of me always will. There were times, just recently, when I wondered if I would ever care so strongly for a man again. I never guessed I would love anyone like this—so totally, so—" She broke off the sentence, not finding the words to adequately express how very much she loved him.

"Don't stop," Gard chided. "Tell me more."

"You're already too conceited," Rachel accused.

"You think so?" He shifted his position, turning onto his side and taking away his shoulder as her pillow. His hand caressed her jaw and cheek as he faced her. "If I am, it's because you've made me so damned happy."

Leaning to her, he kissed her with long, drugging force. When it was over, it just added to the overall glow she felt. Her gray eyes were as soft as velvet as she gazed at him, happy and warm inside.

"Do you realize they're serving dinner, and neither one of us has had anything to eat all day?" she reminded him reluctantly, loathe to leave the bed.

"Yes," Gard said on a heavy sigh, then smiled crookedly. "But I can't say that I like the idea of sitting across the table from nosy Helen and her husband." Rachel made a little face of agreement. "I'd rather keep you all to myself. Why don't we have dinner in the cabin?"

"I'd much prefer that," she agreed huskily.

"As a matter of fact," he went further with the thought, "I can't think of any reason to leave this cabin for the next two days, until the ship puts in at Acapulco."

"I can think of one," Rachel smiled. "All my things are in my cabin. I won't have anything to wear."

"I know," he murmured with a complacently amused gleam in his eye. "It would be terrible if you had to lounge around the cabin stark naked for two days."

The thought brought a little shiver of wicked excitement. "I'm sure you'd hate that," she retorted with a playfully accusing look.

"Like a poor man hates money," Gard mocked. "But—since I don't like to share my toothbrush, I'll let you fetch some of your things tomorrow."

"Thank you," Rachel murmured with false docility.

"In the meantime"—he flipped the sheet aside

and swung out of the bed—"I'll see if I can't get the steward to rustle us up something to eat."

Rachel lay in bed a minute longer, watching him pull on his pants before walking out to the sitting room to phone. With a reluctant sigh she climbed out of bed and made use of his bathroom to wash and freshen up.

When she returned to the bedroom, instead of putting on her grape-colored shift, Rachel picked up his shirt. Its long tails reached nearly to her knees and the shoulder seams fell three inches below the point of her shoulders. The smell of him clung to the material and she hugged it tightly around her, then began to roll up the long sleeves.

There were sounds of his moving about in the sitting room. Rachel walked to the door and posed provocatively in its frame. Gard was standing in the far corner of the room by the drink cabinet.

"How do you like my robe?" she asked, drawing the rake of his glance.

"Nice." But the look in his eyes was more eloquent with approval. "I told you that you didn't need clothes."

She laughed softly and came gliding silently across the room in her bare feet to watch while he finished mixing them fresh drinks. In truth, she couldn't remember the last time she'd been so happy—or even when she'd ever been this happy. She gazed at him, so sure of her love. If she ever lost him, she thought she'd die. The possibility suddenly brought a run of stark terror to her eyes.

"Dinner is on its way, so I thought we'd have

those drinks we never got around to having." He capped the bottle of tonic water and turned to hand Rachel her glass. An alertness flared in his eyes at her stricken expression. "What's the matter?"

"Nothing. I—" She started to shake her head in a vague denial, but the fear that gripped her wouldn't go away. She looked back at him. "I just have this feeling that . . . I'd better grab at all the happiness I can today. Tomorrow it might not be here."

A searing gentleness came into his features. He put an arm around her and brought her close against him, as if reassuring her of the hard vitality of his body. His head was bent close to her downcast face.

"Rachel, I'm not your . . . I'm not Mac." He corrected himself in mid-sentence, making it seem significant that he hadn't said "your husband" as he had been about to say. "Nothing's going to happen."

"I know." She stared at the scattering of silken-fine hairs on his chest, but the tightness in her throat didn't ease.

He tucked a finger under her chin and forced it up. "Do you always worry so much?" he teased to lighten her mood.

"No."

When he kissed her, she almost forgot that odd feeling, but it stayed in the back of her mind throughout the evening. It lent an urgency to her lovemaking when they went to bed that night. While Gard slept, she lay awake for a long time with the heat of his body warming her skin. In the darkness the feeling came back. It seemed like a premonition of some unknown trouble to come. Try as she might, Rachel couldn't shake it off.

Stirring, Rachel struggled against the drugged feeling and forced her sleep-heavy eyes to open. A shaft of sunlight was coming through the drawn curtains and laying a narrow beam on the paneled wall. There was an instant of unfamiliarity with her surroundings until she remembered that she was in Gard's cabin. Her head turned on the pillow, but the bed was empty. Unreasoning alarm shot through her, driving out the heavy thickness of unrestful sleep.

She bolted from the bed, dragging the sheet with her and wrapping it around her nude body, her hand clutching it together above a breast. She rushed to the sitting room door and pulled it open. Before she'd taken a full step inside, she halted at the sight of Hank Scarborough standing next to Gard.

Both men had turned to look when the door had been yanked open. Hank had been twirling his hat on the end of his finger, but he stopped when he saw Rachel in the door with the sheet swaddled around her. Self-consciously she lifted a hand to push at the sleep-tangle of her hair, knowing that Hank had a crystal-clear picture of the situation. Rachel hitched the sheet a little higher.

"Good morning." She broke the silence.

"Being an officer and a gentleman, I should keep my mouth shut," Hank declared with a wry shake of his head. "But if I were Gard, I'd be thinking it's a helluva good morning. And I hope I haven't embarrassed you by saying so."

"You haven't." In fact, his frankness had relaxed her. "I shouldn't have come barging in like this, but I didn't know anyone was here."

"Did you want something?" Gard asked, then slid a quick aside to his friend. "And you're right about the kind of morning it is."

"No, I—" She couldn't comfortably admit that she'd been worried that something had happened when she hadn't found Gard in bed with her—not with Hank standing there. "I just wondered what time it is."

"It's nearly ten o'clock," Gard told her.

"That late?" Her eyes widened.

"You were sleeping so soundly, I didn't have the heart to wake you," he said. "I'll order some coffee and juice."

"All right," Rachel agreed, still slightly stunned that she had slept so late. Her glance darted to Hank. "Excuse me. I think I'd better get cleaned up."

"You've missed breakfast, but we're lying off the Las Hardas Hotel," Hank informed her. "You'll be able to get breakfast at the hotel."

"Thank you." She cast him a quick smile, then moved out of the doorway and closed the door.

Her clothes were draped across a chair in the room. After she had untangled herself from the length of the sheet, Rachel hurriedly dressed. For the time being she had to be satisfied with combing her hair, because all her makeup was in her own cabin, but at least she looked presentable.

Hank had left when she returned to the sitting room. Within seconds she found herself in Gard's arms, receiving the good morning kiss he hadn't given her earlier. His stroking hands rubbed over her body when he finally drew his mouth from her clinging lips. The premonition that had troubled her so much the night before was gone, chased away by the deep glow from his searing kiss.

"You shouldn't have let me sleep so late," Rachel murmured while her fingers busied themselves in a womanly gesture of straightening the collar of his shirt.

"If Hank hadn't shown up, I planned on doing just that," Gard replied. "Although I probably would have crawled back in bed with you to do it."

"Now you tell me." She laughed and eased out of his arms. "When is the coffee coming?"

"Anytime. Why?"

"I thought I'd run down to my cabin and pick up a few things—like my toothbrush," Rachel explained, already moving toward the door.

"Don't take too long," Gard warned. "Or I'll send out a search party to find you."

Rachel had no intention of making a project of it, but even hurrying and packing only the few items she absolutely needed, plus a change of clothes, took her more than a quarter of an hour. When she returned to Gard's cabin, she had to knock twice before he came to the door.

A puzzled frown drew her eyebrows together as he opened it and immediately walked away. She had a brief glimpse of his cold and preoccupied expression.

"How come you took so long to come to the door?" she asked curiously as she quickly followed him into the room. "Is something wrong?"

"I'm on the phone to California." There was a harshness in his voice that chilled her.

Her steps slowed as she watched him walk to the phone and pick up the receiver he'd left lying on the table. A tray with cups and juice was sitting on the long coffee table in front of the sofa. Rachel changed her direction and walked over to it, sitting down so she could observe Gard.

There was very little she could piece together from his side of the conversation, but it was his body language she studied. His head was bent low in an attitude of intense interest. He kept rubbing his forehead and raking his fingers through his hair as if he didn't like what he was hearing. There was a tautness in every line.

That odd feeling began to come back, growing stronger. She poured coffee from the tall pot into a cup and sipped at it. It seemed tasteless. She folded both hands around the cup, as if needing to absorb its warmth to ward off some chill.

The phone was hung up, but his hand stayed on the receiver, gripping it tightly until his knuckles showed white. He seemed to have forgotten she was in the room.

"What is it, Gard?" Rachel asked quietly.

He stirred, seeming to rouse himself out of the dark reverie of his thoughts, and threw her a cold glance. "An emergency." He clipped out the answer and pulled his hand from the phone to comb it through his hair again.

"Is it serious?" she asked when he didn't volunteer more.

"Yes." Again his response was grudgingly given, but this time there was more forthcoming. "Bud—one of the partners in my law firm—was killed in a car accident on the freeway last night."

Even as he spoke the words, Rachel could see that he was trying to reject the truth of them. Quickly she crossed the room and gathered him into her arms. She understood that combination of shock and pain and hurt anger. His arms circled her in a crushing vise as he buried his face in the blackness of her hair.

"Damnit, he had three kids and a wife," he muttered hoarsely.

For long minutes she simply held on to him, knowing that there was no more comfort than that to give. Finally she felt the hard shudder that went through his body, and the accompanying struggle for control as he pulled his arms from around her and gripped her shoulders.

"Look . . ." His gaze remained downcast as he searched to pull his thoughts together. "I'm going to have to see if I can't catch a flight out of Manzanillo back to Los Angeles. Would you mind throwing my things into the suitcases?"

"I'll do it." She nodded with an outward show of calm, but inside there was a clawing panic. Last night she had worried about losing him. Today he was leaving her. They wouldn't have those two more days on the ship as he had talked about. It couldn't be over—not so quickly—not like this.

"Thanks." Gard flashed her a relieved glance and turned to pick up the phone.

Rachel bit at the inside of her lip, then boldly suggested, "Would you like me to fly back with you?"

"No." As if realizing that his rejection was slightly abrupt, Gard softened it with an explanation. "There's nothing you can do, but I appreciate the offer. It's going to be chaotic for a few days, both personally and professionally." He dialed a number and waited while it rang. "Did you say you were staying in Acapulco for a few days?"

"I was, but—I think I'll fly straight back on Saturday." She didn't look forward to those idle days in the Mexican resort city now that she knew Gard would be in Los Angeles.

"Write down your address and phone number so I can call you later next week," he said, then turned away as the party answered the phone on the other end.

While he was busy making inquiries about airline schedules and reservations, Rachel took a pen and notepad from a desk drawer and printed out her name, address, and the telephone numbers at both her home and the office. She slipped it onto the table in front of Gard. He glanced at it and nodded an acknowledgment to her, continuing his conversation without a break.

A feeling of helplessness welled inside her, but there were still his suitcases to be packed. She went into the bedroom they had shared for only one night and took his suitcases from the closet and began to fill them with his clothes.

Half an hour later she was shutting and locking the last suitcase when Gard walked into the bedroom. The troubled, preoccupied expression on his features was briefly replaced with a glance of surprise at the packed suitcases on the bed.

"Are they ready to go?" he asked.

"Everything's all packed," she assured him.

"The steward's on his way." He looked at his watch. "There's an opening on a flight leaving Manzanillo in an hour and a half. If I'm lucky, I'll be able to make it and my connecting flight to Los Angeles."

As she noticed the slip of paper in his hand with her address and phone numbers marked on it, Gard folded it and slipped it into his shirt pocket. There was a knock, followed by the steward entering the cabin.

There were no more moments of privacy left to them as Gard called the steward in to take the luggage. Then they were all trooping out of the cabin and down to the lower deck to take the tender ashore.

As the collection of white block buildings tumbling down the steep sides of the mountain to the bay came closer, Rachel was conscious of the sparkling white beauty of the place, contrasted with the dark red tile roofs. Flowering bushes spilled over the sides of white balconies in scarlet profusion. But she couldn't bring herself to appreciate its aesthetic beauty. She was too conscious of Gard's thigh pressed along hers as they rode on the tender to the yacht harbor.

There was no conversation between them when

they reached shore. Rachel offered to help carry one of his suitcases, but Gard refused and signaled to a hotel employee when they reached the large, landscaped pool area with its bars and dining terraces.

At the hotel lobby Gard finally stopped his hurried pace and turned to her. "I'll catch a cab to the airport from here. There's no need for you to make that ride."

"I don't mind," she insisted, because it was just that many more minutes to spend with him.

"But I do. We'll say good-bye here so I won't have to think about you making the ride back from the airport alone," he stated.

"Okay." She lowered her gaze and tried to keep her composure under control.

"I've got your address and phone number, don't I?" There was an uncertain frown on his forehead as he began to feel in his pockets.

"It's in your shirt pocket," she assured him.

"It'll probably be the middle of the week before things settle back to normal . . . if they ever will." It was an almost cynically bitter phrase he threw on at the last, showing how deeply this loss was cutting into his life.

"I understand," she murmured, but she wanted to be with him.

"Rachel." His hand moved roughly into her hair, cupping her head and holding it while he crushed her lips under her mouth. She slid her hands around his middle, spreading them across his back and pressing herself against the hard outline of his thighs and hips. The ache inside was a raw and painful thing, an emotional tearing that ripped at her heart.

The tears were very close when Gard dragged his mouth from hers. Rachel rested her head against his shoulder and blinked to keep them at bay. She didn't want to cry in front of him. She had never considered herself to be a weak and clinging female, but she didn't want to let him go.

It didn't seem to matter how much she tried to rationalize away this vague fear. Gard wasn't leaving her because it was what he wanted to do. There was an emergency. He had to go. Shutting her eyes for a moment, she felt the light pressure of his mouth moving over her hair.

"This is a helluva way to end our cruise," Gard sighed heavily and lifted his head, taking her by the shoulders and setting her a few inches away from him. For a moment she was the focus of his thoughts, and she could see the darkness of regret in his eyes. "We were running out of time and didn't know it."

"There will be other times," Rachel said because she needed a reassurance of that from him. There was a pooling darkness to her gray eyes, but she managed to keep back the tears and show him a calmly composed expression.

"Yes." The reassurance was absently made as Gard glanced over his shoulder to see the bellman loading his luggage into a taxi. "I'm sorry, Rachel. I have to catch that plane."

"I know." She walked with him out to the taxi, parked under the hotel's covered entrance.

There was one very brief, last kiss, a hard pressure making a fleeting impact on her lips, then Gard was striding to the open door of the taxi, passing a tip to the bellman before folding his long frame into the rear seat of the taxi.

"I'll call you," he said with a hurried wave of his hand as he shut the door.

The promise was too indefinite. She wanted to demand something more precise, a fixed time and place when he would call. Instead Rachel nodded and called, "Have a good flight!"

As the cab pulled away Gard leaned forward to say something to the driver. Rachel watched the taxi until it disappeared. If Gard looked back, she didn't see him. She had the feeling that he'd already forgotten her, his thoughts overtaken by the problems and sorrows awaiting him when he reached Los Angeles.

She turned slowly, walked back through the lobby, and descended to a dining terrace on the lower level. Out in the bay the *Pacific Princess* sat at anchor, sleek and impressive in size even at this distance. With the reflection of sun and water, the ship gleamed blue-white.

For the last six days that ship had been home to her. Its world seemed more real to her than the one in Los Angeles. The emptiness swelled within her because she was here in this world and Gard was flying to the other. But he'd call her.

Aboard ship again, Rachel was surprised to discover how many passengers knew her until she had to begin to field their inquiries about Gard. Their comments and questions varied, some expressing genuine concern and some merely being nosy.

"Where's your husband? We haven't seen him this evening," was the most common in the beginning. Then it became, "We heard there was a family emergency and your husband had to fly home. We hope it isn't serious." Only rarely was Rachel queried about her continued presence on the ship. "How come you didn't leave with him? Couldn't you get a seat on the flight?"

But there was an end to them the next day when the ship reached its destination port of Acapulco and Rachel was able to change her reservations and fly home sooner than she had originally planned.

# Chapter Ten

The buzz of the intercom phone on her desk snapped Rachel sharply out of her absent reverie. She was supposed to be reading through the stack of letters in front of her and affixing her signature to them, but the pile had only been depleted by three. Instead of reading the rest, she had been staring off into space.

Nothing seemed to receive her undivided attention anymore except the ring of the telephone. Each time it rang, at home or at the office, her heart would give a little leap, and every time she answered it, she thought this time it would be Gard.

For the last two weeks she'd lived on that hope and little else. She couldn't eat; she couldn't sleep; she was a basket case of emotions, ready to cry at the drop of a hat. Rachel was beginning to realize that this state of affairs couldn't continue. She had to resolve the matter once and for all and stop living on the edge of her nerves.

There was another impatient buzz of the intercom. No light was blinking to indicate that a phone call was being held on the line for her. Rachel picked up the receiver.

"Yes, Sally, what is it?" she asked her secretary with grudging patience.

"Fan Kemper is here to see you," came the answer. "She says she's taking you to lunch."

After a second's hesitation Rachel simply replied, "Send her in."

Before she had returned the receiver to its cradle, the door to her private office was opened and Fan came sweeping in, exuding energy and bright efficiency. A smile beamed from her friend's face, but there was a critical look in her assessing glance.

"Sorry, Fan, but I can't have lunch with you today," Rachel said and began to write her signature on the letters she should have already signed.

"I know I'm not down on your appointment book, but I thought I'd steal you away from the office." Fan crossed to the desk, undeterred by the refusal. "I've only seen you once since you came back from the cruise—and every time I phone you, we never talk more than five minutes because you're expecting some 'important call.'"

"I had a lot of catching up to do when I came back." It was a vague explanation, accompanied by an equally vague smile in her friend's direction.

"You look awful," Fan announced.

"Thanks." Rachel laughed without amusement.

"You're lucky you got some sun on that cruise.

Without the tan those circles under your eyes would really be noticeable." Fan pulled a side chair closer to the desk and sat in it, leaning forward in an attitude that invited confidence. "You might as well tell me, Rachel. Hasn't he called?"

The "he" was Gard, of course. When she had returned from vacation and seen the Kempers, Rachel had mentioned him. Fan, being Fan, had read through the lines and knew instinctively that the relationship hadn't been as casual as Rachel had tried to imply.

"No, he hasn't called," she admitted, grimly concealing the hurt.

"It's possible he lost your number," Fan reasoned. "And unless he knows your company is called the Country House, he won't be able to find you, since your home number is unlisted."

"I know."

During the last two weeks she'd had countless arguments with herself. She'd come up with all sorts of reasons to explain why Gard hadn't called her as he'd promised, but she could never forget the possibility that he wasn't interested in seeing her again.

True, he'd said a lot of things to lead her to believe otherwise. But men often said things in the heat of passion that meant nothing on reexamination. Pride insisted it had just been a holiday affair, intense while it lasted, but best forgotten by her.

"Rachel, how long are you going to eat your heart out over him before you do something about it?" Fan wanted to know.

"About twenty more minutes," Rachel replied calmly with a glance at her watch.

"What?" Fan sat up straight and blinked at her.

There was a dry curve to Rachel's mouth as she met her friend's puzzled gaze. "That's why I can't go to lunch with you. I'm going to his office this afternoon." She had looked up his name in the telephone directory so many times that she knew his address and phone number by heart. "I have to know where I stand once and for all."

Fan leaned back in her chair and released a sighing breath of satisfaction. "I'm so glad to hear you say that. Would you like me to come with you and lend a little moral support?"

"No. I have to do this on my own," Rachel stated.

"Have you called?" Fan wondered. "Did you make an appointment to see him?"

"No. I thought about it," she admitted. "But if he doesn't want to see me anymore, I didn't want to be pawned off by his secretary or have some impersonal conversation with him on the phone. When I talk to him, I want to be able to see his face." She slashed her name across the last letter. "So I'm just going over to his office and take the chance that he'll be in."

"If he isn't?" Fan studied her with gentle sympathy.

"I don't know." Rachel sighed heavily. "Then I guess it's back to square one."

"John knows him—or at least they've met before," Fan reminded her. "I could always have him come up with some excuse to call him and mention in passing that you are one of John's clients—use the name coincidence that started this whole thing. At least John could find out what his reaction is."

"Thanks." She appreciated her friend's offer to help, but she didn't feel it was right to have them solve her problems. "I'd rather do this without involving you and John."

"If you change your mind, just tell me," Fan insisted, standing up to leave. "And you'd better call me later, because I'll be the one sitting by the phone on pins and needles."

"I will," Rachel promised with a more natural smile curving her mouth and watched her friend leave, spending an idle minute reminding herself how lucky she was to have a friend like Fan Kemper.

At half past one that afternoon Rachel stood outside the entrance to the suite of offices in the posh Wilshire Boulevard address and had cause to wish for the moral support Fan had offered. Her knees felt shaky and her stomach was emptily churning.

The elaborately carved set of double doors presented a formidable barrier to be breached. On the wall beside them there was a rich-looking plaque with brass letters spelling out MACKINLEY, BROWN & THOMPSON, ATTORNEYS-AT-LAW.

A cowardly part of her wanted to turn and walk away, so she could believe a little longer in the variety of excuses she had made to herself on Gard's behalf. Squaring her shoulders, Rachel breathed a deep, steadying breath and reached for a tall brass doorgrip. The door swung silently open under the pull of her hand and she stepped onto the plush pile carpeting of the reception area.

The young girl at the switchboard looked up when she entered and smiled politely. "May I help you?"

"I'd like to see Mr. MacKinley—Mr. Gardner MacKinley," Rachel clarified her answer in case there was more than one MacKinley in the firm.

"Is he expecting you?" the girl inquired.

"No, he isn't, but I need to see him." Which was the truth.

As she punched a set of interoffice numbers, she asked, "What name shall I give him?"

Rachel hesitated, then replied, using her maiden name, "Miss Hendrix." She'd rather he didn't know who she was until he saw her.

She listened while the girl relayed the information. "Yes, Mr. MacKinley, this is Cindy at the reception desk. There's a Miss Hendrix here to see you. She doesn't have an appointment but she says she needs to speak with you." Rachel held her breath during the pause. "I'll tell her. Thank you." The girl pushed another button to end the connection and looked at Rachel with another polite smile. "He's tied up at the moment, but he expects to be free shortly. If you'd care to have a seat, you're welcome to wait."

"Thank you." It was one more hurdle cleared, but the tension increased as Rachel walked over to sit in one of the leather-covered armchairs against a paneled wall.

Three wide hallways led in separate directions from the reception area. Rachel had no idea which one led to Gard's office. Her chair was positioned beside the opening to one of them and provided her a view of the other two. Her heart was thumping in her chest, louder than the clock ticking on the wall. She watched the clicking rotation of the second hand, then realized that would not make the time pass more quickly. She picked up a magazine lying on a walnut table and nervously began to flip through it.

The cords in her neck were knotted with tension and her nerves were stretched raw. Tremors of apprehension were attacking her insides, adding to the overall strain. From the hallway behind her she caught the sound of a woman's low voice, indifferent to the words until a man's voice responded and the man was Gard. Recognition of his voice splintered through her, nearly driving her out of the chair so she could face the sound of his approaching voice.

Through sheer self-control Rachel forced herself to remain seated. The instant he appeared in her side vision, her gaze slid to his familiar form. His mahogany dark hair and muscularly tapered build were exactly the same as she remembered.

She hardly paid any attention at all to the woman he was walking to the door with until she noticed that Gard had his arm around her. Rachel took another look at the woman, feeling her heart being squeezed by jealous pain, and saw how young and wholesomely attractive she was with her gleaming chestnut hair and adoring brown eyes.

Gard's back was to her when he stopped by the door, giving Rachel a clearer view of the woman who had his hand on her waist. In her numbed state it took her a minute to realize the pair were talking. She wanted to cry out when she heard what Gard was saying.

"I'll come over to your place for dinner tonight, then afterward I'm taking you to the Schubert Theater. I pulled some strings and got tickets for tonight's performance. I know you've been wanting to see the play."

"I have," the woman admitted, then bit at her lip and frowned. "What do you think I should wear?"

Gard had taken hold of the woman's hand and was now raising it to his mouth, pressing a warm kiss on the top of it while he eyed her. "A smile," he suggested.

"And nothing else, I suppose." The woman laughed. "Advice like that could get a girl in trouble." She leaned up and kissed him lightly. "I'll see you tonight."

"I'll come early, so pour me a scotch about six o'clock." He pushed open the door and held it for her while she walked through.

Pain was shattering Rachel's heart into a thousand pieces, immobolizing her. Raw anguish clouded her gray eyes, which couldn't tear their gaze from him. When Gard turned away from the door, his idle glance encountered that look.

His dark eyes narrowed in frowning astonishment before a smile began to spread across his features.

"Rachel." There was rough warmth in the way he said her name, then he took a step toward her.

It was too much to see that light darkening his eyes when not a moment before he had been flirting with another woman. Rage followed hot on the heels of her pain. She had wanted to know where she stood with him and now she knew—in line!

Rachel pushed out of the chair and aimed for the door, intent on only one thing—leaving before she made a complete fool of herself. But Gard moved quickly into her path and caught hold of her shoulders.

"What are you doing here?" He held on when she tried to twist out of his grasp, pushing at his arms with her hands.

"I came to find out why you hadn't called," she admitted with bitter anger that slid into sarcasm. "I saw the reason."

"What are you talking about?" he demanded, giving her a hard shake when she continued to struggle.

A glaze of tears was stinging her eyes. She glared through it at the angry and impatient expression chiseled on his features.

"I don't care to take up any more of your valuable time," she flashed bitterly. "I'm sure you have a lot to do before you can keep your dinner engagement tonight."

As understanding dawned in his eyes; they darkened with exasperation. "It isn't what you're thinking. Brenda is Bud's wife, the partner I just lost. She's lonely and needs company."

"Especially at night," Rachel suggested, untouched by his explanation. "Consoling widows must be your specialty."

She nearly succeeded in wrenching free of his hands, but he caught her again and turned her around, half pushing and half carrying her along with him as he headed for the hallway by her chair. The receptionist was watching them with wide-eyed wonder, a silent and curious observer of the virulent scene being played out before her.

"You are going to listen to my explanation whether you like it or not," Gard informed her in an angrily low voice as he marched her past a secretarial pool and a short row of offices.

"Well, I don't like it, and I'm not interested in hearing anything you have to say!" she hissed, conscious of the curious looks they were receiving. She stopped resisting him rather than draw more attention.

"That's too bad," he growled and pushed her into a large, executive-styled office with windows on two sides and a healthy collection of potted plants. "Because you're going to hear it anyway." The door was shut with a resounding click of the latch.

The minute he let go of her, Rachel moved to the center of the room and stopped short of the long oak desk. She was hurting inside and it showed in the wary gray of her eyes. When he came toward her, she stiffened noticeably. His mouth thinned into a grim line and he continued by her to the desk. He picked up the phone and pushed a button.

"Tell Carol to come in and give me a report on her progress so far," Gard instructed and hung up.

Turning, he leaned against the desk and rested a

hip on the edge of it. His level gaze continued to bore into Rachel as he folded his arms and waited silently. Long seconds later there was a light rap on the door.

"Come in." He lifted his voice, granting permission to enter.

A young brunette, obviously Carol, walked in with a pen and notepad in her hand. Her glance darted to Rachel, then swung apprehensively to her employer.

"I'm sorry, but I still haven't been able to locate her," she began her report with an apology. "A couple of people have recognized the name as someone in the business, but they couldn't refer me to anyone. I'm almost through the L's in the Yellow Pages. I never realized there were so many furniture stores in the metropolitan area of Los Angeles."

It was Rachel's turn to stare at Gard, searching his face to make sure she was placing the right meaning on all this. A look of hard satisfaction mixed with the anger smoldering in his eyes.

"Thank you, Carol," he said to the young girl. "You don't have to make any more calls."

"Sir?" She looked worried that he was taking the task from her because she hadn't made any progress.

"Since you've spent so much time on this, I thought you should meet Rachel MacKinley." Gard gestured to indicate Rachel.

"You found her!" Her sudden smile of surprise was also partly relief.

"Yes." He let the girl's assumption stand for the time being while his gaze remained on Rachel. "By the way, Rachel, would you mind telling Carol the name of your furniture company?"

It was suddenly very difficult to speak. Her throat was all tight with emotion. It was obvious that Gard had been looking for her, but she still had some doubts about what that meant.

"The Country House." She supplied the name in a voice that was taut and husky.

"The T's." The girl shook her head in faint amazement.

"Thank you, Carol. That will be all." Gard dismissed the girl. There was another long silence while she exited the private office. "Now do you believe that I've been trying to locate you?" he challenged when they were alone again.

"Yes." It seemed best to keep her answer simple and not jump to any more conclusions.

"I jotted my flight schedules on the back of the slip of paper you gave me with your address and phone numbers on it. It was late when I arrived back in L.A. I didn't pay close attention to what was in my shirt pockets when I emptied them. All I saw were the flight schedules on the paper. I didn't need them anymore, so I threw the paper away. It wasn't until a couple of days later when I was looking for your phone number that I realized what had happened. By then my cleaning lady had already been in and emptied the wastebaskets."

The explanation was delivered in a calm, relatively flat voice. It was a statement of fact that told Rachel nothing about his feelings toward her. Nothing in his look or his attitude offered encouragement.

"I see," she murmured and lowered her gaze to the beige carpet, searching its thick threads as if they held a clue.

"Information informed me that you had a private, unlisted number, so that only left me with the fact that you owned a furniture company," Gard stated. "I pulled one of the junior typists out of the pool and had her start to phone all the stores listed under the furniture section of the Yellow Pages and ask for you."

"I thought it was possible that you had somehow lost my number," Rachel admitted slowly. "That's why I came by today."

"But you also thought it was possible that I didn't *intend* to call you," he accused.

There was a defiant lift of her chin as she met his unwavering gaze. "It was possible."

His chest expanded on a deep, almost angry breath that was heavily released. Gard looked away from her for an instant, then slid his glance back.

"I won't ask why you thought it was possible. I'm liable to lose my temper and break that pretty neck of yours," he muttered, his jaw tightly clenched. "Is it fair to say that you understand why I haven't called you before now?"

"Yes." Rachel nodded.

"Good." Unfolding his arms, he straightened from the desk. "Now, let's see if we can't clear up this matter about Brenda."

"I'd rather just forget it," she insisted, her breath running deep and agitated. "It's none of my business."

"To a point, you're absolutely right. And if you

hadn't insulted Brenda by the implication of your accusations against me, I wouldn't explain a damned thing to you," he informed her roughly. "She buried her husband last week. She puts up a good front, but she's hurting and lonely. Damnit, you should know the feeling! There are times when it helps her to have people around her who were close to Bud. He was my friend as well as my law partner."

"I'm sorry." Rachel felt bad about the thoughts she'd had when she'd seen Gard with that attractive woman—and the things she'd said, out of hurt, when he had explained who the woman was. "I jumped to the wrong conclusion."

"You couldn't have jumped to that conclusion if you hadn't already decided that I didn't care about seeing you again," he countered.

"I hadn't decided that," she denied.

"I'd forgotten," Gard eyed her lazily. "You were prepared to give me the benefit of reasonable doubt. That's why you came to see me, isn't it?"

"Something like that, yes!" Rachel snapped, not liking the feeling of being on the witness stand. "You could have lost my number and I had to know!"

"Yet you were also willing to believe that I had just been stringing you along during the cruise, and that I didn't have any feelings toward you."

"It was possible," she insisted. "How could I be sure what kind of man you are? I haven't known you that long."

"How long do you have to know someone before you can love them?" Gard demanded, coming over to stand in front of her. "Two weeks? Two months? Two years? I recall distinctly that you said you loved me. Didn't you mean it?"

"Yes." Reluctantly she pushed the angry word out.

"Then why is it so hard for you to accept that I love you?" he challenged.

She flashed him a resentful look. "Because you never said you did."

He stared at her for a long minute. "I must have said it at least a thousand times—every time I looked at you and touched you and held you." The insistence of his voice became intimately low.

"You never said it," Rachel repeated with considerably less force. "Not in so many words."

His eyes lightened with warm bemusement as a smile curved his lips. "Rachel, I love you," he said as if repeating it by rote. "There you have it 'in so many words.'"

It hurt almost as much for him to say the words without any feeling. She started to turn away. A low chuckle came from his throat as his arms went around her and gathered her into their tightening circle. She started to elude his mouth but it closed on her lips too quickly.

The persuasive ardor of his warm, possessive kiss melted away her stiffness. Her hands went around his neck as she let the urgency of loving him sweep through her. With wildly sweet certainty Rachel knew she had come home. She lived in the love he gave her, which completed her as a person the same way her love completed him.

"You crazy little fool," he muttered near her ear

while he kept her crushed in his arms. "I was half in love with you from the beginning. It didn't take much of a push to make me fall the rest of the way."

"You knew even then?" She pulled back a little to see his face because she found it incredible that he could have been so sure of his feelings almost from the start.

"Admit it," he chided her. "We were attracted to each other from the beginning. You saw me when I arrived, just the same way I noticed you sitting there outside the terminal."

"That's true," Rachel conceded.

"When you came strolling into what I thought was my cabin and claimed to be Mrs. Gardner MacKinley, I thought it was some practical joke of Hank's and he'd put you up to the charade. Despite your convincing talk about the reissued ticket, I still didn't believe you until you became so indignant at the thought of sharing the cabin with me. I could tell that wasn't an act."

"And I couldn't understand how you could take it all so lightly," she remembered.

"That's just about the time I started to tumble," Gard informed her, brushing his mouth over her cheek and temple as if he didn't want to break contact with her even to talk. "I was intrigued by the idea of sharing a cabin with you and fascinated by the thought that you were Mrs. Gardner MacKinley. I didn't even want to correct people when they mistook you for my wife."

"Neither did I," she admitted, laughing at the discovery that he'd felt the same.

"Remember the cocktail party?" He nibbled at

185

the edge of her lip while his hands tested the feel of her body arched to his length.

"Yes," she murmured.

"When I introduced you as Mrs. MacKinley, that's when I knew for certain that was who I wanted you to be—my wife. She was no longer some faceless woman I hadn't met. She was you—standing in the same room with me—and already possessing my name." He lifted his head about an inch above her lips. "Are you convinced now that I love you?"

"Yes." She was filled with the knowledge, its golden light spreading through every inch of her body.

"Then let's make it legal before something else separates us," he urged.

"I couldn't agree more."

"It's about time," he muttered and covered her mouth with a long kiss, not giving her a chance to worry about anything but loving him.

# THE
# SECOND
# TIME

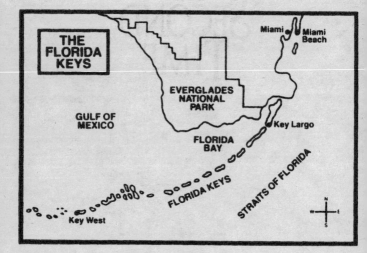

# Chapter One

In the yellowing light of a May morning, it was already hot and the temperature would climb toward the hundred mark in the Florida Keys before the day was over, led by the rising sun. The quiet was broken by the droning whine of a boat's engine as it skimmed over the calm waters. The noise disturbed a pelican from its roost in the mangroves. Its lumbering bulk took wing as the skiff and its two occupants came into view.

There wasn't any breeze, but the speeding craft whipped up a wind that tore the smoke from the cigarette protectively cupped in Slater Mac-Bride's hand almost before he could taste it. Dark sunglasses were curved to his face to reduce the long glare of the angling sunlight reflecting off the water. They concealed his gray eyes, the dark color of gun metal that sometimes silvered with humor, and sometimes smoked with anger. Now they were sweeping the narrow, ever-shifting channels of the Keys' back country with calm but lively interest.

Facing into the wind, his profile was delineated by bold, sure strokes from the slant of his forehead to the straight bridge of his nose and the slight jut of his chin. A lifetime spent under a subtropical sun had tanned his skin the shade of polished teakwood and etched creases at the corners of his eyes. In contrast, the sun had lightened his brown hair, streaking its darkness with paler strands, and giving it the light and dark, woodgrained look. The wind's tearing fingers had raked the hair away from his forehead and aggravated the small cowlick in the front that always gave an unruly touch to the shaggy thickness of his hair, yet not unattractively so.

The skiff sped past another island, one of the maze of coral and oolite formed islands that comprised the Florida Keys. Its shoreline was a tangle of mangrove roots, as if the trees themselves were stretching on tiptoes to avoid the sea water. At this speed, there was only a glimpse of the island and it was gone.

Ahead, Slater MacBride saw a trio of stately white herons wading along a shallow flat. Natives of these waters knew that where there were herons, it was too shallow for a boat. The weathered and decaying hull of a fishing boat that had run aground on the flat protruded from the water, telling a sad tale of someone who hadn't heeded the warning of the herons' presence.

Slater was aware of the meaning of the birds, but he didn't point them out to the man at the controls of the skiff. Jeeter Jones was an experienced guide, and an old family friend. He had made his living for nearly thirty years taking people sportfishing in these waters. Besides, any conversation was nearly impossible with the loud whine of the engine roaring in their ears.

Seconds later, the skiff veered slightly to the right and was aimed toward some unseen channel Jeeter Jones knew was there. The water was crystal clear, the ocean bottom plainly visible a few feet below and the depth lessening. The skiff's engine was pushed to full throttle, planing the boat to skim over the surface. Slater sat back enjoying the fast ride and the tangy sea spray on his face.

For over a hundred years, there had been a MacBride living in the Keys and working in various reputable and disreputable occupations. There had been salvage captains, not above encouraging a wreck or two, fishermen, and rum-runners, and even a relative in the cigar-making industry when it was a flourishing concern in the islands. Adaptability was almost an inbred trait. Locals said a MacBride could turn his hand and make a living at whatever enterprise was the most prosperous at the time—pity, he couldn't save any of it.

Once it had been said about Slater MacBride, too. But ten years ago, all that had changed. Now he was something of a local tycoon, owning prime business property in Key West, a couple of tourist resorts, and a small fleet of shrimp boats. A few of them knew about the girl he'd loved and lost when she chose a wealthy Texas millionaire over him. The scars and bitterness were on the inside; the hurt had gone too deep to ever be truly erased.

As the skiff neared the basin, the engine was

throttled back to almost idling speed. The air stopped its rush and became still, like the flat, slick surface of the water glistening in the sun and blending into the blue sky.

"This here's the place." Jeeter Jones cut the engine and picked up the fiberglass push pole to quietly enter the basin. Late May was the season when the tarpon were abundant and moving. It was the lure of this game fish that had drawn Slater away from his varied business interests, a rare break for him nowadays. "Think you still know how to catch one?" Tufts of graying hair poked out from beneath his sun-and-sea-softened captain's hat. Its texture was wiry as if permanently stiffened by years of salty air.

"You find me one and put me in casting distance, and we'll find out," Slater replied dryly to the challenge to his infrequently used skill.

"Old Pop Canady was down at the marina yesterday afternoon. Did I tell you?" Jeeter expertly poled the skiff into the basin, barely making any noise at all.

"No." Slater no longer stiffened at the mention of the name Canady, but there was an inner resistance, a tightening of nerves.

The guide sent a brief, skimming look at the thirty-five-year-old man he'd known since boyhood, so he was more aware than most of the startling contrast from the devil-may-care young man to the successful entrepreneur sitting in his boat. Most people thought Slater had gotten over what had happened eleven years ago, but Jeeter

10

wasn't so sure. He'd played poker with the man too many times to believe his hard, smooth features weren't hiding something.

If he was right, then Slater deserved to be told the news so he could be prepared for it. And if he was wrong, it would be like water rolling off a duck's back. It wouldn't matter.

"Yeah, Pop was all puffed up and bragging. It seems Dawn is coming home, so he'll be bringing his grandson around to show him to all his friends." Out of the corner of his eye, Jeeter caught the sharp glance Slater threw him, although nothing flickered on his deadpan expression.

"I imagine Pop would be happy about that." Slater managed a noncommittal response and contained any reaction to the disruptive announcement.

Inwardly he was damning the cruelty of his mind that wouldn't let him bury the past. If he closed his eyes, he knew he'd recall the sweet scent of gardenias, waxen white against flaming copper hair. Bitterness choked his throat. Dawn had loved him, but she had married money. At the time he'd had no future, and no prospect of any, and she had wanted more than love. He didn't blame her as much as he used to, but that didn't ease the bitterness her decision had created.

"You knew her husband died a month ago, didn't you?" Jeeter inquired in a casual voice.

"I heard." His gaze remained on the water as if

waiting for the first glimpse of a tarpon's wide oily back rolling out of the water, but he was seeing nothing. "She's coming back a very wealthy widow. Will she be arriving by yacht or a private jet?" A bitter sarcasm was threaded through his taut voice despite his attempt to keep it in check.

"Pop never said," Jeeter admitted, referring to Dawn's father. "I always got the feeling her husband didn't want her having anything to do with her parents, like they wasn't good enough for the likes of him, even if he did marry their daughter. He never did bring her back to visit after they got married."

For his sake, Slater had been glad Dawn had left and not come back. There was a time when he had been driven wild by jealousy at the thought of her lying in Simpson Lord's arms after she'd been in his. It still pained him to remember that last night together when they had made love till morning. He had been so certain that she couldn't love him and leave him after that.

Yet she had dressed and calmly slipped that huge diamond sparkler on her ring finger, reaffirming her intention to marry the wealthy Texan, even though she didn't love him. Until that moment, he had been prepared to believe that her young, eighteen-year-old head had been briefly turned by the gifts and attention Simpson Lord had lavished upon her. He had been angry and incredulous when he realized she intended to go through with the farcical marriage.

Her brash statement that morning continued to

haunt him. "I made up my mind a long time ago that I was going to marry a rich man," Dawn had said. "The second time, I'll marry for love."

No matter how many times he told himself after that, that he was well rid of her, it never stopped him from loving her and wanting her. Dawn—with the red-gold blaze of the sun in her hair and the turquoise blue of the sea in her eyes. She was the sun and the sea to him—the heights and the depths.

Now she was coming back—a rich widow. He clamped his jaws together, wondering if she was coming back to claim the love she had discarded. At that moment, he hated her viciously. Did she think he'd still want her after all this time? Did she think she could stir up old fires and make them flame hot again? A rage seethed through him.

"How long is she staying?" Slater put his terse question to the aging guide.

"Pop never indicated that, but I got the impression he didn't expect her to come for very long—a few days maybe," he said with a vague shrug. "Course, with her money, I expect there's more exciting places to go than Key West in the summer."

"Yeah," Slater muttered a disgruntled agreement and wondered why he didn't feel more relieved.

"Look!" The urgent command from Jeeter was accompanied by a pointing finger, indicating a ten o'clock angle from the bow. "See him?"

Slater had been looking, but not seeing. "No." Then straight ahead, his eye caught the swirl of water as the wide back of a tarpon broke the surface and rolled out of sight. "There's another."

"Looks like a whole school." Jeeter leaned on the push pole to ease the skiff toward the large rolling fish. "I told you this was the place."

"You did."

With his quarry in sight, Slater made another check of his equipment to make certain the leader was knotted tightly and the line was coiled neatly where it wouldn't tangle with his feet. He waited while Jeeter poled closer, trying to concentrate on the task at hand. The fly rod was in his hand, but the excitement of pitting his skill against such a large fish with such light equipment was gone. His pleasure in the morning had faded when the conversation had turned to Dawn.

When the skiff was near enough to make a cast, Slater went through all the right motions. The colored streamer settled onto the calm surface a few inches in front of the tarpon. When the big fish struck, Slater responded automatically, pulling back three quick times to set the hook.

There was a whine of line spinning out of the reel as the tarpon took off. Leaping and twisting out of the water, it shimmered silver against the blue sky. The huge fish was easily trophy size, but there was no sense of elation in Slater. Suddenly, the line went slack, the hook thrown.

"Lost him," Jeeter announced flatly.

"It's always the big ones that get away," Slater

murmured with a degree of bitter irony in his voice.

He was unwillingly made aware of the comparison between the lost tarpon and Dawn. In both instances, they had appeared to be well and truly caught only to spit out the hook before he could reel them in. And he was the one left with a bad taste in his mouth.

Her designer blue jeans rode easily on her hips, the denim material softened and faded from many wearings. The hint of looseness about their fit suggested a weight loss that her already slim figure didn't need. Her tan boots were custom-made from hand tooled leather and the topaz blouse she wore was made from imported silk.

Devoid of any jewelry, Dawn Lord nee Canady stood at the back screen door and stared through the wire mesh at her father so earnestly engaged in a conversation with her son—his grandson—on the rear stoop. He was trying so hard to make up for lost time—for the years when Randy had been growing up without the benefit of a grandfather's company. She felt a twinge of pain—for the guilt that wouldn't let her return to the Keys, and for the pride that had kept her parents from accepting money from her to pay their way to Texas.

As her gaze lingered on Randy, there was a troubled light in the deep blue of her eyes. At ten years old, Randy was tall for his age—tall with unruly dark hair that never would behave, and gray-blue eyes that were more often confused and uncertain than happy. At the moment, they were sparkling with eagerness as Randy finally prodded her father into action.

"Mom!" He glanced toward the screen door and saw her silhouette darkening the mesh. "Gramps and I are going for a walk."

"Okay." She acknowledged the information while her thumbs remained hooked in the belt loops of her jeans, not bothering to wave a farewell as grandfather and grandson wandered out of her view.

"Gramps." Her mother's voice came from behind her, repeating the term as if the sound of it gave her pleasure. "Your father will be busting his buttons if Randy calls him that in front of his friends. He's been showing them pictures of that boy since the day Randy was born. Now, he's finally got the real thing."

"Yes," Dawn murmured, swiveling slightly to glance at her mother when she came to the screen door to stand next to her.

"To tell you the truth, I don't know which of them was more anxious to go for that walk," her mother declared with a silent laugh.

"I know what you mean." Dawn turned away from the door, but she thought she knew who would have won that contest, because she knew why Randy was so eager to explore the town. It worried her.

"There's one slice of Key lime pie left. Are you sure you don't want it?" Her mother offered for the second time. "Your father and Randy will just fight over it when they come back."

"No, honestly I don't have room for another thing," she insisted, pressing a hand against a stomach that was already filled with her mother's home-cooking. "Besides, it's fattening."

Reeta Canady skimmed her with an assessing look. "It seems to me you could stand to gain some weight."

Dawn didn't respond to that. "I'll have a cup of coffee though, if there's any left," she said instead.

"You sit at the table and I'll bring it."

A protest formed, but Dawn sensed her mother welcomed an excuse to wait on her, wanting to spoil her as she always had. Dawn didn't want to take that little pleasure from her mother. She had gone to so much trouble to fix a special lunch to welcome her home, but she still felt Dawn was accustomed to better. Better by whose standards?

Taking a seat, Dawn rested her hands on the table top. Her fingers twisted and weaved together in small movements, nervous movements that betrayed her inner agitation.

Reeta Canady was attuned to all the fine changes in her daughter since the funeral of her son-in-law. The subdued behavior, the weight loss, and the troubled distraction might all be attributable to grief, but Reeta didn't think so. With two cups of coffee poured, she set one on the table in front of Dawn. It was a bit startling to her at times that she had given birth to this stunning and vibrantly beautiful creature. Pulling up another chair, Reeta joined her at the table. There was subconscious satisfaction that she might be able to help her daughter in some way—a daughter who had everything—looks, money, and position.

"Something's bothering you. I can tell," she announced gently. "Would you like to talk about it?"

Dawn flashed her a surprised but grateful glance, then smiled ruefully. "Mother, I just got home less than two hours ago. Let's leave all the confessions until tomorrow and enjoy being together." Her problems would keep, and it wasn't fair to spoil this homecoming day for her mother.

"Where's all your jewelry?" her mother asked, sharply alert to the bareness of Dawn's fingers. "Your wedding ring? And the big solitaire?"

Dawn resisted the impulse to hide her hands in her lap and curved them around the coffee cup instead. Without the rings, her fingers felt oddly light and naked. A long sigh came from her.

"I sold them."

There was a moment of silent shock before her mother managed to ask a confused, "Why?"

The corners of her mouth bowed down in a humorless smile. "I needed the money."

"What are you talking about?" Reeta Canady showed her puzzled surprise, then didn't wait for Dawn to answer as she leaped to a conclusion. "Did Simpson lose all his money? Is that why he had his heart attack?"

"No, Mother," Dawn answered patiently. "If there was anything that caused his heart attack, it was overexertion and playing tennis in the heat of a Houston afternoon. As for his estate, I'm not sure anyone knows the exact figure but it will be in the tens of millions."

"Then, I don't understand." Her mother leaned back in her chair, fully confused. "Why did you need money?"

"It's very simple." She stared into the black coffee in her cup, sightlessly watching its shimmering surface catch the sunlight through the window. "Simpson didn't leave me any—or very little." Which was more precise.

"But—" Her mother faltered over the protest. "—you are his widow. That makes you entitled to a major share of his estate."

"Yes, I could contest the will and demand a widow's share," Dawn admitted. "But I'm not going to do that. Simpson did make a provision for me in his will to receive fifteen thousand dollars a year until Randy comes of age or I remarry. I think he was afraid I might embarrass the Lord family and wind up on the welfare rolls." It was meant as a joke but its humor was weak. In her heart, she knew that hadn't been Simpson's intention although some of his relations believed that.

"It still isn't fair," her mother protested. "You were married to him for eleven years."

"Yes. But we both know I married him because of his money. Simpson knew it, too, but it didn't matter to him as long as he was alive." Taking a sip of her coffee, Dawn felt no bitterness for his decision not to leave her more than a stipend. In a way, there was a certain justice in that. "On the whole, they were good years. Eventually I grew to care a lot about Simpson, even love him a little. I honestly tried to be a good wife to him. I owed him that."

"You were so young," her mother insisted poignantly and reached to cover Dawn's hand, squeezing it in deep affection with a mother's unwillingness to believe the worst of her child.

"That was no excuse." If she had learned anything in these last eleven years, it was the high price of selfishness. So many people had been hurt by it, including herself. "Now I have a chance to start over."

"What will you do?" Reeta asked with worried concern, wanting to help and not knowing how.

"I don't know." Giving rise to her agitation, Dawn pushed away from the table to stand. She wound her arms around herself in an unconsciously protective gesture, and wandered again to the screen door, half-turning to keep her mother within sight. "All the gifts Simpson gave me—the jewels, the furs—were mine to keep. But I certainly didn't need them anymore—or want them. So I sold them. They were worth three times the fifty thousand I got for them, but it's enough to buy a small house."

"Where?"

Her sidelong glance held her mother's for an instant then slid away. "I had planned to stay in Texas so Randy wouldn't have to change schools and leave his friends." Her expression became grim and resentful. "You remember that old saying: Nobody knows you when you're broke? When everyone found out I wasn't the rich widow, you'd be surprised how many friends I suddenly didn't have. Neither did Randy. That's really why I decided to leave Texas—because of Randy."

"What about Randy? How is he taking all this?" An anxious frown creased her forehead as Reeta Canady watched her daughter, feeling her pain and anger.

"It's difficult to say." Dawn sighed again and looked through the screen. "Randy holds so much inside that I don't really know what he's feeling. When Simpson died, he was angry at first, then hurt by his friends' rejection. I'm sure he's confused . . . and desperate."

"Didn't Simpson . . . I mean, in the will, did he—"

"No. Two years ago, Simpson set up a trust to fund Randy's college education but other than that, he left him nothing." Dawn arched her throat, fighting the tightness that gripped it, and shoved her hands deep into the hip pockets of her jeans. "I'm so glad now that Simpson insisted I had to tell Randy the truth when he was small. If I hadn't, I don't know if Randy could have handled all this—I don't know if I could have handled it. Now it's a relief that he's known for a long time that Simpson wasn't his natural father."

Dawn had to give full marks to her late husband for being so good to her son. He hadn't loved him like a father, but he had liked him and been kind to him. His belief in blood ties was too fierce for Simpson to ever consider adopting Randy. Only his flesh and blood would inherit the fortune his family had amassed.

"Does he know who his real father is?" her mother asked hesitantly.

Turning slowly, Dawn retraced her steps to the table and sank down in the chair. "Yes. He asked me, so I told him. I thought he had the right to know the name of his father." It was said flatly, all emotion pulled from her voice.

"I suppose he does." But it bothered Reeta.

"Randy hasn't actually said so, but I know he wants us to move here—to Key West. He's curious about his father. That's why he was so eager to go for a walk with Pop," Dawn explained with a vague weariness. "He's hoping he'll accidentally run into Slater—or see him—anything. He desperately wants a father. It wasn't so bad when Simpson was alive because Randy could pretend he had one. Now—?"

"Will you move here?" She had hardly dared to hope that Dawn, her only child, would consider coming back here where she could see them as often as she liked.

"That depends."

"On what?"

"Slater," Dawn replied, and combed the copper red hair behind her ears with a rake of her long fingernails.

"Are you going to tell him about Randy?" After all these years of silence, Reeta Canady couldn't help being surprised by this change in her daughter's attitude.

"He has a right to know, too," she said with a defensive air.

"You should have told him before," her mother declared in a rare admonishment.

"No!" It was a hard, swift denial that brought Dawn's head up sharply. Then just as quickly, her chin drooped in defeat. "Yes." She breathed out the admission. "I should have told him before, but I thought I knew it all then."

"Don't we all at eighteen," her mother murmured in sympathy.

"I have to tell Slater now. How he takes the news will determine whether we'll stay here or go somewhere else. I don't want Randy to know that. If Slater refused to acknowledge him even privately—and I wouldn't blame him if he did—I'd rather that Randy never learns that. I don't want him to be hurt anymore because of my stupidity." She picked up her cup but the coffee had become cold.

"When were you planning to go see him?" She pitied her daughter because she knew how awkward it was going to be.

"Not for a couple of days. I want to spend some time with you and Pop first." Just in case after she told Slater that the situation would turn too uncomfortable for her to stay. She knew how angry and bitter he had been when she'd jilted him. She couldn't even begin to guess how he'd react when he learned that she'd had his son.

Her mother fingered the handle of her coffee cup. "You do know Slater never married. Maybe . . . the two of you—"

"No, Mother." Dawn rejected that possibility as laughable. "After the way I treated him, there isn't any chance things could ever be the way they were between us. Marriage is out of the question even for Randy's sake. Slater despises me—and I can't say that I blame him."

"I know he judged you harshly," her mother conceded. "But a lot of years have passed."

"Precisely." She seized on the latter statement. "People change, especially after they've been separated a long time. The intensity of feeling isn't there anymore. I know I'm not the same girl that sailed away from here on that yacht eleven years ago."

And she thanked God for that, even though she knew it was too late for her and Slater. She had lost him, and she didn't fool herself into believing she could ever win him back.

But just talking about him and the dilemma of her future provided some measure of relief. She hadn't meant to burden her mother with this discussion so early in her homecoming. Now that it was over, some of her tension had eased.

Picking up her coffee cup, she once again got to her feet. "We'd better get these lunch dishes washed before Randy and Pop come home and it's time to fix supper."

"You don't need to help," her mother protested. "Not your first day home. Sit down and have some more coffee. I'll do them."

"No, Mother," Dawn smiled and continued toward the sink full of dirty dishes. "I've got to get into practice again. After all, I'm not going to have a maid and cook to clean up after me anymore."

"It's good to have you home, Dawn," her mother declared, a little teary-eyed.

"It's good to be home," Dawn affirmed on a deep breath that was more positive in its outlook than her many sighs of troubled confusion.

# Chapter Two

Cycling along the cobbled back streets of Key West, Dawn felt the clock turning back the years to the time when a bicycle had been her main means of transportation around the island. She could almost believe she was back in the past if it weren't for Randy on the bike ahead of her.

"Come on, slowpoke." He looked over his shoulder at her, smiling as he taunted her.

"Go ahead, speedy." She waved him on, knowing he was impatient with her lackadaisical pace. Randy seemed to be going through a phase where he had to race at everything. The faster the better was his motto. "I'll be the tortoise and catch up with you later when you're too pooped to pedal."

His long, sun-browned legs began pumping as hard as he could, gaining speed as Randy pulled back on the handlebars to raise the front wheel. Dawn shook her head in silent amusement, not understanding the excitement he derived from "popping a wheelie." A minute later, he was swooping around a corner and disappearing.

There was little chance of Randy becoming lost since it was an island town. Besides, the last two days he'd done so much exploring both on foot and on bicycle that he fairly well knew his way around.

Dawn had stayed close to home until this afternoon when Randy persuaded her to go biking with him. It was fun riding around her hometown, seeing the changes and the old haunts that hadn't perceptibly changed. At eighteen, Key West hadn't seemed to hold enough of anything for her—life, excitement, or the kind of future she had thought she wanted. Now, it seemed a good place to live and raise her son.

Located at the southernmost tip of the chain of Keys, its protective reefs and deep harbor had given Key West its beginnings as a pirate haven. Over the years there had been changing cultural influences until the town was a peculiar blend of New England fishing village, tourist-resort city, and a touch of elegance from its close neighbor, Cuba.

The blue sea surrounded it, and the blue sky covered it, and the sun warmed it all year round. Its near tropical climate nourished a profusion of plant life that gave the Keys a lushness and sense of mystery. There was a riot of color—the bright blossoms of bougainvillea, hibiscus, and poinciana growing rampantly.

Thick oleanders nearly hid the white picket fence from Dawn's sight. She caught the flash of white out of the corner of her eye and let the bike coast on the nearly level street while her attention strayed to identify it. The short driveway leading back to the house was nearly overgrown.

It was the old Van de Veere place. She and Katy Van de Veere had been close friends in school. Dawn remembered her mother mentioning that they had moved to the mainland a couple of years ago. It was sad to see the old house sitting vacant. She braked her bike to a halt along the side of the road for a longer look at this site from her girlhood days.

There had always seemed to be so much character and charm about the house. Even now, with its yard overgrown with shedding palm trees and choking oleanders, it appeared to steadfastly resist any attempt to suppress it. The style of the sturdy wooden house with its wide veranda was locally known as "Conch" architecture. Many places like this had been renovated into lovely homes. Dawn gazed at it wistfully, wishing she could take the house in hand and turn it into a home for herself and Randy.

There was an almost silent whish of bike wheels behind her. Dawn paid scant attention to the sound until she heard the sudden setting of brakes and tires skidding on the rough edge of the road. She turned in sharp alarm, expecting to see a bicycle spinning on its side and some child sprawled in the street. Instead, Randy came to a dramatic stop beside her, a mischievous grin on his face.

"Did I scare you?" he wanted to know, hoping

her answer would be affirmative. "I'll bet you thought I was going to run into you."

"No, but I did expect to see somebody sprawled in the street with their bike turned over," she said, giving him a reproving look from under the white sun visor cap she wore to shield her eyes from the glare of the sun.

"How come you're hanging around here?" Randy asked, rolling his bike back and forth, already anxious to be moving again.

"I was just looking at the house." Dawn bobbed her head in the direction of the structure, visible through the driveway. "One of my girlfriends used to live here. It's empty now, I guess."

"Boy, it looks like a jungle," he declared, looking at the thick undergrowth that had taken over the yard and was attacking the wide veranda. "It sure would be neat to explore the place."

No sooner was the thought voiced than Randy was riding his bike into the driveway. "Randy, that's private property," Dawn admonished. "You could be arrested for trespassing."

"Ahh, Mom," he complained. "I'm not going to vandalize anything. I just want a closer look. That's all."

A few feet inside the driveway, he stopped the bike and rested a foot on the ground for balance. Satisfied that his intentions were no more than that, Dawn followed him, curious herself to see the place up close.

"Look." Dawn pointed to the narrow slats in

the roof under the eaves. "That's 'Key West air-conditioning,' the old style. Those openings trap the cool breezes and carry them into the house."

"Really?" He eyed her skeptically, not sure she knew what she was talking about.

"Really," she confirmed, smiling but definite, and swung her gaze back to the house. Again, a wistful quality entered her deep blue eyes. "I really love that old house."

Randy was watching her closely, the gleam of an idea silvering through his eyes. "Why don't we buy the place, Mom?" he suggested and rushed on before she could answer. "You said you liked it, and we've got to live somewhere."

"Hold it, fella," she cautioned, fully aware of the desire behind all this. "I can't buy something just because I like it. There's a little matter of price and terms, and the cost of repairs. It's probably more than we can afford."

"We can do a lot of repairs ourselves," Randy insisted blithely. "Gramps would help. You should see the woodworking shop he's got in the garage. I'll bet he could fix just about anything."

"Your grandfather is a fine carpenter." It had been his craft all his life. "But there's plumbing and electrical wiring—and who knows what else."

"You're just guessing." He tried a different tactic. "You don't even know if there's anything wrong with the house at all."

"That's true." She was forced to concede the point. "But we don't have that much money to spend on a place that might cost a lot to maintain." She hated to keep harping on their suddenly limited finances, but Randy needed to learn that the purchase price of an object wasn't the only concern.

"Still, you could check and find out about it, couldn't you?" Randy countered with persuasive ease.

Dawn hesitated for a split second. There wasn't any harm in checking to find out how much was being asked for the house and learning what kind of condition it was in. There were a lot of "ifs" that had to be settled before going further than that.

"I'll see what I can find out," she promised, and signaled that they had lingered there long enough by turning her bike around in the driveway to head onto the street.

At the supper table that evening, Randy monopolized the conversation with a detailed account of their afternoon bike ride and managed to work in a subtle reminder of Dawn's promise.

"We stopped to look at this old house," he told his grandparents. "You should have seen the place. It was all overgrown with weeds and flowers. A girl you went to school with lived there, didn't she?" He pulled her into the conversation.

"It was the old Van de Veere place," Dawn explained while she ladled a spoonful of conch chowder to her soup bowl. "Do you know who owns it now?" She glanced at her mother with idle curiosity.

There was an almost stricken look on her mother's face, but her silence was covered by her husband, whose red hair had long ago turned white. "Doesn't that belong to—"

"I don't think so," Reeta Canady interrupted him quickly, throwing her husband a quelling look that was linked to the glance she darted at Randy. "I think some speculator from the mainland bought it, but I'm sure it's on the market, Dawn. You could check with one of the realtors."

"I'll do that," Dawn said, battening down the suspicions that had sprung to life at her mother's behavior.

"Are you thinking about buying the place?" inquired her father. "It's built solid as a rock."

"Yeah—" Randy rushed in with an affirmative answer.

"At the moment, it's mainly curiosity," she insisted, although the possibility hadn't lost its appeal.

It wasn't until after the meal was finished and Dawn was helping her mother clear the dishes from the table that her suspicions were confirmed. Both Randy and her father were in the garage workshop.

"Who owns the Van de Veere house?" she repeated the question she'd asked earlier.

"Slater MacBride," her mother admitted with a long look. "I nearly shoved a fritter in your father's mouth to shut him up from saying any-

32

thing in front of Randy. I swear he talks and thinks afterwards."

"Why did he buy it?" Dawn wondered aloud as she absently stacked the dishes on the counter next to the sink.

"I imagine just for the investment," her mother shrugged. "He owns quite a bit of property, residential and commercial. Slater has done very well for himself. I—" She saw the pained look on Dawn's face and stopped, changing what she had started to say. "I'm sorry. But who's to say if you had married MacBride instead of Simpson, whether he would have turned out to be the same way," her mother offered in consolation.

"I know," Dawn sighed, but it was a case of knowing now what a precious gift love could be and how foolish she had been to think wealth was more valuable. For a long time, she had been reconciled to living with regret for the rest of her life, but that didn't stop it from hurting once in a while.

"After the wedding, Slater was—almost obsessed with making money," her mother explained with a kind of sadness in her voice and expression. "Every bit of money he earned or could beg, borrow, or steal he put into his deals— gambling everything on venture after venture." She shook her head, as if in reflective despair. "Eventually, I guess it became a habit." Lightly, she trailed her hand over the shimmering firelights in Dawn's hair, a gesture that reminded Dawn instantly of her childhood when her mother had stroked her hair, comforting her over some hurt. "But the money didn't make him any happier than it did you."

"It never makes anybody happy." There was a grim twist of her mouth into a rueful smile.

"Are you going to contact him about the house?"

Dawn turned on the faucets to fill the sink with water. "I don't think Randy will give me a minute's peace until I make some effort to find out about it," she declared on a humorless laugh. "And I guess it will give me a legitimate reason to call him . . . test the water before I have to plunge in."

"It would be a bit awkward to simply walk up to him and inform him about Randy," her mother agreed.

"That is an understatement." But Dawn was fully aware that she had put off contacting Slater long enough. There was no more reason to delay the moment that had to be faced. "I'll telephone him in the morning." Still, she gained herself one more night.

After reading the same paragraph twice without concentrating on what it said, Slater sighed in exasperation and started it a third time. Before he had finished the first sentence, extremely long in typical legal fashion, he was distracted by the opening of the door to his private office. Slater glanced up from the legal contract, irritated by the interruption. Nearly everything irritated him lately.

The instant he recognized his secretary, Helen Greenstone, his attention reverted to the document in his hand. Helen, a woman in her fifties, efficient, capable, new to the area, and a grandmother, walked over to his desk.

"There is fresh coffee made. Shall I bring you a cup, Mr. MacBride?" She was a stickler for formality, insisting on a show of respect for her employer who was nearly young enough to be her son.

"Yes, thank you." He glanced briefly at the correspondence she placed on his desk, letters requiring his signature. The telephone rang. The line of his mouth thinned at the second interruption. "Answer that for me."

Without a word, she reached for the telephone on his desk and punched the necessary line before picking up the receiver. "Mr. MacBride's office. May I help you please?" There was a pause for a response by the calling party. "Mr. MacBride?" She sent a questioning look at him to see if he wanted to take the call.

"Find out who it is." If it wasn't important, he didn't want to be bothered with it at the moment.

"Who's calling, please?" Helen Greenstone requested, then covered the mouthpiece with her hand to muffle her voice. "It's a Mrs. Lord."

Dawn. The identity of the caller shot through him like a lightning bolt, freezing him motionless for a split second. In the next, he wanted to grab the phone from the woman and hear Dawn's voice for himself. Anger tightened him that she could still generate that kind of reaction in him.

"Find out what she wants." Slater denied himself the sound of her voice, not totally trusting himself at that moment.

For the last four days, he'd been wondering if he'd see her or hear from her, if she'd have the nerve to contact him after all this time. Now that it had happened, he realized it had been like watching a burning fuse on a stick of dynamite and waiting for the explosion, not knowing when it would come. It finally had. Now there were the reverberations.

"What did you wish to speak to him about?" Helen asked. "Perhaps I can help you." There was another pause during which she glanced at Slater. "The Van de Veere house? Yes, it's for sale."

A shaft of anger plunged hotly through him at the thought of her calling him about a house!

"I'm certain I can arrange an appointment with Mr. MacBride to show you the house," his secretary stated and opened his appointment book, tapping a finger on the one o'clock slot to see if that met with his approval. He nodded curtly. "Mr. MacBride is free after lunch. Would one o'clock be convenient for you, Mrs. Lord—at the Van de Veere house?" She smiled at the receiver. "Thank you. Good day." She hung up the phone and jotted the meeting on his calendar for the day. "I'll bring you some coffee," she said and started to leave.

"No." It was a brisk refusal, which Slater

quickly followed with an ambiguous explanation. "I've changed my mind. I don't want any."

He focused his gaze on the legal contract he was studying as if it had all his attention. When the door closed behind his secretary, it strayed to the name written on the sheet in his appointment book. Slater stared at it for a long time.

Dawn was slow to replace the telephone receiver on its cradle. Her nerves were so raw she wanted to scream and release some of the tension that was building up inside her. There was a keen sense of hurt, too, because she hadn't expected to be fobbed off onto his secretary. Once she'd identified herself, she had thought she'd be put right through to Slater. Instead, she'd been forced to carry through the charade of looking at the house.

"Who were you talking to just now, Mom?"

Startled, Dawn swung around to stare at her son. She thought he was outside. Had he been listening? Was it merely the gleam of curiosity in his eyes, or the sharpness of foreknowledge? She reached out to smooth the cowlick on his forehead.

"I was making an appointment to see the man about the house you and I looked at yesterday," she admitted, smiling stiffly and excluding the information that the man was his father. A change of subject was needed. "It won't be long and you'll be as tall as I am."

"My dad is tall, isn't he?" The quietly asked question nearly undermined her.

"Yes," Dawn replied with an attempt at smoothness that didn't completely succeed. "Six foot. So you have a few more inches to grow yet."

"When are you going to talk to him about the house?" This time he changed the subject. Or so Dawn hoped.

"One o'clock this afternoon."

"Can I come with you?" he asked.

"No." She smiled to make her refusal seem less important than it was.

There was a flicker of disappointment, but it was soon replaced by a resigned acceptance. "I might go looking around the shops in Old Town after lunch. Is that all right?"

"Sure." Her smile widened with his failure to pursue coming with her.

At lunch, Dawn was too nervous to eat, her stomach churning in anticipation of the meeting with Slater. Pleading a lack of appetite she excused herself from the table and went to her old room to get ready.

It wasn't easy choosing what to wear. The near-tropical summer climate dictated light-weight clothing, but there was still the choice of casual, sporty, sophisticated. Thanks to Simpson's generosity during their marriage, Dawn had an abundant wardrobe to choose from.

After several false starts, she settled on a seer-sucker suit, white with thin blue stripes, and a plain silk blouse in sapphire blue. Her sandaled heels and purse were a matching shade of blue to complete the ensemble. Luckily Dawn had kept the good pieces of costume jewelry, selling only the gold and the jewels, so she slipped a couple of rings on her fingers and a pair of earrings.

The mirror said the finished product looked subtly elegant and slightly businesslike. The curling thickness of her rich auburn tresses lay casually about her shoulders to soften the effect. Her expression looked a little tense, a tautness to her mouth, but it was to be expected under the circumstances.

When she left the house, she waved at her mother who anxiously wished her good luck. The moral support was gratefully received. There was no sign of Randy as she reversed her car out of the driveway, so she wasn't forced to tell him again that she didn't want his company.

If it hadn't been for the afternoon heat, the distance to the Van de Veere house could easily have been walked, but Dawn didn't want to spoil the freshness of her appearance. The dashboard clock in her car, another gift from Simpson his estate hadn't been able to claim, showed two minutes before the hour when she turned into the driveway.

There was no other vehicle parked there, and no sign that anyone was around—or had been around. As she climbed out of the car, her nerves were jumping and her breath was running shallow and fast. The sidewalk to the front door was nearly impassable. Dawn had to lift encroaching branches and vines aside to reach the steps.

A breeze stirred the palm, the spiked fronds

rustling together. There was a reassuring solidness to the veranda floor as she crossed it to try the front door. It was locked, eliminating the possibility that Slater was inside waiting for her. Dawn turned, looking back to the driveway and suddenly wondering if he would come at all. Or would he thwart her by sending someone else to show her the house? A quiver of unease went through her.

From the street, there was a loud purr of a powerful car engine approaching the house. When a low, sleek Corvette turned into the driveway, a tingle of mixed relief trailed over her nerves. It stopped behind her car and the motor was killed. The minute the driver stepped out, Dawn no longer had to wonder whether Slater would come himself. He was here.

Long and lean, his familiar body had retained that easy flow of movement that came with being in prime physical condition. His profile was strongly cut and sun-bronzed, and his gilded brown hair was slightly rumpled by a playing wind. A pair of sunglasses hid his eyes, but she knew he'd seen her standing on the wide veranda.

There was an instant's pause before he removed them and tossed them through the opened car window onto the seat. Without another glance in her direction, Slater wound his way through the tangle of underbrush encroaching on the path to the steps.

In those first seconds, she was struck by all the

things that were familiar about him. But as he came closer, she became aware of the changes. No more faded jeans, worn soft to hug his thighs, no more T-shirts stretched thin to mold his flatly muscled chest and shoulders, no more soiled sneakers without socks on his feet.

The way he was dressed was a stark contrast to the past. From the fine leather of his polished shoes to the continental cut of his brown slacks and the print silk shirt tapered to fit, Slater MacBride was the model of what the successful man looked like . . . casual—the shirt unbuttoned at the throat—and confident.

The softness of youth was gone from his features, that love of a good time which had once creased it with eagerness. Maturity had brought a hard definition to the male angles of his face, adding more emphasis to virility than to mere handsomeness.

But all the changes were unquestionably improvements. All her senses, everything inside her seemed to rush out, reaching for him. It was like a torrent being unleashed, a torrent of love and regret that seemed to spill from her in waves, yet she never moved, never took a step forward to greet him, and never changed her expression. The tumultuous reaction was all contained inside. Dawn had learned too well, during her marriage to Simpson, how to hide her true feelings.

When she finally met the flint-gray in his eyes, she was glad she hadn't begun the meeting on an emotional note. The aloofness in his gaze was chilling. When she finally spoke, she felt she was literally breaking the ice.

"Hello, Slater." Her voice was smooth and even. "It's good to see you looking so well."

"Thank you." He inclined his head at the compliment with a thick trace of mockery. "Or, perhaps I should say 'thanks to you.'" The barbed correction was accompanied by a challenging flick of his brow, but he continued smoothly without waiting for a response. "I'd like to take the opportunity to offer you my condolences on the untimely death of your husband."

She doubted it was a sincere offer of sympathy, but she didn't question it. "Thank you," she murmured.

His gaze made a sweep of her. "I expected to find you elegantly clad in black, Mrs. Lord—the grieving widow mourning for her beloved husband." There was a mocking twist of his mouth. "But these days, I guess not even the rich follow the custom of wearing black."

"That's true," she admitted, refusing to take offense at his thinly veiled jibes. She had not arranged to meet him to take part in a war of words, with herself constantly on the defensive, so she was determined not to parry any of his sharp thrusts. "It's no longer considered improper to wear other colors."

"Pity. You would be stunning in black," he murmured with a lazy glance at her fiery mane of hair, but his coolness took any hint of a compliment from his voice.

Dawn was stiff, trying to keep in check the natural instinct to defend herself from his subtle attack. "I'll try to remember that," was the most indifferent reply she could make, but even it betrayed that his stinging comments were getting through.

"You have a slight accent," Slater observed.

"Have I?"

"After living so long in Texas, I guess it's to be expected," he said with an uncaring shrug, then smiled. "But you don't need to be concerned. A little drawl is very sexy, but then—it goes with the body, doesn't it?"

Despite the rake of his eyes, Dawn had the feeling Slater didn't find her at all sexually appealing. It seemed he had crushed out every feeling for her. Had she really thought it would be otherwise? She dug her long nails into her palm, resisting the impulse to slap him and hurt him physically the way he was hurting her mentally. Any other response was impossible so she made none.

Her silence seemed to irritate him, however briefly. "I believe you were interested in this house." He reached in his pocket for the key and moved past her to unlock the front door. "I only acquired the property recently so I haven't had the opportunity to have the yard cleaned up and the house put in order. Naturally the price will be reduced to compensate for its neglected condition." Pausing, he pushed the door open and turned to hold her gaze. "That is, if you are actually interested in purchasing it?"

It was the skepticism in his eyes that prompted Dawn to put him through the formality of showing her the house, although she had serious doubts that a sale would ever come to pass. For a moment she wanted to forget about her true purpose in meeting him and avoid all this unpleasantness. But she recognized it was a selfishly motivated desire. There was Randy's need to consider as well.

"I am interested," she stated and walked past him to enter the house, stale and musty from being shut up for so long—like their relationship. Perhaps an airing was all that was needed for them, too. Dawn suspected that was purely wishful thinking.

# Chapter Three

Dust had naturally accumulated on the window-sills and floors. A cupboard door or two in the kitchen had swelled shut, but there were no major things wrong. None of the ceilings showed any signs of roof leakage. There weren't any rust stains from leaky water pipes. Without furniture in the rooms or curtains at the windows, the house had a starkness to it, but now and then Dawn caught traces of the character she remembered as Slater toured her through the rooms.

Coming full circle back to the living room, Slater paused inside the arched doorway. Behind his lazy regard of her, there was an intensity that had persisted each time he looked at her. It made Dawn uncomfortable and tense, as if she never dared to relax. She made a show of ignoring him, her glance wandering around the room instead.

"Trying to decide which wall to hang your Picasso on?" Slater queried mockingly. "It might look out of place in these simple surroundings."

"Why should it?" She swung around to face him, half the width of the empty room separating them. "The ceramic cat Picasso designed for

Hemingway is displayed in the house where he lived here in Key West." She was tired of his constant jibes about money and cultural status. "There's a whole colony of artists and craftsmen here."

"But not jetsetters, or the wealthy elite," Slater countered. There was a lazy curve to his mouth, but it held more mockery than amusement. "Their gathering place is Key Largo. Maybe that's why I have trouble believing you are actually serious about buying this house. Or are you trying to make this area the new 'in' place for rich snowbirds?" His taunting voice continued to challenge her. "How much time will you spend here? A week a year? Two weeks?"

"Key West is my hometown," Dawn reminded him. "Why is it so impossible to think that I might want to live here?"

"Maybe because you've stayed away for ten years."

"Eleven," she corrected.

A shoulder lifted in an uncaring shrug. "Who's counting?" It was obvious he wasn't. That hurt almost more than anything else he'd said.

"You're right." Her voice went flat.

"Why did you really want to see this house, Mrs. Lord?" he challenged.

He deliberately kept using her married name, constantly reminding Dawn of her perfidy. She wanted to scream at him to stop it, the sound of it scraping over her raw nerves, but she didn't.

"I've already told you," she insisted stiffly.

"It's a lovely old home," Slater said idly. "A

bargain. I guess that's the problem. I don't see you as a bargain-hunter—" There was an abrupt pause. "I guess you are at that. You like to look over the merchandise and shop for the best deals, don't you?"

"What am I supposed to say to that?" she demanded, bristling at his constant harangue.

"If the shoe fits?" he murmured and left the rest of the old saying unfinished.

"Sometimes people outgrow old shoes." It was the closest she'd come to denying his veiled accusations against her character.

Now that she had finally risen to his baiting remarks Slater seemed to tire of the sport. "About this house—" he began. "You have seen the condition it's in. If you're serious about buying, we'll get down to the business of price and terms. Even if you don't choose to live in it, the property would be a sound investment."

"I'm considering possibly moving here permanently," Dawn stated, drawing his sharpened glance.

"Depending on what?" Slater sensed the unspoken qualification in her announcement.

"Depending on you." The conversation had finally come around to the subject she needed to discuss with him, and she drew her first calm breath, the moment finally coming.

But the calm didn't last more than a second. The stale air became suddenly charged with a volatile energy. Slater discarded his pose of lazy mockery as his features hardened in contemptuous anger and his gray eyes smouldered.

"That's rich!" He breathed out the harsh words, his jaw rigidly clenched. "You don't give a damn about me! You don't care about anybody but yourself and what you want!"

Her gaze faltered under the censorious glare of his. She tightened her grip on the blue purse, glancing at her whitened knuckles briefly.

"I don't blame you for thinking that way about me. Heaven knows I've given you cause," Dawn admitted, managing to keep her voice even. "What I did was wrong. I know that now. And I'm sorry."

"And what does that mean?" He moved toward her, one slow step gliding into the next.

It wasn't until he stopped inches in front of her that Dawn realized how much he had kept his distance from her. Now he was all too close, so tall, wider in the shoulders than she remembered. She felt the rush of adrenaline through her veins, heightening all her senses.

"It means I'm truly sorry I hurt you." There was no adequate elaboration she could make on the apology to convince him she was sincere.

His mouth was pulled straight in a hard line, a muscle jumping on the high ridge of his jaw. "I'm sorry I hurt you," Slater repeated her words in a tautly flat voice. "As if I'd been knocked down and skinned my knee." He dismissed the apology as small compensation for the pain she had caused him. "I loved you." The declaration was pushed through his teeth, fierce and low. "When you married him, you took everything—my heart,

my pride, my all. You left me barren and empty—
like this house! Crying out for—for you!"

The sting of tears was in her eyes, sharp remorse twisting like a knife in her heart. Dawn
met the harshness of his gaze without blinking.
At the time, she had been too selfish to see the full
consequences of her action, the ripple effect her
decision had made, first striking Slater, then
Simpson, Randy, even her parents.

"I know," she said. "I had hoped time would
have healed some of the pain." Or at least tempered some of his anger, but it hadn't.

"Why?" Slater demanded. "Did you think you
could come back and pick up where we left off? Did
you think you could kiss away the hurt that was
left and make it better?" His hands gripped her
arms, his fingers digging into the seersucker
sleeves of her light jacket. "Why don't you see if it
works?"

The snarling challenge was no sooner issued
than Slater was pulling her roughly against him
to have it carried through. An arm was hooked
behind her waist while eleven years of bitterness,
anger, and loathing came crushing down on her
mouth. Dawn was rigid against this punishing
sexual assault, powerless but unyielding.

The hardness of his mouth ground her lips
against her teeth, not taking any effort to make
the bruising kiss anything but unpleasant. The
humiliating sensation was so at odds with the
stimulating scent of spicy male cologne that as-
sailed her nose, and with the evocative familiari-

ty of his lean, muscled body molded so tightly to hers.

There was only one purpose to this embrace—to hurt and degrade her mentally and physically the way she had injured him. And Slater was resorting to the base tactic of sexual force to accomplish it. Even while Dawn hated him for treating her so brutally, she couldn't cast stones with a free conscience.

The grinding pressure of his mouth gradually eased as he slowly broke the contact. Dawn remained motionless, a prisoner in his arms. Her eyes closed as she tried to piece together her pride. His fanning breath was warm and moist against her sore lips, his breathing labored and uneven.

"Damn you." There was frustration in the hoarseness of his low curse as if the result of his abusive kiss hadn't been as satisfying as he had expected it to be.

Slowly Dawn raised her lashes to look at him. He was so close she could count the number of tiny white suncreases around his half-closed eyes. Mixed in with the bitter pain, she could see the want that was darkening his gray eyes. Her breath caught in her throat.

His hand moved slowly along her spine, no longer imprisoning but exploring instead with almost reluctant interest. She was conscious of the feel of his body shaped so fully to hers and the ache of desire in his eyes. Memories came rushing back of a time when his touch had excited her beyond all measure, making it easy to forget something so unpleasant as the events of a minute ago. The protective tension faded, taking the stiffness from her limbs, letting her go soft against him.

"Why did you have to come back?" he groaned in a kind of despair. "I was just getting to the point where I could hear your name without going to pieces."

"I was such a fool, Slater." Caught in the emotional moment, Dawn nearly sobbed out the admission.

When her arms went around his neck to make her a participant instead of a victim of his embrace, it was only instinct that prompted her fingers to retain their grip on her clutch purse. This time eleven years of hunger were unleashed when his mouth moved onto her swollen lips. The rawness of his need evoked a tumultuous response that sent her heart soaring.

She strained to fulfill it, wanting to give back more than she got. She was the aggressor. Her fingers curled into the virile thickness of his hair, forcing his head to increase its angle and the pressure of his kiss, while the driving probe of her tongue pushed its way between his lips to intimately deepen the kiss. She could feel the hammering of his heart, only a beat behind the racing tempo of her own.

His hands were caressing, roaming at will over her back and shoulders and stirring up passions that had lain dormant for so long. It was not that Simpson had been sexually unsatisfying as a lover, but there had not been this volatility that was created by the combination of physical and emotional desire. Time hadn't altered this feeling they shared. Dawn recognized that, and there was a wild singing in her veins at the discovery that she found what she thought had been irrevocably lost.

Abruptly, almost violently, Slater was pulling her arms from around his neck and pushing her from him. Dawn was stunned by the fury she saw in his expression. Cold and bitter rejection was taking the place of the desire that had glittered in his eyes.

"Your husband has only been in the ground a month and already you're trying to seduce another man into your bed," accused Slater. "But you're not going to sucker me a second time, *Mrs. Lord.*"

"No. Slater—" She was wounded by his sarcasm, which was for once totally unjustified. Regardless of what he thought, that hadn't been her intention in meeting him.

"You warned me eleven years ago." There was disgust in his sweeping visual assessment of her. "But I didn't think even you would have the gall to do it. 'The second time for love,' isn't that what you said? But first you were going to marry money." His mouth curled with contempt.

"Don't." It was a quiet protest, because there was no point in going into all that.

But Slater took no notice of it. "Well, you've got your money now, don't you?" he taunted. "The Widow Lord and all her Texas millions."

Dawn didn't correct his impression that Simpson had bequeathed her the bulk of his estate. Her wealth, or lack of it, wasn't the issue that had brought her here, so she didn't want the distraction of discussing it. Besides, it wasn't any of Slater's business.

"You came back to see if that love you threw away eleven years ago was still around. Did you really think I'd want you?" There was a rigid movement of his head, a kind of negative shake that was heavy with disdain. "You can take your money and your love—and you know what you can do with it!"

Dawn spoke quickly when he started to swing away to leave. "That isn't why I came back, Slater."

"Isn't it?" His mouth was slanted in a cruelly mocking line.

"There are a lot of reasons why I haven't been back before now, but there is only one reason why I wanted to see you privately today," she stated, a steadiness finally returning to her voice after the passionately disturbing kiss. "When I told you that I hoped you wouldn't be so bitter after this much time, it was the truth. Not because I wanted to pick up where we left off. I don't expect us to be lovers. I doubt if we can even be friends."

"I'm glad you see that so clearly, because you destroyed any future for us eleven years ago," he returned grimly. "Don't forget to shut the door when you leave."

"Wait." Her voice checked the stride he had

taken toward the door. Impatience vibrated in his glance as Slater half-turned. "There's something I have to tell you."

"I can't think of anything you have to tell me that I would be interested to hear," he stated flatly, and started again for the door.

"Not even about your son?" Dawn asked and watched him freeze, then slowly turn to face her.

His probing gaze was hard with anger. "What is that supposed to mean?" he demanded with an openly skeptical expression.

"I'm talking about Randy—my son. *Our* son." Her voice remained level, containing a degree of false calm under his narrowing gaze. "You are his father."

The silence lengthened into interminable seconds without his expression changing from its hard and doubting contempt. "You haven't changed a bit." His low pronouncement reached out to strike her down. "You'll use any trick in the book to get what you want. Even to the extent of trying to tie me to you by pretending I fathered your son." He shook his head, suddenly becoming totally indifferent. "It won't work."

"Randy is your son," Dawn insisted, but Slater was already striding to the door. She started after him. "If you'd just let me explain—"

The door was pulled shut behind his retreating figure, ending her sentence before it was finished. Dawn stopped and stared at the door, stunned by his reaction to the news. She had prepared herself mentally for bitterness, anger, and outrage—even doubt—but she hadn't expected Slater to dismiss it as an impossibility and refuse to listen to what she had to say.

A despairing depression settled heavily onto her shoulders. Dawn turned, her gaze running sightlessly around the empty room. Dust particles danced in the sunlight streaming through a window. What proof could she show Slater that he would believe? If he refused to hear her out, what could she do?

Outside, a car engine growled to life and accelerated, its transmission being shifted into reverse gear. There was something final about the fading sound of Slater's driving away. Unsure what her next move would be, Dawn walked to the door through which Slater had so recently exited the house. The self-locking latch clicked as she closed it and crossed the veranda.

Her thoughts were as crowded and tangled as the lush, green foliage pressing in on all sides. No solution worked its way through her troubled confusion to show her a clear path. Dawn followed the weed-riddled sidewalk to the driveway and her parked car.

Reeta Canady heard the car turn into the driveway and was out the back door before Dawn could slide from behind the wheel. She knew her daughter's decision to live permanently in Key West was riding on the outcome of this meeting with Slater MacBride. And she was anxious to know the result, wanting her daughter and grandchild to stay and crossing her fingers that it would come to pass.

"What happened?" Her searching gaze made a hurried inspection of her daughter's troubled countenance as she tried to guess what it meant.

"Where's Randy?" Dawn asked, glancing around for her son. This was one conversation she didn't want him to accidentally overhear. Until she had decided how to handle this situation, she didn't want Randy to know anything about her meeting with his natural father.

"I saw him ride by on his bike about an hour ago with two other boys his age. I knew it wouldn't be long before he made some friends here," her mother replied, anxious to assert something positive into the negative atmosphere she felt. "I don't expect he'll be back until supper time."

His usual parking stall was unoccupied when Slater returned to the building in Old Town that housed his office. The area was cluttered with tourists, young and old alike. Slater was too preoccupied to take notice of any of them, his expression grim and haunted as he rode the brake and swung the low-slung sportscar into its stall.

With a turn of the key, he switched off the powerful engine. Its demise finally brought an end to the invisible fire that had been burning at his heels, driving him out of the house and away from Dawn. If he had stayed any longer, she would have gotten to him again.

From the moment he'd set eyes on her when he stepped out of the car, the same old excitement had started rising in him. He'd known that he didn't dare get near enough to touch her. But the temptation had been stronger than his willpower could resist.

It had been curiosity that had prompted him to keep the appointment, a desire to prove that he no longer wanted her. But it had backfired in his face. The long abstinence had not eased his craving for her. Like an alcoholic who didn't dare take another sip, he should never have taken that first kiss. He was hooked all over again. Slater hated himself for that, and he hated her, too, in that strange way when a man loves too deeply.

Impatience and frustration marked his movements as Slater stepped crisply out of the car. His coiled muscles rippled with the containment of volatile energy in his whipped-lean body. He started toward his office.

A young boy had stopped his bike behind the black sportscar and appeared to be admiring its sleek lines. He smiled quickly at Slater when he drew nearer. "Hi." It was a bright greeting, issued with guilty swiftness as if the boy was being caught doing something he shouldn't.

Slater nodded to him curtly, not in the mood to converse with some juvenile. But the bold youth didn't take the hint.

"Is this your car?" he asked, setting the kickstand so the bike stood upright on its own.

Slater's first impulse was to ignore the question and keep walking. But he was slowed by a twinge of guilt at the unfairness of taking out his bad temper by being rude to the boy.

"Yes, it is." Politeness put little warmth in his voice, but he did respond.

His gaze made a flicking, uninterested study of the boy, a gangly mixture of arms and legs with dark, russet-brown hair and light blue eyes. Although the bike was dented and rusted in spots, it was obviously rented, because the boy was dressed in expensive clothes, exclusive labels plainly displayed on the knit shirt and designer denim jeans. The youth was obviously the son of some wealthy tourist. It was an observance Slater made without caring much about the conclusion he had reached. Taking note of such details had become second nature to him.

"Boy, it's really something," the lad exclaimed. "How fast will it go?"

This fascination with speed brought a brief twitch of amusement to Slater's mouth. It was typical of the young, the demand for action and excitement.

"Fast enough," he returned, aware the boy's glance was continually darting to him. Something wasn't quite right here. Although the boy was expressing interest in the sportscar, he seemed more intent on studying him. Slater observed a hint of strain and tension in the boy's features. Did it come from excitement or the manifestation of nervousness?

"I'd sure like to have a car like this when I'm older," the boy said in a voice that held a poignant ring of longing.

Bothered by something he couldn't identify, Slater narrowed his study of the boy. Before he could reply, he was hailed by a voice coming from up the street.

"Hey, MacBride!"

He turned to observe the approach of his long-time friend and local fishing guide, Jeeter Jones. With the spry, rolling step of a seaman, Jeeter closed the distance between them. His leathered face was cracked by a greeting smile.

"How are you doing, Jeeter?" Slater felt a surge of impatience at this second delay and wished he had not stopped to speak to this boy. It wasn't company he wanted. It was privacy to deal with the emotions meeting Dawn again had aroused.

"Thought I'd come by and see if I couldn't talk you into buying me a cup of coffee," Jeeter explained and glanced curiously at the boy, who was taking advantage of Slater's distraction to stare raptly at him. "Who's your young friend?" Something about the boy struck a familiar chord and Jeeter darted a quick look at Slater and found it repeated.

With the arrival of Jeeter Jones, Slater had forgotten about that earlier moment when something about the boy had bothered him. His mildly indifferent glance slid to the youth.

"He was admiring my car," Slater explained, then addressed the boy, remembering his previous comment about owning a car like it someday. "Maybe your father will buy you one when you're older." Judging from the way the boy was dressed, his parents could afford it.

There was a sudden flood of red into the boy's cheeks. "Yeah," he mumbled the answer and turned quickly to his bike, hiding the betraying surge of embarrassment. Kicking the stand back, he hopped onto the seat and pedaled away.

The abruptness of his departure pulled Slater's gaze after him. The boy didn't travel far, stopping at the first street vendor he reached. As he looked over the assortment of cookies and cold drinks, the boy stole a glance over his shoulder at Slater and quickly averted his gaze when he saw Slater watching him.

A snorting sound, like a contained laugh, came from Jeeter Jones. "I knew you'd sown some wild seeds in your time, MacBride, but I didn't expect to see the crop maturing so close to home."

Slater swung his gaze around to subject Jeeter to his piercing scrutiny. "What are you talking about?"

"That boy," Jeeter said. "He's darn near the spittin' image of you right down to the cowlicks in his hair. What is he? Some cousin of yours?"

Too stunned to reply, Slater stared at his friend for a blank second. Then his head jerked around to stare at the boy still hovering about the vendor's cart. It wasn't possible! Dawn had been lying. He would have bet his life on it. But—he had to find out. Whipping off his dark glasses, he jammed them into his shirt pocket so they wouldn't shade something from his sight and prevent him from seeing something he should.

Turning away from Jeeter, he broke into a jog. "Hey! What about the coffee?" Jeeter protested in a startled voice.

"Another time." The answer was thrown over his shoulder, his gaze not straying from the boy, who noticed his approach and appeared to tense up. Slater lengthened his stride and weaved through the few pedestrians in his path.

There was a pallor beneath the boy's tanned face as he hurriedly dug into the pocket of his jeans to pay for the limeade he'd ordered. He was still trying to count out the money when Slater arrived at the cart.

Taking two dollar bills from his pocket, Slater laid them atop the cart. "I'll buy his, Rufus," he told the man. "Give me a limeade, too."

After an interested glance that took in both Slater and the boy, the vendor gave a small shrug and turned to fill a plastic glass with the chilled, fresh-squeezed juice.

"I've got the money to pay for my own, sir," the boy declared, suddenly very stiff and warily nervous with Slater there.

"I know." His eyes were taking in the youth-softened yet strongly chiseled lines of the boy's features, the trace of blue in his gray eyes, and the mop of dark hair that rebelled against any orderly style. "What's your name?" He picked up the two glasses, but withheld giving one to the boy.

"Randy," he mumbled, trying but not quite meeting Slater's look.

"Your full name," Slater prompted and offered one of the glasses.

There was a moment of indecision before the

boy answered. "Randy MacBride Lord." Then he looked up to watch Slater's reaction, wary and defensive.

The answer confirmed what Slater had doubted all along. The sudden burden of it removed all emotion from him, wiping him clean like a blackboard.

"Do you know who I am?" he asked with a lack of expression that bordered on a deceptive nonchalance.

Again, he was subjected to a measuring study by the boy before Randy affirmed his knowledge with a slow nod of his head. It was followed by an equally hesitant—"You're Slater MacBride"—as if Randy didn't want to admit how much he knew.

"I met your mother today," Slater said.

"I know," Randy said, then explained, "I saw your car parked in the driveway behind hers when I rode by the house on my bike. Did she—" he faltered, lowering his gaze to nervously study the handlebars of his bike, "—did she . . . tell you about me?"

"Yes." Slater released a bitter, laughing breath that held no humor. "It seems I'm the last one to know." He noticed the moisture gathering in Randy's eyes and his desperate attempt to hide the tears. It tugged at something in his heart. A new gentleness entered his voice when Slater spoke again. "I think it's time you and I talked about a few things."

"Yes, sir." There was a hopeful tremor in Randy's voice.

"Why don't you lock up your bike in that rackstand over there?" Slater nodded to one positioned at the corner. "Then we'll go walk somewhere and find a place to drink our limeade."

"Okay." Randy pushed his bike toward the stand with a betraying eagerness.

# Chapter Four

Her shoulder-length red hair was tied atop her head in a short ponytail to keep the hot weight of it off her neck while she helped her mother fix the evening meal. Dawn dabbed at the perspiration beading in the hollow of her throat from the heat of the stove. She poked a fork into the potatoes to test whether they were done. It broke into pieces at the touch of the fork tines. She turned off the burner beneath the pan.

"The potatoes are almost mush," she announced to her mother and turned. "Any sign of Randy yet?"

Her mother peered out the window above the sink where she was tearing lettuce leaves to make a salad. "I don't see him. Maybe he's in the garage with your father."

"I'll see." Dawn moved away from the stove and walked to the screen door.

Outside, she made a quick scan of the backyard, looking for Randy's bike. There were hammering sounds coming from the garage and Dawn headed toward the raised door. The garage was so crowded with pieces of wood, slabs of cypress trunks, and objects in various stages of completion that there wasn't any room for a car.

Without attempting to work her way through the obstacle course of nails, sawdust, and the lumber-strewn floor, Dawn paused inside the opening and called to her father, raising her voice to make herself heard above the racket of his hammering. "Hey, Pop!"

He straightened from his workbench and turned, taking a mouthful of nails from his mouth. "Time for supper?" he guessed.

"Yes. But I'm looking for Randy. Has he come home yet?" she frowned.

"Haven't seen him all afternoon," he said with a shake of his head, then laid his tools on the counter and turned to walk through the maze on a path only he could discern. "I'm going to get all this cleaned up someday. Problem is, I've run out of friends to give all this stuff to."

Dawn glanced at the cypress clock propped against a wall and a uniquely styled chair with a cypress slab seat, two of the rare pieces that were finished and now gathering dust. "Instead of giving them away, you should sell them," she advised. The garage contained everything from handmade furniture to lamps to polished pieces of driftwood and sculptures made out of shells and carved wood.

"It wouldn't be fair." He shrugged aside the craftsmanship of the products. "It's just something I do to pass the time."

"Puttering or not, it's better than some of the stuff I've seen in the shops," Dawn declared, then turned her gaze toward the driveway. "I wonder where Randy is."

Her father laid a hand on her shoulder in an affectionate gesture that also pushed her toward the house. "He'll be here directly. He probably just lost track of the time. But don't worry, that bottomless stomach of his will soon be reminding him it's supper time."

Dawn let herself be guided to the house, but she was still bothered by Randy's absence.

A quarter of an hour later, all the food was ready to be dished up and served. Her father had returned to the kitchen from washing his hands and took his customary chair at the head of the table. Dawn was growing impatient and irritated at her son's tardiness.

"Isn't Randy here yet?" her father asked.

"No." Her hands were on her hips, betraying the suppressed anger with her stance, as she looked out the rear screen door for the umpteenth time.

"It's all right," her mother insisted. "We can keep the food hot a while longer."

"It is not all right, Mother," Dawn retorted. "Randy knows what time we have supper. It's rude and thoughtless of him to keep us waiting."

"I'm sure he's probably having such a good time playing with his new friends that he just hasn't realized how late it is." Her mother provided an excuse for the absent Randy. "It isn't like him to deliberately stay gone without a reason."

Once Dawn would have agreed with that, because Randy had always been well-mannered and considerate of others. But, since Simpson had died, there had been a couple of isolated incidents when Randy had been deliberately uncaring of the inconvenience he had caused others. She didn't know whether it was a phase he was going through or if he was testing her authority now that Simpson wasn't around to enforce the rules.

"We've already waited supper almost an hour for him," Dawn reminded her mother. "It will be ruined if you try to keep it hot any longer. You two go ahead and eat. I'm going out to look for Randy."

"There's no need for that," her father inserted. "Sooner or later, he's going to come home. When he does, he'll have to eat a cold supper. That will be a good lesson for a boy with Randy's appetite."

But if it was discipline he was unconsciously seeking by staying away—proof that Dawn cared enough for him—then the passive punishment of a cold supper would not accomplish anything. She couldn't begin to guess the motive behind his absence, if there was one, but she intended to find out.

"Maybe so, but I'm going out to look for him just the same," she stated.

"Aren't you going to have supper with us first?" her mother protested as Dawn started out the door.

"No," she paused long enough to answer. "And

don't bother to save anything for Randy and me. I'll fix us something to eat when we come back."

The three most logical places where Randy might be tarrying were the beach, the marina, or the area of Old Town. All of them were within walking distance, but Dawn decided she could cover the areas more quickly by car.

The first two were easy. She drove slowly past the public beach areas. Most of the bathers had forsaken the sand now that the sun was hanging low in the sky and the dinner hour had arrived. The same was true at the marina. The fishermen had already come in with their day's catches and dispersed. Dawn didn't find Randy among the few people still lingering in the two areas.

Old Town proved to be too congested with foot and wheel traffic. The sidewalk restaurants were crowded with customers combining the outdoor dining experience with people-watching. There were too many directions to look at the same time and still keep her attention on the road.

Giving up, Dawn parked the car and continued her search on foot. The more she looked, the more irritated she became. Always the thought was at the back of her mind that Randy might already be home while she was out here walking the streets looking for him. It didn't improve her temper.

Intent on some boys Randy's age engaged in horseplay across the street, Dawn didn't see the tropically dressed pair of tourists until she had bumped into the man. At the last second, she tried to avoid the collision by stepping sideways, but she careened off the bikestand right into the man.

The impact staggered her. She stepped all over the man's toes as she attempted to regain her balance. Finally his steadying hands managed to right her and get her sandaled feet off his toes.

"I'm sorry," Dawn apologized profusely to the middle-aged man. "I'm afraid I wasn't watching where I was going."

"No harm done," he insisted with only a trace of a wince from the injury to his exposed toes in the leather beach thongs. The lovely sight before him seemed ample compensation for any harm she had done to him. His onlooking wife was forgotten as the male tourist got an eyeful of Dawn in her white shorts and clinging knit tank-top.

"Come on, Herb," his wife snapped in irritation at the way he was ogling Dawn.

With a shrugging smile of regret, he stepped to the side to let Dawn pass by, stealing a glance at her rear view before his wife tugged him forward.

Her shin throbbed from its collision with the bikestand. Dawn paused to rub it and glance at the guilty object that had bruised it. Her gaze fastened on the old bike parked in the rack. It looked just like the one Randy had been using. Surely no two bikes would have matching dents and that funny rust pattern on the front fender. A closer look at the lock securing it to the stand confirmed that it was Randy's. Her father's initials were engraved into the base.

She straightened, looking intently up and down the street. Randy was around here somewhere, and not on his way home. But where? She'd looked in nearly every shop and walked all the streets.

Dawn had barely asked herself the question when she came up with the answer. "Mallory Pier, of course," she murmured.

It had become the evening gathering place and center of activity until the sun went down. She struck out for the pier, certain now that she would find Randy there.

When she reached it, the pier was already crowded with people. There was an almost festival atmosphere about the place. Everyone came to watch the sun make its daily spectacular descent into the Gulf of Mexico. It was an ideal setting with a backdrop of all water and sky.

The mood of the revelers didn't touch Dawn, too intent on finding her errant son to care about the party atmosphere. All sorts of amateur entertainers were displaying their talents to the assembled crowd. Passing a juggler, Dawn continued looking into faces. There were so many young people around that their features seemed to blur together, making her wonder if she'd be able to recognize Randy in this sea of teenagers and pre-teens.

Her patience had nearly worn thin when she finally saw him. He was standing at the end of a group, munching on a conch fritter and laughing at the antics of a mime. Randy said something to the man beside him, drawing the sparkling impatience of her gaze to him.

The anger drained from her with a rush as she recognized Slater. For an instant, he was all she could see. As if sensing he was being watched, his gaze suddenly scanned the crowd around him and came to a stop on her. She could almost feel the boring thrust of his gaze impaling her.

A thousand questions whirled around in her mind, all centered on finding the two of them together. There was only one way she could learn the answer. Dawn started forward, circling around the mime to approach them.

Randy wasn't aware of her presence until he happened to look up and noticed Slater staring at someone. He turned, seeing her when she was nearly to him. Surprise flickered across his face.

"Mom. What are you doing here?" Randy voiced it, then seemed to suddenly realize who else was standing with him, and looked anxiously from one to the other.

The gray of Slater's eyes was as hard as flintstone. It was difficult for Dawn to reply normally when she was so aware of the bitter anger that had marked the end of their last meeting. There was a prickling sensitivity along her nerve ends.

"I've been looking all over for you, Randy. Your grandparents waited supper for nearly an hour," she informed him, capable of only a mild rebuke now that she saw the reason that had detained him.

"Gosh, Mom," Randy frowned in sincere contrition, and looked guiltily at the half-eaten conch fritter that had taken the edge off his appetite. "I didn't realize it was that late. I'm sorry."

"I'm sure you are," Dawn conceded. "The next time you need to keep better track of the time."

"I will. It's just that—" he paused to throw a glance at the silent man beside him, "—we've been talking . . . about things," he finished lamely.

"I know." It was a noncommittal answer, but it finally turned her attention to Slater.

All the while she had been talking to Randy she had been conscious of the angry vibrations emanating from Slater. She was conscious, too, of her slightly disheveled appearance. She wasn't the picture of sophistication and confidence that she had been this afternoon.

Wisps of hair were curling damply against the sides of her face and along her neck. Her skin was glowing with a fine sheen of perspiration after the blocks she'd walked looking for Randy. The brevity of her white shorts showed the shapely length of her tanned legs and the slim curve of her hips. The loden green tank top did more than expose her golden-brown shoulders. The knit material clung to her skin, outlining the points of her breasts that had hardened under his regard.

Instead of being proud that her figure hadn't sagged and lost its firmness after childbirth, Dawn was self-conscious of her definitely female shape. It wasn't as if she had dressed this way in an attempt to lure Slater's interest. She hadn't even known Randy was with him. Yet, after his accusation this afternoon that she wanted him back, her scantily clad appearance might be interpreted as an attempt to arouse his prurient interest.

"I hope you weren't worried about me, Mom," Randy said anxiously.

Dawn didn't respond to that directly because she knew she had been unjustly angry. It hadn't been a ploy to gain her attention that had kept him from coming home, but the excitement of finally meeting his natural father and being with him that had made Randy forget the time.

"I knew you didn't have lights or reflectors on your bike," she said as an excuse for her concern. "I didn't want you riding it after dark."

"I'm sorry, Mom." He shifted uncomfortably, shrugging his shoulders as he glanced down at his feet.

Through the entire conversation, Slater had remained silent. Now he turned slightly at an angle that brought him near to Dawn and facing Randy.

"The sun is on its way down. You'd better get your bike and start for your grandparents' house," he advised Randy in a calm, even voice.

His attention was focused entirely on Randy so there was no warning as his fingers clamped themselves around her wrist. Her pulse skittered wildly under the firm grip of his hand. She stiffened in raw tension, but didn't pull away.

She understood the silent message conveyed by his detaining hand. Randy was to leave, but she was to remain. She felt hot and cold all at the same time, dreading the conversation that was to come yet hoping at last he would listen to her.

"I told them not to wait supper for you," she said to Randy, fighting to keep the nervousness out of her voice. "So when you get home, you'll have to fix yourself something to eat. Don't let your grandmother do it for you either."

He had started to take a step, then stopped, reading between the lines of her remarks. "Aren't you coming, Mom?" Randy frowned.

"I'll be home a little later on," she said. "You just be sure to go straight home."

"I will," he promised, but he looked at her a little uncertainly before finally trotting away.

For long, charged seconds, she watched the point where Randy had disappeared into the crowd on the pier until she finally saw him exiting the dock. All the while, she was conscious of the clamp of Slater's strong fingers keeping her at his side.

When she was satisfied Randy intended to obey her directions, she let her glance slide to Slater's profile etched against a purpling sky. He, too, was observing Randy's departure. The questions she had wanted to ask when she'd first seen them together came rushing back.

"Why—?" Dawn stopped and chose another. "How did Randy find—"

"He saw my car parked in the driveway of the Van de Veere house. He was waiting for me when

I drove back to the office," Slater answered her question before she had a chance to finish it. "He'd already looked the address up in the phone book."

"But how did he know—" She was frowning.

"He overheard you making the appointment with my secretary to meet me there." Again, he accurately guessed what she had been about to ask.

"So he had been listening," Dawn murmured to herself, remembering her uncertainty at the time. Instead of relaxing his hold on her wrist, he tightened it and started forward, forcing her to come with him. "You're hurting me," she protested and twisted her arm, trying to force him to loosen his grip rather than actually attempting to break it.

The pressure eased slightly, letting the blood flow again. "We're going to my office—where we can talk in private," Slater announced in a voice that was deadly flat.

There was no opportunity to voice her agreement with his desire for a less public place to hold their discussion. He obviously took it for granted. Dawn quickened her steps to keep pace with his longer strides as he led the way through the crowd of evening revelers.

It was a relatively short distance from Mallory Pier to his office. When they reached it, he released her wrist to unlock the door. In a show of her own free will, Dawn barely gave him a chance to open the door before she was brushing past him to walk inside so he would know this was a conversation she sought, and not one that was being forced on her.

She paused inside the small reception area, unsure which door opened into his private office. Slater extended a hand, indicating the one directly in front of her. She walked to it and went inside. Her curious glance inspected the room, Key West in flavor with its trophy-sized marlin mounted and hanging on a wall. There was an airy openness to the room with its whitewashed walls and unshuttered windows. She noted, too, the framed plaques and awards scattered around that attested to his success and contributions to the community.

The top of his desk was cleared, except for a stack of telephone messages in the center of it. Slater ignored them and walked to a rattan table that concealed a small, counter-high refrigerator. He removed a container of ice cubes and dropped two into a glass, then splashed some bourbon over the top of them. Turning, he glanced at Dawn, a raised eyebrow inquiring whether she wanted a drink.

"No, thank you," she refused and remained standing when Slater showed no intention of taking a seat.

He downed half the bourbon in one swallow, then studied the rest. The continued silence produced a heightening tension that became harder to break the longer it lasted. Dawn didn't feel it was her place to speak first. He had refused to listen to her when she had tried to tell him about

Randy this afternoon. Pride insisted he had to ask for the explanation this time.

Slater gave her a long, measuring look. "Don't you think you're a bit old to go running around in public like that?" he criticized.

Stung, Dawn retorted, "Since when is a woman old at thirty?" But she reached up to unconsciously loosen the string binding her hair in its ponytail and combed it free with her fingers.

He watched the action, especially the way the upward reach of her arm stretched the knit fabric of the tanktop across her breasts and their button-hard nipples. The sight disturbed him more than he cared to admit.

"I wasn't referring to your hairstyle," Slater murmured dryly. "There's something innocent about a teenager running around braless. An older woman ends up looking cheap and easy."

"That's one man's opinion." Dawn refused to be drawn into a debate over the issue. His opinion of her was so low he'd find fault with her no matter how conservatively she was dressed. "I doubt if you'd approve of anything I wore. This afternoon you were critical because I wasn't dressed in black."

"You can't claim to look like a widow mourning the death of her husband—not in that outfit with all your assets on display," he snapped in disgust.

"I thought we were here to discuss Randy," she fired back. "If all you want to talk about is the way I dress, then I don't see any point in continuing this conversation." She turned on her heel, knowing he wouldn't let her leave.

"Dammit! You know it's Randy." The admission was reluctantly pulled from him.

Slowly Dawn turned back to face him. This time his gaze swung away from the steadiness of hers. "He is your son," she reaffirmed what Slater hadn't been willing to listen to earlier in the day.

"Did you put him up to it?" Slater swirled the bourbon in his glass.

"Up to what?" she frowned.

"Did you put him up to waiting for me here at the office after we talked today?" Slater elaborated on his question, eyeing her in a sidelong look.

"No, I did not." Her denial was forceful and indignant. "It was all Randy's idea. I knew nothing about it, and if I had, I would have prevented it."

"Why?" His head came up as he demanded an explanation of her statement.

"Because I didn't want him to meet you until we had come to some kind of understanding," Dawn stated, protective of her child.

"An understanding about what?" Slater challenged. "The identity of his father? Granted, I thought you were lying to me this afternoon, but I am capable of accepting the evidence of my own eyes. There isn't much doubt that he's my son. Even Jeeter saw the resemblance."

She was momentarily distracted by the familiarity of the name before she remembered the crusty fishing guide, Jeeter Jones. Then her thoughts focused back on the issue at hand.

"Until this afternoon, it never occurred to me that you might deny the possibility you had fathered my child," Dawn admitted. "I never thought there would be any question about that." She paused to draw a breath, glancing down at her hands. "But I knew how much you despised me. It doesn't matter how you feel about me, but I'm not going to let you try to get back at me by hurting Randy. I won't let you take out your anger on him."

A silent rage trembled through him before Slater finally exploded. "For eleven years, you keep the existence of our son a secret from me! My son! You've kept him from me all this time— and you stand there and justify it by saying you are afraid I'll hurt him?! My own child?!"

His outrage put her fears to rest, even making them appear foolish in retrospect, but they had been very real to her for a long time.

"I didn't know how you'd react when you found out," she admitted. "And I didn't want to take any chances of Randy being hurt." She felt almost weak with relief. "It could have been easy for you to use him as a weapon against me."

Slater was slowly bringing his temper under control. He bolted down the rest of his drink and turned to refill the glass, a whiteness continuing to show along the taut line of his mouth. "If you weren't the mother of my son, I think I could kill

79

you for even suggesting I'd do that," he muttered thickly.

But his threat struck a responsive chord in her own feelings and reassured as opposed to frightening her. This strong love for their son was a primitive bond they shared in common. It suddenly became easier to talk.

"I suppose he asked you a lot of questions today," Dawn surmised.

"No. Mostly Randy just talked . . . about himself, school, things he liked to do . . . and I just listened." He stared at his drink, but didn't taste it. "How long has he known that Simpson wasn't his father?" It was close to being a loaded question.

"Since I felt he was old enough to understand. He was around five years old at the time. I explained only as much as I thought he could comprehend, then waited for him to come to me with questions when they occurred to him. So actually, his knowledge of you was gained over a period of years."

"He's known about me all this time. And you're only now bothering to inform me about his existence. Didn't I have the right to know before this?" he accused harshly.

"Yes, you did." But it had taken her a long time to arrive at that conclusion.

"Then why didn't you tell me?" Slater demanded. "For eleven years, another man raised my son. There's eleven years out of his life that I'll never have!" He was growing angry at the injustice of it. "I thought there wasn't any more you could take from me. But you took my son!"

"If I had known I was pregnant with our child, I never would have married Simpson," Dawn countered to deflect some of his anger. "But I didn't know it. And when I discovered I was pregnant, I thought it was my husband's baby. And I was glad, because I was finally giving something back to him after all I had taken."

"So you passed him off as Simpson's child," he accused.

"I believed he was." She remembered how happy she had been when the doctor had confirmed her suspicions only a couple of months after the wedding. She had been so eager to tell Simpson the news, knowing that he had given up any hope of having an heir and guessing how much he secretly hoped for one whenever he played with his nieces or nephews. She recalled, also, how confused she had been when he had failed to express delight at her news.

"How long before you realized he wasn't?" Slater wanted to know.

"Almost right away," Dawn admitted with poignant recollection. "Simpson told me." Her mouth twisted with the irony of it. "A week after I told him the happy tidings, he came back to tell me his."

"Which was?"

# Chapter Five

"Simpson couldn't have children." Her voice was low with the remembered shock of that moment. "Some childhood fever had left him sterile. It was a small detail he hadn't considered important enough to tell me before the wedding. When I informed him we were expecting a baby, he didn't tell me about his sterility until he had reconfirmed it with his doctor in case some miracle had happened."

"Why didn't you get an annulment?" Slater challenged and watched with narrowed and critical eyes.

"And do what?" Dawn asked, because it had occurred to her at the time. "Come back here to you? Pregnant and divorced? After what I'd done to you, you might not have wanted me back. You might not have believed it was your child I was carrying. Even if you had, how would you have taken care of us? You didn't have a steady job, and all you owned was a broken-down old boat and the clothes on your back."

"And you didn't have any faith in my ability to take care of you," he declared grimly, tipping his head back to toss down the second drink. "If I had been Simpson and discovered my loving wife was going to have another's man's child, I would have thrown you out."

"Thank heaven you weren't Simpson," Dawn murmured with a trace of resentment for his callous attitude. "He had more than enough grounds for divorce, but he was willing to forgive and forget."

Only later had she learned that there never had been a divorce in the Lord family, and Simpson had been a great one for upholding the family tradition. Still, even if he had felt honor-bound to continue their marriage, it didn't alter the love and understanding he had shown her, and the kindness he had shown her son. She couldn't have asked more from a man than Simpson had given her.

"So you stayed with him." A humorless sound like a laugh lifted the corners of his mouth, widening it into a derisive smile. "Why not? He was filthy rich. That's why you married him—to get your hands on his money." He lifted his glass in a mock salute. "I never did congratulate you on your success."

Dawn ignored the latter, failing again to correct his impression that she had been left a wealthy widow. "That's why I married him," she admitted. "But his money had very little to do with the reason I stayed with him, beyond assuring my child would be well cared for. After Simpson explained that he couldn't be the father of the child I was carrying, I had to tell him about you. He already knew. I think he even knew why I married him but it didn't matter. You can imagine how I felt."

"No, I can't imagine how you felt." Slater shook his head, his voice running low with contempt. He deliberately refused to understand or even concede she was capable of remorse.

Nothing would be gained by responding to his caustic retort. Dawn felt more could be accomplished by trying to make him understand the reasons behind some of her actions.

"I remember Simpson telling me that, in a way, he was glad he couldn't produce children because he wasn't obligated to make an advantageous business marriage to consolidate wealth since it would require an heir. He was free to marry the girl he loved, which was me." She bowed her head slightly as she spoke. "He loved me enough to accept another man's child into his home. I know you'll find this hard to believe, Slater, but by then, I was tired of hurting people. After hurting so many, I couldn't hurt Simpson more than I already had. I couldn't give him my love, because you had it, but I decided that I could give him happiness. So, yes, I stayed with him—out of a mixture of gratitude and guilt—and I worked at being a good wife to bring him some of the happiness he deserved."

"And you gave him my son," Slater shot the accusation at her, ignoring all else she had told him. "I suppose Simpson passed Randy off as his own."

"No. For Randy's sake, he let him take the

family surname, but Simpson never legally adopted him. And it's your name that is listed as father on his birth certificate," Dawn explained. "Simpson played the role of Dutch uncle to Randy, but he never usurped your position as his father. He was adamant about that."

Her answer brought a moment's silence. When Slater finally spoke, it was with considerably less heat and bitterness. "I guess I owe him something for that." He set his empty glass on the rattan table and squared around to face her. "Which brings us back to Randy, and what's to be done now."

"Not having a father never bothered Randy too much while Simpson was alive." She threaded her fingers together, spreading them and studying the straight patterns they made. "He needs a father. He needs you." She looked at him, folding her fingers together in a prayerful attitude that asked for a truce between them.

His gray eyes glittered in a cold, calculating study of her. "I can't help wondering why you waited until after Simpson was dead before you suddenly decided that Randy needed a father. It can't be that you were waiting until he died. The man's been dead for more than two months."

"Do you think I should have flown out here the day after his funeral?" Dawn bristled at his veiled attack. "There was a small matter of putting affairs in order, not to mention the shock of losing someone I had grown to care about."

"Of course." But it was a response that mocked her explanation. Slater wandered idly toward her, that cool, assessing gaze of his continuing to study her. "At first I had the crazy idea that you'd come back for a much more personal reason. I suppose it shows the size of my ego that I thought you were here to see if we couldn't get back together again. The second time you were going to marry for love—that's what you told me the morning you left. And I wanted to believe that you still cherished some love for me." His voice was growing harder and colder.

How could she tell him that she did when she didn't know how much of her desire was rooted in nostalgia? Both of them had changed so much. It wasn't possible to feel the same. But there was unquestionably smoke coming from an old fire and the ashes were still hot.

"Then I found out about Randy," he said in a tone that indicated the knowledge had changed his thinking. "So you're here, claiming he needs a father." His gaze made a slow sweep of her, taking in every curve of her body. "And there you stand—a sexy, young widow with money to burn and no one to tell her how she should spend it, and with eleven years of having to be a good wife behind her. A half-grown son is bound to be an encumbrance."

"That's not true," Dawn protested, stung by his implication.

"Isn't it?" Slater challenged, stopping in front of her. "You say he needs a father. Are you planning to dump him on me so you can go out and have your fun? It must be difficult to go husband-hunting with a brat in tow. How much easier it is to pawn him off onto someone else."

She was trembling with anger, too incensed to voice any kind of denial to such totally false and denigrating accusations. The recourse left to her was completely instinctive, the impulse to strike the words from his mouth.

The lightning arc of her hand aimed for his cheek, striking it with all the force she could put behind it. The blow turned his head to the side, the impact stinging the palm of her hand. Her own temper made her indifferent to the retaliating anger that darkened his expression. If anything, she felt satisfaction seeing the white mark on his jaw slowly turning red where she had struck him.

Dawn had acted with no thought of the consequences, forgetting that violence was invariably answered with violence. She was forcibly reminded of it when her arms were seized and she was yanked roughly against him, his fingers digging into her soft flesh. The murderous light smouldering in his eyes brought a flicker of alarm to her expression.

The glimpse of it made Slater pause. An expression that was both wry and bitter with regret swept across his features, but his gaze continued to bore into her. The grip of his hands had pulled her onto her toes and arched her body against the length of his. Sensitive nerve endings picked up the sensation of her bare thighs pressed to the cotton texture of his slacks and the solidness of his hip bones ground against hers. The peaks of her breasts were flattened to the hard wall of his chest. Dawn was hardly drawing a breath while her heart beat unevenly, not certain what would happen next.

His mouth thinned into a grim line as he released a disgusted breath that warmed her face. "Ours always was a very *physical* relationship," Slater muttered thickly as if that explained this mutual show of violence. "We still can't seem to communicate on any other level."

Her glance slid to the discolored area on his cheek where she had hit him, and taken pleasure in it. Dawn was sorry now, but—as always it seemed—her regret came too late. Her hands rested loosely on his rib cage, no longer resisting his closeness. Even as she silently acknowledged the accuracy of his statement, she was cognizant of the necessary qualification it needed.

"But we never used to try to hurt each other," she reminded him.

"No, we didn't," he agreed.

A darkness blazed in his eyes, but it was no longer sparked by anger. She could feel the burning heat of it moving over her face and neck. It warmed her in a way that was all too familiar. Without seeming to loosen his grip, his hold on her shifted. One hand curled into her hair at the back of her neck while the other glided down her back.

A half-smothered groan came from his throat as he bent his head toward her. Dawn smelled the whiskey on his breath and turned her lips from him at the last second, letting his mouth graze her cheek.

"You're crazy drunk," she warned him, not because she didn't want his kiss. She did. But she remembered too clearly how their brief, torrid embrace this afternoon had turned him bitter and angry with regret. She didn't want to put either of them through that again.

"Yes, I'm crazy drunk." His mouth, his nose, his chin kept moving over the side of her averted face, nuzzling and exploring what territory was accessible to him. "I'm like a wino who's been on the wagon for eleven years. Then he finds a bottle of wine—the same vintage as the one he took his last drink from—and he wonders if it still has that same wild and sweet bouquet. One little taste, he says." He lipped her ear, drawing a shudder of pleasure from Dawn, and took the lobe between his teeth in a sensual love-bite. "One little taste and that's all. He won't take any more, so he thinks. But all it takes is one taste, and the wino discovers he won't be satisfied until he has the whole bottle." His mouth hovered against the corner of her lips. "You're my bottle of wine, Dawn. I've already had the first taste— the one kiss. I won't be satisfied until I've taken it all."

It was a husky entreaty to give it to him. Inside she was a trembling mass, needing him as much as he claimed to need her. It didn't take much effort to turn that short inch to bring her lips into contact with his mouth. At first their mouths brushed over each other in a feather kiss that heightened the sensitivity of their lips.

When the anticipation level had reached a fever-pitch that had them straining against each other, his mouth rolled onto hers, opening to consume it whole. Her reaching hands went around his middle and flattened across his back, trying to defy physical laws and bring them still closer together.

For endless, whirling minutes, they kissed passionately, devouring each other, his hands roaming, touching, and molding her to fit to his hard contours. When their lips finally untangled so each could draw a labored breath, there was the rawness of dissatisfaction. Slater buried his face in the curve of her neck where her pulse was throbbing madly.

"You don't know the hell I've gone through," he muttered with an ache in his voice, "knowing you legally belonged in another man's bed—and picturing you lying in his arms."

"And you don't know what the agony was like for me—" she whispered to let him know he wasn't the only one who had been haunted by images, "—lying with him and having him touch me and kiss me all the while wishing it was you. Worse, I never stopped wishing it was you."

"What are you wishing now?" His hand had found its way to the bare skin at the small of her back. Slater lifted his head to bring his face inches above hers while he studied her. The black pupils of his eyes had widened until only a silver ring showed around them.

"I'm wishing that you'd love me." In every sense of the word, she meant it, but it seemed unnecessary to elaborate.

It was a wish that seemed destined, at last, to be fulfilled as the crushing weight of his mouth rocked onto her lips. They parted to invite a deepening of the kiss to its fullest intimacy. When her feet were lifted off the floor by his carrying arms, Dawn felt weightless.

She was barely conscious of the lengthening shadows outside the office windows as the darkness of dusk settled over the building. It was only a short distance to the sofa from where they had been standing. Slater set her down on a cushion, his hands lifting the bottom of her tanktop and pulling it over her head as they came away.

Her deep blue eyes were heavy with desire as he leaned toward her and let a hand slide onto her naked breast. She was reaching for him to draw him down on the cushion with her as she lay back. It was imperative that nothing come between them—not the past or the future—or the silken shirt covering his chest from her seeking fingers.

While his lips made exciting forays from her throat to her maturely rounded breasts, she was tugging at the shirt buttons to unfasten them. As soon as his shirt was hanging open, her hands slipped inside to feel the heat of his skin. It was a sensation she didn't have a chance to enjoy for long as his teasing tongue had her writhing with another need.

Actions and sensations all began to flow into

one another—his hand pushing the elastic waistband of her shorts over her hipbone; the searing taste of his kiss drinking deeply of her love; the weight of his flatly muscled body settling onto her; naked flesh against naked flesh; and the golden fire in her loins consuming all thought but the pleasure that came from giving love and receiving it. The sound of her name coming from his lips became her only touch with reality. It was repeated over and over, interspliced with love words that were too quickly lost.

How long she lay afterwards in the possessive clasp of his circling arms, their bodies squeezed together by the narrow width of the sofa, Dawn couldn't have said. But in its own way, this holding of each other was equally as pleasing as the sexual gratification had been. His musky body smell was all around her, warm and enveloping.

"It's been so long since I've felt like this." She traced the hard edge of his jaw with the tip of her finger, feeling the faint bristle that had scraped the skin around her mouth and left it tender.

Slater lightly captured her fingers and lifted them to his mouth, drawing her glance to its male line as he pressed her fingers to it. When she looked at him fully, his expression seemed unnaturally somber. He held her gaze, the gray of his eyes probing in its search for something.

"You got your wish, didn't you?" His comment sounded casual. Dawn wasn't able to detect any hint of bitter mockery.

She nodded once. "It was your wish, too, wasn't it?" she asked.

"Yes." Slater glanced at her ringless fingers. "I've wished for this a long time." His look was almost gentle, a tinge of sadness in it, but no regret that Dawn could see. A muscle flexed in the arm she was lying on. "Move," he said. "My arm's going to sleep."

Reluctantly she propped herself up on an elbow to take her weight off his arm. Instead of merely changing position, Slater sat up and reached for his trousers. She released an inaudible sigh. This moment of supreme closeness had to come to an end sometime, but she had wanted it to last a little longer. But no one could hold on to this rare kind of happiness forever.

By the time she had pulled the hem of her tanktop down around her waist, Slater was standing by the desk. He switched on a tall lamp, chasing away the intimacy of near darkness with the sudden glare of light. Shirtless, the upper half of his body had a sun-bronzed sheen to it that rippled with the play of his muscles as he turned his back to her and reached for something on the desk.

"Cigarette?" he asked with a glance over his shoulder.

"No thanks." Dawn bent down to slip on her sandals, hooking a finger in the back strap to ease it over her heel. She heard the snap of a cigarette lighter, and the click of it being shut.

When she straightened, he was leaning against

the edge of the desk, half-sitting on it while he watched her. There was something unnerving about his absent stare. She sensed that he had withdrawn from her and become preoccupied with his own secret thoughts. She couldn't stand not knowing what was going on in his head.

"Penny for your thoughts?" she said with a quick smile to make her curiosity appear more casual.

His mouth twitched almost into a smile. "You could have bought them for that once, but I'm worth more than that now." The drawled response eased much of her concern.

"I noticed all your business trophies on the walls." Dawn glanced briefly at the plaques of achievement.

"I don't claim to be in Simpson Lord's league yet," Slater stated dryly and flicked the ash from the end of his cigarette. "But he had a couple of generations' headstart on me."

It had not been spoken entirely in jest. There was a competitive edge in the words, as if the worth of a man was judged by the amount of money in his bankbook. Dawn had learned the hard way it was a false standard to use in the search for happiness. And she didn't want Slater to think she still believed that was important.

"That doesn't matter to me, Slater," she insisted quickly.

Again his mouth slanted with a crooked smile. "That's right. This time it's for love, isn't it?" he mocked. Before she could respond to that vague jibe, the muted ring of a telephone sounded in the outer office area. He picked up the receiver on his desk. "MacBride," he said into the phone. Without speaking again to the calling party, he straightened from the desk and held out the receiver to her. "It's for you."

Briefly startled by his announcement, she crossed quickly to the desk to take the phone from his hand. "Hello?"

"Dawn?" It was her mother's voice on the other end of the wire. "I'm sorry to call you but it was getting so late and I—" She trailed off lamely without completing the sentence.

"It's all right," Dawn assured her that she wasn't upset by the phone call.

"I just wasn't sure how late you would be— whether I should wait up for you or leave the housekey under the mat outside the door," her mother explained so Dawn wouldn't think she was trying to dictate what hour she should come home.

"I'll be there shortly," Dawn promised, guessing that Randy was probably as anxious as her mother to find out what had transpired during the long discussion with Slater. She couldn't very well tell either of them how much had been said without words.

"All right. I hope I didn't interrupt anything important," her mother added.

"You didn't. Good-bye." She waited until her mother had echoed the word before hanging up the phone. She glanced at Slater as he paused near the desk to grind out his cigarette butt in the ashtray. "That was—"

"—your mother," he interrupted to finish the sentence and identify the voice he'd heard.

"You recognized her voice," she realized.

"I suppose the clucking mother hen was checking up on her missing chick," Slater guessed with a smoothness that bothered her.

"In a way," Dawn admitted, and glanced at the darkness outside the window panes. "It's later than I realized."

He looked at his watch. "Past your parents' bedtime," he acknowledged. "I suppose they're anxious to lock up the doors and turn in."

"Yes." There was something about this conversation that she didn't like, although it seemed innocent enough on the surface.

"Do you suppose they've guessed what we've been doing all this time?" he asked, then answered his own question. "I don't imagine they have. They were always a few minutes late on the scene, whether it was your mother waiting on the porch five minutes before you were supposed to be home or your father not finding us on my boat until the next morning. Was that the night Randy was conceived?"

He was dredging up too many memories and appearing to taunt her with them. Her mind was whirling, trying to keep pace with the changing direction of his sentences.

"It must have been," she nodded.

Slater turned from her and she found herself facing the muscled smoothness of his tanned back. "You'd better go," he said. "You promised your mother you'd be home shortly."

"Yes." But she didn't make any move to leave, not wanting to go now that everything between them suddenly seemed so unsettled. "Slater." She came up to his side and laid her hand on the taut, sinewed muscles of his upper arm.

With grudging slowness, he faced her and looked down the straight bridge of his nose at her. There was indecision in his eyes, an inner war being waged with himself. Dawn swayed toward him, in some way wanting to reassure him.

The little movement brought his arms around her to catch her to him, and gather her hard to his body. His mouth was coming down as he muttered roughly, "Damn you for twisting me up into knots like this."

There was something hard and demanding in his rough kiss that hadn't been there before, as if he was trying to exorcise her ghost from his system. Dawn pulled away from his mouth and stared at him in hurt and half-angry confusion.

Instantly he released her and moved away, but she had a glimpse of the darkening frown gathering on his forehead.

"I'm sorry, Dawn." But he didn't say for what. "Go," he urged with absent gruffness. "Before your mother starts getting worried."

She hesitated a second more then walked to the door, letting his apology take the place of an explanation for the time being. She had the inner door open and was halfway out of it when Slater added, "I'll talk to you tomorrow."

He tossed the remark after her with an absent

indifference. Dawn saw it as a desire to continue their relationship, however reluctantly it was expressed. There had been a few minutes when she had thought it was going to fall apart all over again.

When she stepped into the clear night, bright stars shone in the sky overhead, and a big, old moon rode high above the horizon. A cool sea breeze drifted off the water to scent the languid air. It was a long time since she had noticed such things.

# Chapter Six

All the breakfast dishes were washed and returned to their respective places in the kitchen cupboard, except for a coffee cup. It was sitting on the table where her father was still reading the morning paper. Dawn hummed along with the song being played on the radio while she swept the kitchen floor, tapping her father's shoes so he would move his feet and allow the broom to reach the area under him.

Her mother was hurrying around drawing all the window shades and drapes to trap the lingering coolness of the night air inside the house. Randy was outside, playing by the garage. Every once in a while, Dawn heard the basketball hitting the backboard her father had installed above the garage door.

As she swept the dust into a small pile, Dawn was absently amazed at how easily she had reverted to the habit of doing household chores after so many years of having them done for her by others. Maybe she'd tire of them, but right now she didn't resent doing them at all. Maybe that acceptance came with maturity, too.

When she reached for the dustpan, a car roared into the driveway. Instantly the dustpan was forgotten and the broom was hurriedly propped against a cabinet counter as Dawn rushed to the back door. Her face lit up when she saw the shiny black Corvette. She pushed the door open and stepped onto the back stoop. Randy was already running to greet Slater, so she waited there, taking the couple of extra minutes to smooth her watersilk blouse inside the waistband of her tangerine slacks.

There was a suggestion of impatience in the line of his long, muscled body as Slater paused to greet Randy. He smiled, but Dawn noticed the smile didn't reach his eyes. Her expression sobered slightly, her gaze becoming more watchful.

When he started toward the house, his strongly cut features seemed close to wearing a brooding scowl. He looked up to see her standing at the railing around the stoop, and just as quickly, his glance skipped away. Another bad sign. Dawn fought to hold the bitter disappointment and hurt away from her expression.

"Good morning," she greeted him with what she hoped was calmness.

"Morning," he returned, the omission of an adjective making it starkly apparent there was nothing "good" in it as far as he was concerned.

A surge of stubbornness made Dawn confront him with his obviously sour mood. "You're grumpy this morning," she challenged to identify the reason.

His eyes were like gray stones, hard and impenetrable when they finally met her searching gaze. The lack of any emotion in them seemed to confirm her suspicion that Slater was wishing last night hadn't happened for them, regardless of what he'd said at the time. Her lips compressed into a taut line.

"I guess I haven't had my morning quota of caffeine," Slater countered her challenge with an obvious lie.

"We still have some coffee left over from breakfast. Why don't you come in and have a cup?" Dawn invited, conscious that Randy was trailing along at Slater's heels, making any open discussion impossible while he was there.

"Fine." It was a clipped answer of acceptance.

Pivoting, Dawn led the way into the house, feeling the tension mount in her system. Both her parents were in the kitchen when they entered it. Slater had obviously been the subject of their conversation since both fell into a guilty silence.

"Have a seat." Dawn coolly waved a hand at the chairs around the kitchen table. "I'll pour your coffee."

"Hello, Slater." Her father wasn't sure how to handle the situation, whether to greet him as a longtime family friend or a mere acquaintance. Dawn had been very circumspect about the information she'd given her mother last night, downplaying her meeting with Slater. Now she was glad she hadn't sounded too optimistic. "I'd ask how business is—" her father continued

"—but every time I turn around I hear 'MacBride owns this' or you sold that or you're making a ton of money from something else."

"I can't complain." But Slater didn't return the courtesy by inquiring how her father was doing, nor did he offer any encouragement for the conversation to continue.

As Dawn took a cup from the cupboard and filled it with coffee, she heard the scrape of a chair leg. Randy had brought the basketball into the house and was absently bouncing it on the linoleum floor. It was nearly as irritating as drumming fingers.

"Not in the house, Randy," she reminded him as she carried Slater's cup of coffee to the table.

"Sorry, Mom. I forgot." He hooked the ball under his arm and hovered next to Slater's chair. "Do you wanta come out and watch me shoot a few baskets after you drink your coffee? I'm pretty good." Randy seemed to be the only one who wasn't conscious of the brittle atmosphere in the kitchen.

"We'll see." Slater avoided a commitment.

"I'm on my way to the grocery store," her mother announced. "Is there anything you need, Dawn?"

"No." She walked back to the kitchen counter to pour herself a cup of the strong, black coffee.

There was the rustle of the newspaper being folded and set aside as her father took a clue from his wife's departure. "Got some work I need to get finished in the garage," he said and followed his wife out the back door.

"You should see the stuff Gramps makes in his workshop." It didn't occur to Randy that his presence might not be wanted. "He's been letting me help him, and showing me how to do stuff. I found this piece of driftwood that we're going to make into a lamp. It's got a real weird shape. Do you want to come out and see it?"

"Not now!" His voice was harsh with impatience.

Dawn saw the hurt frown cloud Randy's features. She was instantly angry. "Slater," she spoke his name in sharp rebuke.

This time the angry impatience on his features was directed at himself. He sliced a grimly apologetic glance at Randy. "I'm sorry. I had no cause to snap at you." Slater sighed heavily and rubbed a hand across his forehead. "I'm not feeling in the best of moods this morning."

"That's okay." Randy was quick to dismiss his rudeness as he worked to acquire a pseudo-adult air for a man-to-man comment. "What cha got? A hangover?"

Slater's gaze flicked briefly to Dawn. "You could say that," he murmured with a wry, biting twist of humor to his mouth.

The look immediately reminded her of the analogy he'd made between himself and an alcoholic. An auburn brow shot up. "From too much vintage wine?" she taunted coolly and sat across the table from him.

"Yes." There was considerably less humor in the curve of his mouth, his eyes darkening in withdrawal from this word-game. He continued to study her as he spoke to his son. "Why don't you run outside, Randy, so I can talk privately with your mother. I'll be out after I finish my coffee."

Randy didn't like being excluded again, but his relationship with his father was too new for him to risk testing it by refusing to leave. Glumly he walked to the door.

"Don't be too long," was the closest he came to a protest.

Keeping her eyes downcast, Dawn looked into the mirror-black surface of her coffee and waited for the sound of the door latching securely behind Randy. Her nerves felt raw from this constant exposure to Slater's ever-reoccurring resentment toward her.

"We never did get around to having our talk last night," he said, breaking the heavy silence that had descended on the room with Randy's departure.

"I guess we didn't." She continued to stare at her cup. For a while last night, she hadn't thought there was anything left to discuss. Obviously she was wrong.

"Just what is it you want from me?" Slater demanded.

Her head came up sharply, her gaze flying to the chilling set of his hard features. "If you have to ask—" Dawn checked the angry words.

Nothing would be gained by losing her temper and lashing out at him. It was apparent that he was shutting out those moments when love had blazed so brilliantly. She struggled to do the same and respond to his questions as if it hadn't happened.

"I want you to be a father to Randy—to be there when he needs you." That had been her original desire when she had returned to Key West. She hadn't dared hope for more than that. Foolishly she had begun to believe there could be.

"Are you planning to stay here?" He sounded like an interrogator who had no stake in her answer.

"Yes—providing, of course, that we come to some kind of truce where Randy is concerned." Too agitated to remain seated, Dawn stood up and carried her full cup of coffee back to the counter by the pot, setting it down. "Naturally, I don't intend to live with my parents. That's why I was interested in purchasing the Van de Veere house—providing the price was reasonable." She kept her back to the table, unable to look at him while she endured this farcical conversation. "How much is it?"

When she turned, she was startled to discover Slater was standing only a few feet from her. He had moved so quietly she hadn't been aware he'd followed her.

After he had quoted a price well within range of what she could afford to pay, he added, "So we won't have to waste time haggling over the price, I'll drop it another two thousand."

"Sold." It was totally a reflex movement that prompted Dawn to extend a hand to shake on the deal.

Slater just looked at it, then slowly raised his

glance to her face. White and trembling from this deliberate affront, Dawn held her head high, falling back on pride now that all else had failed her. But moisture gathered in her eyes to blur her vision and there was a traitorous quiver of her chin.

"Damn you," she cursed hoarsely, and swung away to grip the edge of the counter. "And damn you for being a man. You're schooled from the cradle not to show your feelings. And girls are encouraged to cry when they're hurt. It isn't fair," Dawn protested in a choked voice, and brushed impatiently at a tear that slipped off her lashes. "What happened? Last night I thought—"

"Do you think one night with you can make up for the thousands I spent alone?" He bitterly hurled the angry words to cut off her sentence.

Her head jerked as if she had been slapped. But the demand served to check her tears. "No, I don't." Her voice lost its husky waver although it remained tight. "It happened too soon. I should have known it did. You've hated me for so long. Not even you can reverse directions overnight." The corners of her mouth curled into a sad, laughing smile. "There's something in that old saying about 'the cold light of day,' isn't there?"

"Maybe it's myself I'm not liking very much this morning," Slater offered grimly. Dawn turned slowly to look at him and discover what he meant by that statement. He moved closer, stopping when his legs brushed against hers, in effect pinning her between himself and the counter. "I had sworn if you ever came back, I wouldn't have anything to do with you. I wasn't even going to give you the time of day. It lowers a man's opinion of himself when he learns he hasn't the strength to resist the temptation of a woman's body." Self-derision deepened the corners of his mouth. "And I'm too old and too experienced to claim that you seduced me. I was more than willing—I was eager."

"Now you're sorry." That's what hurt.

"I don't know what I am," he declared with a grim shake of his head. "One minute I want to hurt you before you can hurt me, and in the next, I just want to love you."

Dawn wished he wasn't standing so near. She didn't want to feel the muscled columns of his thighs or the slight thrust of his hips. It was all too evocative and intimate.

"I'll tell you what," she began. "Until you decide which way you want it to be, why don't you go back on the wagon?" She stepped sideways to end the contact with him although her senses continued to clamor from it. "In the meantime, we'll keep everything on a strictly business level."

"That's roughly what I was going to suggest," Slater said, and didn't sound too happy that she had proposed it first.

"About the house—how long will it take to have the papers drawn so we can close the sale?" Now that she had changed the subject, Dawn stayed with it. "There's no need to discuss terms. I'll pay cash."

"Of course," he murmured dryly. "I can write up the contract today, but you'll need the abstract examined and brought up to date."

"How long before I can take possession?" she asked.

"As far as I'm concerned, you can move into the house this afternoon if you want. All the paper work and deeds should be ready within a week." Slater paused, studying her a second. "You don't have to buy the house. It's just sitting empty. You and Randy are welcome to live in it—for as long as you want."

"For nothing?" Dawn was certain there had to be some kind of strings attached.

"For nothing," he assured her.

"No thanks," she refused his apparently generous offer. "I'd rather not be under any obligation to you. I prefer to buy it rather than have people talking about me as Slater MacBride's kept woman."

"Randy is my son," Slater reminded her. "I offered the house so I could contribute something toward his support. I was not trying to put you in my debt."

"Perhaps you weren't," she conceded. "But just the same, I'd rather purchase the house outright. We'll probably move into it as soon as possible."

"I can arrange to have a crew go over there and clean the place up for you," he said.

"There's no need. I'll handle it myself," Dawn insisted. "I'll stop by your office early this afternoon to sign the necessary papers and make a down payment. You can leave them with your secretary—along with the doorkey."

"I'll do that." It was all very curt and professional. "I'll go out and see Randy before I leave."

Dawn watched him walk out the door. On the surface, it seemed to be a sound and workable proposal, but she knew it was doomed to failure. They shared too many intimate memories to ever sustain a business relationship without personalities interfering. They were just kidding themselves.

Dawn had put most of her household and personal possessions in storage before she left Texas. After she had signed the papers for the house, she arranged to have them shipped to Key West. While she waited for them to arrive, there was a great deal of work to be done on the property, both outside and in. Viewing it as a kind of therapy to take her mind off Slater, Dawn threw herself into it with all her energies.

The overgrown yard was chosen as the first task. Randy teased her that she intended to wage war with it when he saw the tools she had raided from her father's equipment shed. There was the usual assemblage of garden tools, such as rakes, hoes, and spades, plus more lethal items— hatchets, machetes, and a double-bladed axe. She loaded them into a wheelbarrow and, together, she and Randy wheeled it over to their new house in the cool of early morning.

Dressed in combat gear consisting of long-sleeved shirts, sturdy denims, boots, and gloves to protect their bodies from the sharp and sometimes thorny underbrush, they attacked the front yard in earnest, using the sidewalk as their route of entry. By late morning, they had made a sizable and hard-fought dent in it. But the heat and the humidity were beginning to wear them down.

Randy had stripped down to the waist, sweat streaming down his shoulders and wetting the thick hair on his forehead. A kerchief was tied around it, creating a sweatband to keep the stinging perspiration out of his eyes. Another wheelbarrow load of palm fronds and tangled vines had to be pushed to the growing pile of debris in the driveway. The muscles in his young arms bulged as he lifted the handles and began driving it forward.

Hot and frazzled, Dawn leaned on her rake. A scarf was tied around her hair. She tipped her head back and squinted at the sun high overhead, trying to judge the time. She hadn't risked wearing her watch for fear she'd catch it on some brush and lose it. The plan had been to work until noon, then quit before the full heat of the day hit them. It had to be close to that now, she decided.

She shifted her grip on the rake and winced in pain. Gingerly she pulled off the glove on her right hand and examined the blister on her palm.

It looked raw and angry. She heard the rattle of the wheelbarrow as its load was dumped and turned to call to Randy.

"Bring a bandage from the first aid kit when you come." Her voice croaked on a weary note.

Stopping, Randy turned and jogged the short distance to the veranda where the first aid kit and water jug sat side by side in the shade. Dawn marveled at the resiliency of youth that Randy still had the energy to move out of a dragging walk.

Enough of the yard had been cleared to enable her to have only a partially obscured view of the street. A flash of black caught her eye, attracted by the sound of a passing car. Only it wasn't passing. Dawn recognized the black Corvette as it swung into the driveway, just managing to stop short of the brush pile.

Even though Dawn was too tired to care about her appearance, she was conscious of it. Her face was streaked with dust and pollen. Stickers and broken twigs were hooked onto her clothes. In this old shirt of her father's, she knew she looked shapeless. Even the crowning glory of her hair was hidden under the dirty scarf. For some strange reason, it was her chipped nails and blistered palms that bothered her the most. There wasn't time to slip her glove back on, and it would have been too painful anyway, so she simply let her hand hang by her side, hoping he wouldn't notice it.

His brows were drawn together in a frown as

his gaze swept the yard, his long, free-swinging strides carrying him to where she was standing. "Where are your workmen? Have they broken for lunch already?"

"We are the workmen," she said, including Randy with a gesture of her gloved hand as he joined them.

"You aren't planning to clean up this yard by yourselves?" He looked at her as if she'd lost her senses.

Dawn was hot and tired enough to wonder if she had. "We're both young and able-bodied. All it takes is a little muscle."

"A weak mind and a strong back, that's what it takes," Slater corrected with a trace of exasperation.

"A little physical labor doesn't hurt anybody," she insisted, and smiled briefly at her son. "Besides, this is going to be our new home. We have to put some effort into making it that." She felt it would be a good lesson for Randy; instill in him a sense of ownership because he had helped with it.

"Here's your bandage, Mom." He offered it to her.

"Physical labor doesn't hurt anybody, huh?" Slater mocked and took the bandage from Randy. His seeking glance noticed the gloveless hand at her side. "A blister?" he guessed.

"Yes. It's just a little sore." She wouldn't admit that it was throbbing painfully since it had been exposed to the air.

Turning her hand palm-upward, she showed him the fiery red sore. His gaze flicked sharply to her face. "You crazy little fool," he muttered angrily under his breath. "You'll be lucky if you don't get infection in it."

"It isn't that bad." But Dawn winced as his finger probed around the edges of it, his touch basically gentle although it imparted pain. He firmly held her hand so she couldn't pull it away from him.

"Do you have any antiseptic with you?" he asked.

"In the first aid kit," she nodded.

"Go get it for me, Randy," he ordered. "Before we put a bandage on it, it needs to be cleansed and treated."

As Randy trotted off again, Dawn didn't want to pursue the subject of her blister, certain it would only invite a lecture from Slater. And if she chose to clean the yard herself instead of having it done, it was entirely her own business. But she wasn't in the mood to argue with him over that point.

"Why did you stop by?" she asked. "Do you have the final papers ready for the house?"

"No, they should be finished tomorrow," he said, then explained, "I had the afternoon free so I stopped by your parents' house to see if Randy wanted to go out on the boat with me. I promised to take him snorkeling some time."

"He'd like that." As sticky and overheated as she felt, the invitation sounded heavenly.

"Do you mean he doesn't have to work in the yard this afternoon?" There was a devilish twinkle in his gray eyes that laughingly mocked her.

"Regardless of what you think, I'm not so foolish as to work outside in the heat of the afternoon," Dawn retorted.

"Why don't you come with us?" Slater invited unexpectedly.

"No." Her refusal was quick, perhaps too quick.

"Why not?" he challenged, deliberately argumentative to wear down her resistance. "With Randy along as chaperon, I'll have to lay off the booze." She stiffened self-consciously at the oblique reference to her, knowing full well it was what she had wanted to avoid when she had initially turned down the invitation. "Sorry. I guess that joke was in poor taste."

"It doesn't matter," she murmured.

"I'd still like you to come with us," he said more quietly. "Being the father of a ten-year-old boy is still new to me. It gets a bit awkward between us sometimes. I'm never sure what I should say to him, or what we're supposed to talk about. I think it would be easier on Randy if you came along to smooth out the rough spots."

She listened to the run of his voice, hearing its calm reasoning and persuasive tone. It made sense. Plus it had been years since she had gone snorkeling in these clear waters. The combination made for an irresistible appeal.

"I'll come," she agreed.

Randy came trotting up, slowing to walk heavily the last couple of steps. "I brought the whole kit 'cause I wasn't sure which you wanted," he said to Slater and opened the box to show him the contents.

"How would you like to go snorkeling this afternoon?" Slater asked as he removed a bottle of disinfectant to cleanse the blistered sore.

"Really?" Randy perked up with interest.

"Your mother's going to come with us." He doused the area as Dawn hissed in a breath at the burning sting it made.

"Great!" His enthusiasm at the news was a total endorsement of the plan.

Slater dabbed on some antiseptic before pressing the adhesive bandage over the sore. "Get all these tools put away and I'll give you a ride home so you can get cleaned up and ready to go."

In record time it seemed, the car was rolling to a stop in her parents' driveway. The motor idled while Slater waited for them to climb out.

"I'll be back in an hour," he said.

"We'll be ready," Dawn promised, although it just barely gave them time to shower, change, and grab a bite of lunch.

As he backed out of the driveway, she curved an arm around Randy's shoulders and turned them both toward the house. When the sound of the motor had faded away, Randy tipped his head back to look at her with an anxious frown.

"Do you think he likes me?" he asked earnestly. "I mean *really* likes me—not just because he should 'cause he's my father." He didn't pause for Dawn to answer. "I want him to like me so much, but sometimes I get all tongue-tied and can't think of anything to say."

Her expression softened. "I'll bet he has that same problem, too."

"I doubt it." He scuffed the toe of his shoe in the gravel.

"I wouldn't worry about it, though," Dawn insisted. "After you get to know each other better, all the awkwardness will go away."

Randy's concern was almost an echo of the sentiment Slater had expressed to her earlier, and confirmed that her presence would be useful. It wasn't something she was just pretending so she would have an excuse to spend an afternoon with Slater.

# Chapter Seven

The class of boats tied up at the marina ran the full gamut from sport fishermen with fly bridges to catamarans to houseboats, and anything and everything in between. Dawn silently admired the sleek lines of the thirty-foot cabin cruiser they approached. Slater had already pointed it out as belonging to him.

When she was close enough to read the lettering on the side, she looked at it and laughed, *"Homesick?* What kind of name is that for a boat?"

Instead of being offended, Slater treated her to an indulgent look. "Whenever I get fed up with the business grind and wish I was back lazing around and living off the sea, I take the boat out for a couple of hours—or a couple of days. In other words, I get 'homesick.'"

The explanation silenced her amusement at the name. She knew the drastic change his lifestyle had undergone, and the transition couldn't have been an easy one. She was glad he hadn't severed all ties with the sea. He had loved it so, familiar with its every mood. It was natural for him to

117

miss it, and the *Homesick* would take him back to it whenever he wanted to go.

After they were on board, Slater glanced at Randy. "Do you want to cast off the lines while I start the engines?"

"Sure," he agreed quickly, then snapped a salute. "I mean, aye-aye, sir."

Slater saluted him back, smiling faintly, then headed to the cruiser's bridge area. Dawn followed him, lifting the hair out of her eyes when the wind off the sea blew it across her face. Over her black swimsuit with its swirling tiger-eye pattern, she wore a white lace beach jacket, belted at the waist. She stood to one side of Slater, out of his way, and looked out at the vast expanse of water shimmering under a high sun.

"Whatever happened to the *Seaspray*?" The minute she asked the question, she regretted it. Memories of that boat were all tied up and intertwined with the memory of their romance.

There was a long second when he appeared to be preoccupied checking gauges. "Initially I was going to do something dramatic," he said, looking out to see how Randy was doing but not glancing at her. There was no inflection in his voice that might have indicated he was disturbed by the question. She could just as easily have asked him about the weather. "—like towing her into deep water and sinking her to the bottom, hoping she'd take your ghost with her. In the end, I sold her to some guy from New York and used the money to buy a partnership in a shrimp boat.

From there, I started building my little empire."
The last phrase was used wryly, managing to
emphasize the smallness of his wealth in propor-
tion to someone of Simpson Lord's calibre.

"I'm glad you sold her," Dawn said because she
felt some kind of response was necessary.

"A month after he bought her, the guy ran her
into a reef," Slater informed her. "The *Seaspray*
broke up and went to the bottom. But she didn't
take your ghost with her."

Maybe it was the blandness in his announcement that made her suddenly so restless. Dawn
really didn't know. "I'll go see if Randy needs any
help," she murmured and moved away.

The boat's engines were kept a notch or two
above idle speed until they had cleared the harbor, then Slater opened them up. The racing wind
seemed to blow away Dawn's tension and allowed
her to relax and enjoy the ride.

After Slater pointed out their destination on a
nautical chart, she and Randy plotted a course to
it. Each took a turn at the controls, and the hour it
took to reach the spot on the map flashed by.

They anchored the cruiser in the deep water
just off a coral reef and swam ashore. It only took
Randy a few lessons to become accustomed to the
use of the snorkeling equipment before he was
initiated to the underwater beauty of a coral reef.

For Dawn, it was a matter of rediscovering all
the little delights. It was a sport of wondrous
beauty and serenity, the waters crystal clear and
the colors of the fish and strange plant life dis-

playing a rainbow brilliance. She was totally at peace—most of the time.

With a ten-year-old boy on the scene, there was bound to be some horseplay in the water. Usually it was between Randy and Slater but occasionally she was drawn into the playful fray. It just added to the fun of the afternoon.

All too soon it seemed, Slater was signaling them it was time to swim back to the boat. He was already on board when Dawn climbed the swimming ladder. Reaching down, he grabbed hold of her arm and hauled her onto the deck. Water streamed off of her as she looked up at him, smiling, a little out of breath from that last long swim, but blissfully contented.

His gaze glittered warmly onto her upturned face. "Enjoy yourself?"

"Yes," she breathed out the very definite answer. "I'd forgotten how wonderful it is out there."

She moved away so he could help Randy aboard. Exhausted but happy, she sank onto the aft deck, her legs curled to the side, and picked up a towel to towel-dry her hair. Randy was bubbling with enthusiasm over the adventure, talking non-stop from the second his feet touched the deck.

When he finally had to stop for a breath, Slater inserted, "It's late. If you two are going to get home in time for supper, we're going to have to get under way pretty soon."

"I'll help," Randy volunteered.

Dawn didn't even make an attempt to move,

except to straighten her legs out and lie back to let the sun evaporate the salt water from her skin. When she heard the fore and aft anchors being raised, she smiled and settled more comfortably on the hard deck. With two males on board, her help wasn't needed. She intended to simply lie there and soak up the sunshine.

The deck vibrated pleasantly with the purring throb of the engines. Her eyes were closed against the bright light of the sun. She was conscious of the boat's movement and the warmth of the sun on her skin, tempered by the coolness of an eddying wind. For a time she'd heard Slater and Randy conversing back and forth, but now there was only the sound of the boat and the splash of the water.

Something—a sixth sense maybe—seemed to warn her that she wasn't alone. She let her lashes raise just a crack and looked through the slitted opening. Slater was standing at her feet, silently looking at her. Her eyes opened a little wider.

A disturbing heat began to warm her blood. The way he was looking at her gave Dawn the uncanny feeling that in his mind, he was covering her. Without half-trying, she could feel the heat of his sun-warmed body against her skin and the pressure of his mouth on her lips, and the excitement building in her limbs.

It was a mental seduction, and all the more disturbing because of its intensity. It was like a spell being cast on her. Dawn knew she had to break it or it might cease to be mental.

She moved, shifting onto her side first to grab her beach jacket then rising to her feet. Without trying to make it seem deliberate, she turned her back to him while she turned out the jacket to locate the sleeves.

"Are we nearly there?" she asked to shatter the unbearable silence.

"About twenty minutes out."

His hands touched her waist, then slid around to the front to draw her backward against his length. Her heart did a funny little flip against her rib cage as one hand slid low on her stomach and the other curved to the underswell of her breasts. Spontaneous longing quivered through her. He bent his head and nibbled at her bare shoulder, adding to the effects the arousing caress of his hands created. Her fingers curled onto his forearms and weakly attempted to pull his hands away.

"You swore off drinking, Slater," Dawn reminded him in a voice that was all husky and disturbed.

"Yes, I swore off drinking," he admitted, his mouth moving near her ear, stimulating its sensitive shell-opening. "But there's no harm in caressing the bottle the wine comes in."

She turned into him, using her arms to wedge a space between them. "What will that accomplish?" Frustration flashed in the blue of her eyes as she discovered it was no less stimulating to feel her hips arched against his hard, male outline.

"I don't know." He locked his hands together in

the small of her back and eyed her lazily. "But you're going to ache almost as much as I will."

His mouth skimmed her face but didn't taste her intoxicating lips. She guessed he was testing his self-control and tried not to let him see that hers was stretched to the limit. When he finally drew away, she had the satisfaction of noting he was breathing no easier than she was. But there was also no question that he had aroused an ache that was slow to fade.

After they had docked the boat at the marina, they trooped to the car, none of them talking very much—not even Randy. He squeezed into the back of the Corvette and slumped tiredly.

"Boy, am I beat," he murmured.

"After working all morning and swimming all afternoon, you should be." Dawn knew she wasn't far away from exhaustion as she slid into the passenger seat. She was running on nerves, alert to every movement of Slater. "You'll have to get to bed early tonight," she told Randy. "It's work again in the morning."

"Don't listen to her, Randy," Slater advised and inserted the key in the ignition. "You don't have to work in the morning." Dawn opened her mouth to protest this usurpation of her authority. Father or not, he had no right to countermand her orders without discussing it with her in private first. "Neither do you," he glanced at her, a small smile showing.

"I wasn't aware you had the authority to give me the day off," she replied a trifle stiffly.

"Let's just say that tomorrow you don't have to work in the yard," he said as if that avoided a confrontation.

"And why don't I?" Dawn challenged.

"Because while you two were getting cleaned up this noon, I took a crew of laborers over and had them finish the yard this afternoon."

"You had no right to do that!" Her stunned surprise was giving way to anger.

"Maybe I had no right to do it, but it's done," he stated. "If I had known you were going to try to clear that underbrush yourself, I would have done it to start out with—before you ever bought the house." He sliced her a short look. "I don't like the idea of either one of you handling all those sharp knives and blades. One careless mistake and you could cut yourself open to the bone."

"You could have discussed this with me first." She didn't argue against his logic, because she had been leery about Randy handling some of the sharper tools.

"I remember what it's like to argue with you when your mind's made up about something," Slater said dryly and shifted into reverse gear. "It's easier to have the discussion after the fact."

"I'm glad you hired those guys," Randy yawned from the back seat. "That was hard work."

"And it didn't hurt you a bit," Dawn flashed.

"I never said it did," Randy defended himself. "I'm just glad I don't have to do it again tomorrow morning."

"If you want to teach him work ethics, have him scrub floors or wash windows," Slater advised. "Going back to the basics is very noble, but there comes a point where it can be carried too far. A woman and a child clearing a jungle is taking it too far."

"So maybe it was," she admitted grudgingly, aware it had been a penny-pinching decision. "But since you took it upon yourself to hire those workmen, you can pay them, too."

"I planned on it." There was a trace of amusement in his voice. "You never did like letting go of your money, did you?"

"No." She turned her head to look out the side window, subsiding into silence.

Her mother looked around the front room with an approving nod. "It's looking so nice, Dawn."

"It's really beginning to look like a home, isn't it?" she said with satisfaction.

Half of their personal belongings had arrived by truck the same day Dawn received the deed to the house. The furniture and linen didn't arrive until the following week, and it took nearly the whole of another to get everything unpacked and organized.

In retrospect, it probably would have been best if she and Randy hadn't moved in until after everything was done. But Dawn had wanted them to be on their own, even if it meant living in the house while she was still trying to bring order to the chaos. Trying to juggle meals, dishwashing, bedmaking, and daily cleaning with the uncrating of boxes had only prolonged the day when it would all be done.

"And it's all going to look so much better when these drapes are hung," Dawn declared, walking over to the green and white sofa to pick up a freshly ironed panel. "They look beautiful, Mother."

"That material didn't turn out to be the easiest to sew, but I think they turned out rather well," she replied modestly.

The windows in the front room were odd-sized. After several fruitless shopping trips, Dawn had been finally forced to accept the drapes in the front room would have to be custom-made. She was spared the exorbitant price a decorator would have charged when her mother volunteered to make them.

"Those windows have been bare for so long." Dawn held the drape up, picturing the soft green color against the white walls. She looked at her mother and smiled. "Just imagine, I'll have privacy tonight. No one will be able to see in."

"Are you going to put them up tonight? Do you want me to stay and help you?" her mother offered.

"No, I can manage. You've done more than enough," Dawn insisted.

"If you're sure—" She didn't persist in her offer. "—I need to get home and start supper for your father. Randy's helping him in the garage. He's welcome to eat with us so you don't have to stop to fix him anything."

"No thanks." If she let her mother have her way, Randy would eat with them every night.

"It's time he learned he has to come home for supper."

"I'll send him home," her mother promised reluctantly and walked to the door. "Call if you need anything."

"I will."

Her mother's car hadn't left the driveway before Dawn was hauling the small stepladder into the living room so she could hang the pleated drapes at the windows. The two small side windows were a snap, but the large front window proved to be more of a hassle than she expected.

That area of the floor was warped, which meant the ladder wasn't balanced on all four legs so it rocked with each shift of her weight. Add to that, the drapes were wider by necessity and more awkward to handle because so much had to be held on her arm. She only had one hand free to fit the hook into its sliding eye-bracket, and to reach that she had to balance a knee on top of the ladder and stretch on tiptoe. It wasn't a position that promoted security. Dawn wished now that the ceilings that gave the house so much character weren't quite so high.

After much struggling, balancing, and stretching, she got one half of the front window set hung. There was still the other half to go. She moved the ladder over and observed how much it rocked. She debated waiting until Randy came home so he could hold the ladder steady, then decided to try it.

She tugged at the hem of her jean shorts and

gathered up the large panel, laying it over her arm. Her bare feet gripped the slatted steps of the ladder while it seesawed under her moving weight. Dawn took her time, testing the swaying rock of the ladder so she wouldn't accidentally overbalance the wrong way.

Then the slow process began of stretching and aiming for the eye, trying to hook it before it slid away and not losing her balance when the ladder rocked to a different three-point stance. It was nerve-wracking. When she heard footsteps crossing the veranda, Dawn sighed with relief.

As soon as the front door opened, she called, "Will you come over here and hold this ladder steady so I can finish hanging these drapes?"

She expected a grumble of protest from Randy, but none was voiced as she fumbled one-handed with the next hook to hold it in a position of readiness. When she felt a hand gripping the ladder, she made the final stretch for the bracket.

Suddenly there was a hand stroking the back of her thigh. Her eyes widened in shock at such familiarity from her son. She let go of the hook and swung her arm around to knock away his hand, turning to look at the same time.

"Randy!" His name was out of her mouth before Dawn saw Slater standing beside the ladder. "It's you!" She was almost relieved as her heart started beating again.

"I should hope it's me and not our son." There was something lazy and warm about the way he was looking at her. It did things to her pulse that still hadn't recovered from her initial start.

Since they had moved into the house, Slater had dropped by unannounced a couple of times, but Dawn had been expecting Randy and simply hadn't anticipated it might be anyone else. On his previous visits, Randy had always been at home. It was the first time they'd been alone since that night in his office.

"I didn't hear your car." Dawn noticed the way his dark hair gleamed with sun-burnished lights streaking through it. She wanted to reach down and smooth his unruly forelock the way she so often did Randy's.

"That's because I walked," Slater replied.

"If you're here to see Randy, he hasn't come home yet." Dawn turned back to the window and adjusted the drape material folded over her arm.

How many times had she seen Slater in the last two weeks? Easily more than a half a dozen times, sometimes on a matter related to the house and others when he'd come to see Randy. Even when the terms had been friendly, there had been a tension between them. It was difficult to be with him without wanting to touch and be closer.

"I suspected he wasn't." His voice was dry with amusement at her obvious announcement. Its tone altered when he added, "The drapes really make the room look different."

"They look good, don't they?" she said with smiling pride in the result, and grasped the hook she had dropped earlier to aim it for the eye bracket.

Just as she stretched for it, his hand trailed down the silken-smooth back of her leg. His touch went through her nerve ends like liquid lightning. She missed the bracket.

"Will you stop that?" she demanded.

"You have nice legs," Slater remarked with no remorse.

"Thank you." The compliment was almost as awkward to handle as his wayward hand.

His playful orneriness was unsettling. Her task was a difficult one requiring concentration and coordination. Slater was affecting both. She started to reach for the bracket again, then paused to look over her shoulder at him.

"Don't touch my leg. Okay?" she asked for his word, not liking the little silver light that danced in his charcoal-dark eyes.

"Okay," he agreed smoothly. Satisfied that he meant it, Dawn focused her gaze on the target and made her move for it. "You do have nice legs," Slater repeated. "Dirty feet, but nice legs." He ran a finger down the ticklish sole of her bare foot.

It was like testing her reflexes—all movement was involuntary. Her knee jerked, changing the center of her balance and tipping her forward. She yelped and grabbed for the top of the ladder to keep from going headfirst through the window.

The momentary fright had her heart beating like a racing motor. Her breath was coming in little gasps. It wasn't until her senses started quieting down that she felt his hand gripping the back pocket of her jean shorts. Obviously Slater had grabbed her to prevent her from pitching forward. But his efforts to save her weren't appreciated since he had been the cause in the first place.

She'd had to let go of everything. The unhung drape material was swinging drunkenly from the rod, attached to it by the first few hooks. She knew she wouldn't get the material folded so neatly again, which meant the material would be more cumbersome on her arm.

"Damn you, Slater MacBride," Dawn swore angrily. "You know the bottoms of my feet are ticklish."

"I think I'd forgotten *how* ticklish you are." There was a throaty chuckle in his voice. "Sorry. I won't do it again."

"You'd better not," she warned, unimpressed by his apology and its accompanying promise. "If you do that again, I'm liable to get myself killed."

"I certainly don't want that to happen," Slater murmured with an obvious effort to contain his amusement.

Dawn began hauling up the dangling portion of the drape panel and looping it over her arm. In her irritable mood, she didn't take as much care as she might have to keep the material from wrinkling.

"Will you just hold the ladder and keep your hands to yourself?" she demanded. "Don't touch me anywhere."

"I'll be as still as a mouse," he assured her.

Her first tries were tentative, not completely trusting him. Gradually, Dawn realized he intended to keep his word. The work went smoother after that.

When she had threaded the last hook through its eyes, she let her aching arms fall to her side and gazed with satisfaction at the smoothly hanging drapes with their crisp pleats spaced in neat rows. Not once had Slater intervened or even broken the silence. With the job done, she'd lost her irritation with him.

"They look great, don't they?" Dawn was eager to hear someone's opinion other than her own.

"Perfect," Slater agreed.

Unbending her knee, Dawn straightened her leg so her foot could find the ladder rung and join its twin. Her hands gripped the flat top of the ladder for balance so she could begin her descent.

With the first step, an arm hooked her legs and tugged her off balance so she was turning. A second arm circled her hips to finish the turn and lift her off the ladder. Her startled outcry was ignored and Dawn had to grab for his shoulders to keep from overbalancing.

Held high in the air by strong arms that hugged her hips to his chest, Dawn was helpless to do anything about it. She looked down at Slater's laughing features. The physical contact she'd longed for and the possessive gleam in his eyes made it impossible for her to even fake anger.

"Will you put me down?" There was a breathless catch in her voice.

"I don't think so." He was eye-level with her breasts that were angled away from him by her arched back, but he seemed quite fascinated by their nearness, and their movements under her cotton-thin blouse.

Dawn knew he was staring at them to disturb. It was confirmed when his glance flickered upward to measure her reaction. And there was one. Her lips were parted and her eyes were darkening with want. But she was too aware of recent bad experiences in his arms to give rein to her own desires.

"For a reformed alcoholic, you certainly play around with fire a lot." It was a husky accusation, a veiled attempt to remind him of his resolution concerning her.

His grip loosened, letting her slide down a few inches. "But there was a condition to my abstinence," Slater reminded her and nuzzled the blouse buttons that fastened the material across the valley between her breasts.

"What?" It was hard to think when sensation was trying to dominate her thought process.

His mouth shifted its area of interest to rub over the material covering the rounded sides of her breasts. "I said I'd stay away from you until I decided what I wanted." His murmuring voice was partially muffled by the cloth.

"And you decided?" Her eyes were closed and her head was bent toward him as her hands curled around his neck.

Slater eased her a little farther down to nuzzle the hollow of her throat, his lips and breath warm against her skin. "There was more agony doing without you, so I've decided to learn to live with my addiction."

She was lowered the last few inches until her toes touched the floor while he continued to nibble on her neck and to rub her jaw. Happiness soared through her at the news that he was bringing a close to his inner conflict.

"I thought you'd never make up your mind," she declared throatily.

"You don't know what it's been like for me since you came back," he asserted. "You're all I thought about. When I wasn't around you, I wanted to be. I dragged out closing the sale of the house just so I could have a legitimate reason to talk to you privately—away from Randy. I couldn't hold an intelligent conversation with anybody for more than five minutes without my mind wandering off with thoughts of you." His breath mingled with hers as his mouth became poised just above her lips. "It came down to a simple understanding. You're here—and I want you."

Her fingers tunneled into the thickness of his hair to force his head down. The union of their lips was a hungry testament of their need for each other that could not be culminated in a merely sexual act. Their bodies strained for more intimate contact, reaching wildly for the ultimate closeness that could never be adequately achieved.

As if coming from a great distance, there was the sound of running footsteps. The significance was lost on the entwined couple until the front door burst open and the intrusion startled them into breaking off the torrid kiss.

# Chapter Eight

Randy halted abruptly, holding the door open and looking a little embarrassed as if he wasn't sure whether he should stay or go. Slater recovered first and withdrew his arms from around Dawn. Self-consciously, she smoothed the front of her blouse where it had ridden up.

"Grandma said I was to come home for supper," Randy said.

"Yes," Dawn nodded a little jerkily.

"I was just helping your mother off the stepladder," Slater explained.

Randy suddenly grinned and let go of the door, his light eyes glittering knowingly. "Next you'll be trying to convince me you two were practicing mouth-to-mouth resuscitation. I've been around, you know."

Slater laughed silently and glanced at Dawn. "Smart kid. Yours?"

"No, yours," she countered, smiling now, too.

"It's time the three of us had a discussion." He took her hand and drew her with him as he crossed to the sofa. Randy ambled over in the same direction and flopped in the armchair, eyeing them curiously.

"A discussion about what?" Dawn inquired into the subject matter as she settled onto a seat cushion beside Slater.

"I have a small problem, which I believe Randy shares," he said. She frowned slightly because the conversation wasn't taking the turn she expected. "We're father and son, but it's awkward for either of us to openly claim the relationship. We constantly would have to explain why his name is different from mine. It's probably more awkward for Randy because kids tend to call others names that can hurt."

A glance at Randy noted the tightness around his mouth, an admission that what Slater was saying was true. Dawn had known it was a potential problem, but she hadn't realized it had already surfaced.

"I've come up with a way to solve the problem," Slater announced.

"You have?" Randy gave him a wide-eyed look that was full of hope.

"Your mother and I can get married and have your name legally changed to mine." A faint satisfied smile curved his mouth as he explained his solution.

"That's great!" Randy declared, but Dawn kept her silence, stunned—not by his backhanded proposal—but his justification to Randy for their marriage. Then Randy laughed loudly. "When you do that, my name will legally be Randy MacBride MacBride. I'll be a MacBride twice."

"I guess you will." Slater smiled along with him.

Dawn finally found her voice. "I thought this was supposed to be a discussion between the three of us. It sounds like the two of you have made a decision without even asking my opinion," she pointed out. "It is going to affect me."

"I wanted to hear what Randy thought of my solution before I asked you about it—privately," he stressed the latter, an engaging smile deepening the corners of his mouth.

"Randy—" she turned to her son, struggling to keep calm until she found out what Slater had to say, "—why don't you go get cleaned up for supper."

This was a discussion she didn't want postponed. She needed her suspicions put to rest, and soon, or they'd eat away at her.

"Okay." He pushed out of the chair and paused. "You know you think it's a good idea, too."

"Go," she urged without denying his statement.

Her gaze followed him as he left the room and lunged up the stairs, taking the steps two at a time. She waited until she heard him in the upstairs bathroom before she glanced at Slater.

"Did you mean that about getting married?" she asked, with a searching look.

"Like Randy said, it's a good idea," he repeated while his fingers curled tighter around her hand.

"It's never any good for two people to get married for the sake of a child," she insisted, wanting him to give her a better reason than that. "It wouldn't be any good for us, either, even if it makes the situation easier for Randy."

"It'll be good." He slipped an arm around her waist and pulled at her hand to draw her closer to him.

Her free hand pushed at his shoulder to keep from being drawn into his embrace while she turned her face away from his descending mouth. "I have to know why you want to marry me—whether it's only because of Randy." She wouldn't be persuaded into accepting by his kisses.

When she drew her head back to look at him, Slater sighed heavily and didn't try to pursue his quarry. "Don't you know?" There was a half-teasing light in his eyes. "Maybe I want to marry you for your money?"

Dawn went white. "If that's supposed to be a joke, I don't think it's very funny."

"I don't suppose it is," he agreed, the light fading. "It would be poetic justice, wouldn't it? This would be my first time at the marriage altar, so I should be wedding money—according to you."

Hurt that he would continue with this terrible joke—if it was a joke—Dawn tried to twist her hand out of his grasp and pull it free. Slater just laughed in his throat and gathered her into his arms.

"You didn't think I was serious?" He rebuked her for questioning his motive while his gaze burned possessively over her features. "I thought I'd made it plain before Randy ever walked in the door how I felt about you." His lips brushed her cheek in a gentle and reassuring caress.

"It was cruel to tease me like that." There was a hint of desperation in the way her arms went around him to cling. If it hadn't been for her own guilty conscience about the way she had treated him long ago, she probably would have laughed off his joking suggestion. "I'm too sensitive, I guess."

"It was a foolish way for me to let you know that I was putting all that kind of thinking behind us." Slater took part of the blame. "But it's something we both have to tread lightly around, it seems."

Dawn suspected he was right. There were too many years of hurt that couldn't be wiped out with the wave of any magic wand—even love. But understanding that would carry them a long way in overcoming it.

"I'm still curious about something." She reluctantly drew back so she could see his face, but this time made no attempt to expand the circle of his arms.

"What's that?" He playfully kissed the tip of her nose.

"Why did you allow Randy to think we were getting married because of him?" she asked.

"Because I wanted him to see how our marriage would benefit him, then gradually ease him into discovering that he was going to have to share a lot of your time with me." A sudden smile flashed across his features. "And I wanted him on my side just in case you got stubborn and thought we should wait awhile before tying the knot."

"Trying to gang up on me, were you?" Dawn accused with a provocative look through the tops of her lashes.

"That's one of the benefits of having a son. We'll always have you outnumbered," he warned. "Speaking of numbers, I have something to give you."

Releasing her, he stretched out a leg and reached inside his pants pocket. She caught a gleam of shiny metal as he reached for her left hand.

"Numbers equals digits equals fingers," Slater explained his word association and slipped an engagement ring on her finger. "A sapphire—to match your eyes."

"It's beautiful." Dawn stared at it, adequate words escaping her, but the brilliant shimmer in her blue eyes rivaled the deep color of the sparkling stone when she finally looked at him.

"I remembered that Simpson had given you a diamond and I didn't want to follow in his footsteps," he admitted.

Dawn wished he hadn't mentioned him. It tarnished some of the joy in the moment, but she couldn't block the memory of him out of her life. It was time both of them began treating his name as belonging to a mutual acquaintance.

"He always followed in yours," Dawn corrected him.

"I'm glad you quit wearing his rings," he said.

Before she could explain that she had sold them, Randy chose that moment to clump loudly down the steps. He halted on the last one and called, "Is it safe to come down?" This time he gave them forewarning before bursting into the room.

"It's safe," Slater chuckled.

He bounded jauntily into the room, his gaze darting from one to the other. "Well? What did she say?"

"Take a look." Slater lifted her left hand for Randy's inspection of the engagement ring.

"Great! Now that we've got that out of the way, what's for supper?" His hunger took precedence over any prolonged celebration of their engagement.

The abrupt change of subject startled a laugh from her. "Oh, Randy," she declared in amusement.

"Well?" The challenging inflection of his voice made it a defensive word. "You told me to get cleaned up for supper, so what are we going to eat—and when? I'm starving."

"You're always starving," Dawn insisted with an indulgent look.

"He takes after me," Slater murmured and bit at the lobe of her ear. "I'm hungry, too." But the growling sound of his voice spoke of an appetite that had nothing to do with food.

A response to that was impossible with Randy listening in, so Dawn attempted to deal with her son first. "I haven't started anything for supper so you have your choice of hamburger—or hamburger."

"That's a lot of choice," Slater laughed. "How are we supposed to make up our minds?"

"Let's have hamburgers," she suggested with a laugh.

"How long's it going to take?" Randy asked.

"If I had two handsome helpers, I bet supper would be on the table in half an hour. How hungry are you?" Dawn challenged.

It looked as if Randy's appetite was fading, but Slater rolled to his feet and clamped a hand on the boy's shoulder. "You've got your two volunteers."

She stood up. "The kitchen is that way." She pointed to the hallway behind them. Slater turned Randy around and marched him toward it while Dawn brought up the rear.

"What do you want us to do?" Slater asked.

"Randy can set the table and you—" she opened the refrigerator and tossed him the packet of hamburger, "—can grill the hamburgers."

"What are you going to do?" Randy protested what he saw as an unfair division of labor.

"I'm going to put the frozen french fries in the oven and make a salad," she said and took a head of lettuce out of the refrigerator's vegetable bin.

Slater exchanged a glance with Randy. "She's a regular general handing out orders." He slid her a look as he formed the hamburger into patties. "Do I have your permission to wear the pants in our family?"

Pausing by the stove where Slater was working, Dawn turned the oven on to heat. Her arm brushed slightly against his, attracting his downward sideglance.

"You can wear the pants." She saucily gave him permission.

Before she could elude the retaliation she expected, he hooked an arm around her waist and hugged her to his side. He bent his head near her ear. She tipped her cheek up to him, expecting a kiss.

Instead, Slater murmured, for her hearing alone, "I don't care who wears the pants as long as neither one of us wears them to bed." As he let his hand fall from her waist, he playfully pinched her bottom.

"Ouch!" But she was laughing as she quickly backed away from him.

"Hey, I've been wondering." Randy frowned as he circled the table, dispensing plates at the three place settings. "Where are we going to live after you two get married?"

Dawn had been riding so high on her newfound happiness that she hadn't thought about such details. "The house, we just bought it." She hated the idea of moving out of it when they had barely settled in.

"Considering that I have only a one-bedroom apartment, I think we would all be more comfortable if I moved in here." Slater eliminated her concern.

"Well, when are you going to get married?" Randy asked.

"As soon as possible." Both answered the question simultaneously, then looked at each other and laughed at their mutual haste.

"We'll probably get married the end of the week," Slater was more specific. "I should be able to arrange to get away from the business for a couple of days. That, combined with the week-end, should enable us to take a short honey-moon." He looked at Dawn, silently seeking her approval of his plan. "I thought we could go away on my boat."

"I'd like that," she nodded, her face beaming with a smile because they had once spent so much of their time together on his old boat.

"Can I come, too?" Randy thought it sounded like fun.

"Absolutely not," Slater laughed. "The three of us will go out for a weekend *after* your mother and I have our honeymoon. How's that?"

"Since I don't have any choice, I guess it has to be okay," he declared with a dismal shrug of his shoulders. "The table's all set. I'm done."

"I don't see the salt and pepper," Dawn noticed. "What about ketchup and mustard? All those things are part of setting the table."

"Aw, Mom," Randy grumbled, but added the missing items to the table.

Less than half an hour after the three of them converged on the kitchen, they were sitting down to the meal. When Randy reached for his third hamburger, Slater eyed him skeptically then glanced at Dawn.

"Does he always eat like that or haven't you fed him the last couple of days?" he asked, more to tease Randy than anything else.

She just smiled. "Wait until you find out how expensive it is to feed a growing boy." Once that hadn't been of any concern to her until she had to start managing on a limited budget. With the food on her plate gone, Dawn stood up to carry it to the sink. "Coffee?"

"Sounds good," Slater nodded.

"Do I have to help with dishes?" Randy wanted to know.

"Not tonight," Dawn told him as she set her plate in the sink and took down two cups from the cupboard.

"Then is it all right if I go over to Gramps'?" he asked, already pushing his chair back from the table. "We're making a table."

"What about your hamburger?" Slater glanced at the sandwich Randy had just taken with only one bite gone from it.

"Oh, I'll eat it on the way," he said, unconcerned.

"You can go," Dawn excused him from the table. He grabbed up the sandwich and bolted for the door. "Don't forget to be home before dark!" she called after him. There was a wry shake of her head as she carried the filled coffee cups to the table. "He eats and never stops; he runs and never walks."

"All I can say is—" Slater waited until she had set the cups on the table, then grabbed her hand and pulled her onto his lap, "—alone at last."

"I thought you wanted coffee." She linked her hands behind his neck and settled comfortably against his chest. Her finger felt pleasantly heavy with the weight of her engagement ring.

"To tell you the truth—" he ran his hand up her thigh and over her hip to her waist, "—that isn't what I'm thirsty for."

The driving pressure of his kiss drank deeply from her lips. It ignited a ground swell of desire that flamed through her veins. The completeness of her love was almost shattering to behold. The heat surged through her limbs, melting bones and flesh. His roaming hand cupped itself to the underswell of her breast, his thumb stroking the tip in heady stimulation, her thin blouse holding back none of the delicious sensations.

With a bang of the screen door, Randy charged into the house and came to a sliding stop. "Whoops!" His ears reddened at the sight of them.

"I thought you went to your grandparents'," Slater said with a trace of exasperation, but continued to hold Dawn on his lap.

"I did—I am," Randy was flustered. "I just came back to see if it was all right for me to tell them that you're getting married."

"Of course, you can tell them," Dawn replied.

"Okay." His mouth twitched in a hesitant smile as he backed to the door. "Bye."

When the door had closed, Slater studied her wryly. "You know what's going to happen in about ten minutes, don't you?"

"What's that?" She smoothed her hand over the slanting line of his jaw.

"Your mother is either going to call or come over so she can be the first to congratulate us."

"You're probably right." Her mouth lifted in a crooked smile. "Pop will probably come over, too."

"Which means they won't leave until dark," Slater concluded. "What's Randy's bedtime?"

"Eleven o'clock."

An exaggerated groan came from his throat before he smothered it by kissing her fiercely. She felt his frustration and echoed it with her own. They'd been apart so long that he was impatient with anything that kept them apart any longer.

His tongue licked at her lips, sensuously going over their outline, then threading its way between them. She was filled with the taste of him, so heady and male. The buttons of her blouse were unfastened one by one, and his invading hand pushed the material aside to explore the bared flesh. There was an involuntary tightening of her stomach muscles at the touch of his hand.

A storm shower of kisses moistly covered her face, closing her eyes while Dawn trembled in the throes of growing passion. It stopped so Slater could view the prize he held in his lap. Through the slits of her lashes, she saw the pleased look in his heavily lidded eyes and took pleasure in her womanly shape.

Her back was arched slightly by the pressure of his arm as he bent his head to kiss the pouting tip of a breast, briefly taking it between his teeth and tracing its hardness with his tongue. Her hands tightened around his neck in instant reaction. A half-satisfied smile played with the corners of his mouth as he turned away to rub his cheek against hers, his breath stirring the hair near her ear.

"Are you sure you don't want to change your mind about getting married on Friday?" he murmured against her skin. "The ceremony isn't going to be up to your standards, you know."

"What do you mean?" Dawn was too bemused by his kisses and caressing hands to devote her whole attention to what he was saying.

Talk seemed unnecessary at a time like this. Of course, that wasn't all he was doing. His hands continued their roaming ways, stroking thigh and hipbone, sensually rubbing and familiarizing themselves with the shape of her.

"There won't be time to make it a lavish affair with hundreds of guests. The wedding party will consist of you and me—and your parents, I suppose, as our witnesses. You'll be lucky to find a wedding dress, let alone a trousseau. There won't be tons of wedding gifts to open, nor a grand reception." Slater continued rubbing his mouth over her cheek, not letting the conversation interfere with his loveplay. "Just a quickie marriage."

"It sounds perfect." She didn't need to tell him that she'd been through all that. "I've become very fond of simple things."

"Meaning me?" He took a tenderly punishing bite of her ear in revenge and Dawn wiggled at the peculiar blend of exquisite pleasure and pain his love-nip induced.

"You're far from simple," she insisted huskily. "As a matter of fact, I think you're very complicated. It's going to take me the rest of my life to figure you out."

"Just so long as you remember it is for the rest of your life," Slater murmured and rolled his mouth across her lips in a sealing kiss.

"I do." Dawn lovingly trailed a finger over his tanned cheekbone down to his mouth, running it over its masculine firmness. "At this moment, Friday seems far away. But I know it's going to be hectic getting the blood tests, applying for the license and arranging for a minister, not to mention finishing all the things I have to do here in the house—and moving your things in."

"And me," he added.

"And moving you in, too," she smiled.

"You can always hire someone to do it for you instead of trying to do all this housework, unpacking, and moving yourself," Slater pointed out.

"But I like doing it myself," Dawn insisted.

"Right now it's all a novelty to you, but you'll get tired of it," he predicted. Then his expression grew serious, his gaze narrowing to bore deeply. "What happens when the newness wears off, Dawn? You're used to the excitement of big city life. What happens when this life become too tame and boring?"

"It won't happen." She didn't even have to think about her answer.

She was very positive about it because she had experienced both kinds of life and knew the advantages and disadvantages of both. Now she knew precisely what she wanted.

"It better not." His arms tightened around her, crushing her to his ribs while he roughly kissed her lips.

The roughness fled quickly as desire took hold and made it a moistly heated exchange. Her position in his lap became a dissatisfying one, too passive when she wanted to be an active participant in this embrace.

"Dawn!!" The sound of her name ended on a high, questioning note. She instantly recognized the voice as belonging to her mother, and she was calling from the living room. Neither had heard the front door open.

Quickly she catapulted herself off of Slater's lap and began buttoning her blouse. "It's mother," she hissed needlessly, trying to put her clothes into some kind of order before she responded to the calling voice.

"So much for being alone," he murmured dryly, and watched her frantic efforts with a trace of amusement. "It lasted just long enough for us to get hot and bothered—and not long enough to do anything about it."

She flashed him a glance that held both amusement and a trace of embarrassment at his frank assessment. Another call came from the living room, and Dawn couldn't delay answering any longer.

"We're in the kitchen, Mother!" she called, and grabbed up some dishes to carry them to the sink. She threw a glance over her shoulder at Slater, still seated in the chair. "Aren't you going to help?"

"I think it's best if I stay seated," he replied and chuckled at the faint blush that tinted her cheeks.

"Randy just told us the news." Her mother started talking excitedly before she even walked into the kitchen. She beamed at both of them. "I'm so happy for you. Randy said the wedding was going to be Friday and I just knew that couldn't be right, so I came over—"

"It's going to be Friday," Dawn inserted.

"But there's so much to do beforehand," her mother protested.

"Not really. It's going to be a very simple ceremony—with just you and Pops—and Randy, of course," she explained as she carried a cup of coffee to the table for her mother.

"Even at that, there's still things to be done." A little agitated, she sat down and began listing them, ticking them off her fingers as she thought of them. "An announcement has to be placed in the paper. And flowers to be ordered. Even if you don't carry a bouquet, you'll at least want a corsage. And a wedding cake; you'll want a small one if nothing else."

"Just a small one," Dawn conceded, caught up in the snowball.

"And as for the reception afterward—" her mother began.

"We'll have drinks on my boat after the ceremony," Slater interrupted.

"And what will you wear? You'll want to buy a new dress," her mother continued. "And Randy—he's outgrowing all his clothes."

Turning his head, Slater glanced at Dawn. "What was that you said about 'simple'?" he mocked the growing length of the list.

# Chapter Nine

In sleep, Dawn lay on her stomach with her cheek burrowed into the pillow. Her hand felt its way across the bunk's mattress to locate Slater, but the space beside her was empty. The information registered in her subconscious, prodding her awake.

Frowning sleepily, she turned her head and looked at the hollowed-out place where Slater had been sleeping. His head had left an impression in the pillow and the musky smell of him clung to the sheets.

Sunshine came through the portals, finishing the rousing process; Dawn rolled onto her back and pushed the copper hair away from her face as she listened intently for some sound of Slater moving about on the boat. When she heard his tuneless whistle, she smiled and pulled the light cover up, tucking it under her arms, conscious of the pleasantly rough sensation of cotton sheets against her naked skin.

A languid contentment seemed to have taken all the strength from her muscles, as well as any inclination to leave the bed where she had enjoyed so much loving last night. Her smile deepened at the satisfying memory of it. Just thinking about it produced a little quiver of excitement.

She hugged the cover more tightly across her breasts and glanced at the gold wedding band that had joined the sapphire engagement ring on her finger. "Mrs. MacBride," Dawn murmured, liking the sound of it and feeling like a giddy schoolgirl for trying it out.

Since Slater dominated the subject of her thoughts, her curiosity naturally ran to what he was doing. She could hear him whistling, but there wasn't any sound of him moving about on deck. But there were odd thumps and clunks, and a soft scraping sound that puzzled her.

Between the wondering and the desire to be with him, she tossed back the light cover and swung out of the wide bunk. His white terrycloth robe hung on a hook. Dawn hesitated, then slipped it on and tied the swaddling bulk around her. She glanced at her reflection in the oval mirror. The provocative gleam that entered her blue eyes indicated a satisfaction with the resulting look.

As she passed through the small galley, she noticed the pot of coffee on the stove and an empty cup sitting on the counter beside it. She stopped and poured a cup for Slater and one for herself before proceeding up the hatchway to the deck. Trying to keep an eye on the cups, she glanced around to locate Slater.

"Good morning?" She didn't see him. "How about some coffee?" She wrinkled her nose as she caught the acrid smell of marine enamel.

"Good morning," Slater answered.

When she glanced in the direction of his voice, Dawn saw him hanging over the side of the boat, secured by some sort of rope swing. She frowned curiously and started across the deck to see what he was doing. At the moment, all she could see was his head and the top part of his bare chest.

"What are you doing?" The paint smell grew stronger as she approached. "Is this any way to spend your honeymoon? Painting a boat?"

"You get away from here." He motioned her backward with a wave of his paintbrush. "This is supposed to be a surprise, so you can't look yet. I'll be through in a minute."

"A surprise?" Dawn halted, then took a couple of steps sideways to sit in a deck chair. "What are you doing?"

"What does it look like I'm doing?" Slater countered with a smug little smile.

She was aware of his concentration, and the almost painstaking strokes he seemed to be making. "It looks like you're writing something." Her eyes widened at the conclusion that followed that. "Are you changing the name of the boat?"

"Clever girl," he smiled.

A little thrill went through her, guessing that he must be naming it after her if it was supposed to be a surprise. "What if *Homesick* doesn't like it?" she said, giving the boat an identity.

"She'll have to like it," Slater replied, "She doesn't have any choice."

"Your coffee is going to get cold if you don't hurry," she warned, nearly eaten up with curiosity herself.

He didn't answer immediately as he concentrated on the last bit of lettering. Then a smile was breaking across his face. "All done." He looked at her for an instant, then shifted his position to haul himself on board.

An invitation wasn't required as Dawn set the coffee cups on the deck and hurried to the side. Slater was clad only in a pair of cutoff jeans, the legs frayed to form a rough fringe. His outstretched arm checked her haste.

"Careful," he advised. "You don't want to get any wet paint on you."

His word of caution prompted her to look where she was putting her hands before she leaned forward to peer over the side. It took her a minute to read the lettering upside-down. There was a sudden rush of tears as she straightened and turned to Slater.

*"The Second Time."* Her voice choked on a bubble of emotion. "Oh, Slater." Her chin quivered and she tried to laugh at her overly sentimental response.

"It is the second time—for us—and being together on a boat," He quietly reinforced his choice with an explanation, and reached for her left hand, rolling his thumb across her wedding rings. "Only this time, it's my ring you're wearing in the morning."

She wrapped her arms around his bare middle and hugged him close, resting her cheek against his flatly muscled chest and closing her eyes. "Thank you for *The Second Time*. It's a wonderful wedding present for both of us."

He tucked a hand under her chin and lifted it to kiss her mouth, with long, drugging warmth. When he finally raised his head, it was to lazily study her upturned face.

"I suppose you know how sexy you look in my robe," he murmured and let his gaze trail downward to the gaping front and the exposed swell of her breasts.

Dawn started to deny any foreknowledge, then grinned saucily. "Yes."

"Brazen hussy," he accused mockingly and kissed her hard, then let her go. "I'll have that cup of coffee now."

"Tease," she accused, but let him take her by the hand and lead her back to the deck chair, where he pulled one alongside of hers.

After they were seated with their respective cups in hand, their fingers stayed linked in loving companionship. All around them was stillness, the quiet lapping of water against the boat's hull interrupted only by the distant cry of a bird.

The boat was anchored inside the entrance to a small sheltered cove of an uninhabited key away from the more frequently traveled water routes. Slater had sailed to it last night, so Dawn had seen little of it in the dark.

With a midmorning sun shining on its sandy

shore, she was taking her first good look at it. It seemed a tropical paradise with its blue waters and swaying palms. Although it appeared uninhabited at first glance, Dawn revised that opinion as she began noticing the variety of birds—long-legged herons, squatty white pelicans, and a roseate spoonbill, as well as a circling osprey.

"No wonder Audubon spent so much time in the Keys," she murmured. "It's teeming with exotic birdlife." Turning her head, she glanced at Slater. "Why don't we spend our honeymoon here instead of hopping around to other places? It's so beautiful and peaceful."

"We can." He drained his coffee cup and set it on the deck. "Want to go for a swim before breakfast?"

"Sure." She started to stand up. "Just give me a minute to change into my swimsuit."

His fingers tightened their link with hers. "Why bother?" he challenged. "We've got the place all to ourselves so why not swim in the nude?"

"Why not? I will if you will," she said with a little shrug and stood up. "Deal?"

"It's a deal," he agreed, but he was suspicious of the little gleam in her eyes.

"I'll race you to the beach," Dawn challenged. "Last one there has to cook breakfast."

With a quick tug of the sash, the robe fell open and Dawn slipped out of it. Slater was still unzipping his cutoffs when she dove over the side and struck out for shore. The time it took him to strip was the handicap she needed. Even though she was a strong swimmer, she was no match for Slater.

Even with the headstart, he nearly caught up with her. She waded onto the sand only two steps ahead of him. Breathless from the exertion, she collapsed onto the smooth sand and lay back on her elbows. Her blue eyes were sparkling with triumphant laughter that she didn't have the wind to voice.

"You have to cook . . . breakfast," she informed him between gulps for air.

"You cheated." He dropped onto the sand beside her, breathing hard, water dripping from him.

"Now why should you complain because I can undress faster than you?" Dawn blinked her eyes at him with mock innocence. "I should think a man would be overjoyed about that."

"You think so, eh?" Slater shifted to lean over her in a threatening posture.

But the leap of awareness in her senses was not caused by alarm. She lifted her chin to gladly take the kiss he pressed onto her mouth. The weight of his chest collapsed the support of her elbows, sinking her slowly backward on the sand, the wet, warmth length of his body stretching out alongside hers.

Her arms curved around him, a hand exploring the sinewed ridges of his backbone. When he dragged his mouth away, his gaze burned a look over her face and chest. She ran the tip of her tongue across her lips.

"You taste like salt," she identified the briny substance that had moistened his kiss.

"So do you," he murmured. "But I always did like the taste of salt on my food." As if to prove it, he began to show her how much he enjoyed her salty flavor.

It was an idyllic time, hours lazily drifting into one another. They swam, fished, tramped the island, snorkeled, sun-bathed, and made love. If it weren't for the nightly ship-to-shore calls they made to talk to Randy and for Slater to check with his office, it was as if they were isolated from the rest of the world.

In a bulky gray sweatshirt and a headband keeping the copper-red hair off her neck, Dawn gazed at the tranquil cove. A late afternoon sun had created a new pattern of shadows, which she studied, intent on memorizing the way it looked.

A pair of arms stole around her waist, but she knew their feel. Her hands gripped them and helped them to tighten their circle while she tipped her head to the side and give Slater free access to the curve of her neck.

"Mmm, delicious," he murmured, nibbling on it. "Unfortunately—" he sighed, "—it doesn't take the place of food. Let's have an early dinner."

Dawn carried his suggestion one step further. "Let's build a fire on the beach and have a cookout."

There was a short silence while he considered her suggestion. "Why not," he agreed. "Get the stuff together so we can load it into the rubber dinghy."

After they got the food and utensils ashore, Slater gathered driftwood and built a fire while Dawn wrapped the potatoes, vegetables, and yellowtail fish in individual foil packets for roasting on the coals. The meal was ready in time for them to eat by the light of a lingering sun. Then they settled back with a cup of campfire coffee to watch the orange ball of flame sink into the ocean. The sunset splashed the sky with corals and pinks and lavenders.

A breeze stirred to life with the setting of the sun, cool as it came off the waters. The warmth from the flickering fire was just enough to ward off any chill. Dawn leaned back in Slater's arms and used his chest for a pillow while she waited for the moonrise to silver the cove.

"That sunset was specially ordered," Slater said, his breath stirring her hair as he tipped his head slightly down. "Did you like it?"

"It was beautiful," she assured him, although by now her mind had begun wandering down another path, one far from the island. "How much do you think it would cost to lease one of those shops in Old Town?"

"I don't know." He sounded amused by her question from left field. "I imagine it would depend on a lot of things—the square footage of floor space, location, the condition of the building. Why?"

"I've been thinking about leasing some space, and opening a shop. My father makes some beautiful things and I know they would sell if they were marketed right. Heaven knows, he has enough inventory in his garage to stock the place," she added wryly.

Slater shifted to the side in order to better see her face. "I'm surprised. I always thought your father was too proud and stubborn to let someone else—even his daughter—provide the financing to set him up in business."

"I wasn't thinking of setting him up in business. I thought I'd operate the shop. Maybe my mother could work part-time in it." She considered that possibility. "That way both of them would be earning some extra money to supplement their pension."

"Why would you want to operate the shop?" There was a frown in his voice.

"Don't tell me you're one of those husbands who believes a wife's place is at home?" Dawn teased.

"The idea isn't totally unpleasant," he admitted dryly. "But that doesn't answer my question."

"It's very simple. I want to earn some money. No woman wants to ask her husband for every penny of her spending money," she defended her stand.

He chuckled in vague confusion, his chest moving under her head. "You're worried about asking me for spending money?" He was amused by the thought. "What about the Lord family fortunes? There must be a moldy dollar or two lying around, doing nothing."

She laughed, suddenly understanding why he was puzzled. "I forgot to tell you. Simpson didn't leave me anything when he died. Oh, he did arrange for me to receive a yearly living allowance, but that stopped when I married you."

"What?" It was a low, surprised question.

"It's true," she assured him. "I was told I could contest the will since I was legally his wife and I hadn't signed any marriage contract that negated my claim to his estate. But it just didn't seem to matter anymore."

"Where did you get the money for the house?" he asked in that same slightly disbelieving voice.

"I sold all the jewelry Simpson had given me. He also set up a trust fund for Randy's college education," Dawn added. "So, at least, we won't have to worry about that expense."

"No."

A pale, fatly shaped crescent moon rested above the horizon. "Look, there's the moon." She called Slater's attention to it. "It's beautiful, isn't it?"

"Yes."

She snuggled into his arms and pulled them more tightly around her waist. "It's too bad we can't stay here forever," she sighed.

"You can't have everything, Dawn." He unwrapped his arms from around her and gripped her shoulders to sit her up. "It's time we were getting the dinghy loaded and headed back for the boat."

"So soon?" she protested and stayed curled on

the sand while Slater rolled to his feet and kicked out the fire.

"Yes, so soon."

"Spoilsport," she accused and held out her hand so he could pull her up.

There was a split-second hesitation before he grasped it and hauled her to her feet. But it didn't flow into an embrace as she thought it might. Instead Slater walked over and picked up the basket loaded with dirty dishes and gear.

"It is early." Dawn shook out the blanket and began to fold it.

"It will be early in the morning when we leave, too," he replied.

"Leave?" She stared at him. "To go where?"

"Back to Key West." His features were in shadow, the pale moon not providing sufficient light to let her see his expression.

"But I thought we didn't have to go back for another two days," she frowned and trailed after him when he headed for the dinghy, grounded on the beach a few yards away.

"Something's come up and I'm needed back at the office." It was a very uncommunicative answer.

"But—when you talked to Mrs. Greenstone this afternoon—afterward you said everything was running smoothly." Dawn was positive he hadn't mentioned there were any problems.

"Dawn—" he stopped and turned to look at her, the utmost of patience in his tone, "—things can be running smoothly, but there still can be an item that requires my personal attention. There wasn't any reason to mention it earlier, because I didn't want to spoil your last evening."

"Well, it's spoiled," she declared, but mainly by his attitude.

"You knew we had to go back sometime," he stated.

"Of course, I did. I'm not a child," she retorted, a little snappishly. "And you didn't have to keep it from me as if I were a child."

"Have it your way," Slater muttered and turned away to stow the basket in the dinghy.

It was a short, and very silent, ride back to the boat. Dawn glanced at the name gleaming on the white hull—*The Second Time*. It had a bitter ring to it somehow.

In the same tense silence, they unpacked the dishes and utensils from the cookout. When Slater went up on deck, Dawn went into the head and used the shower. The cleansing spray seemed to drive out her moody resentment. By the time she had toweled dry, she was regretting her participation in this silent war. She didn't want their last evening to come to a close on such a sour note.

Hoping it would spark a more pleasant memory, she grabbed his terrycloth robe and tied it around her. As she started down the narrow companionway, she noticed Slater sitting at the table in the galley. A briefcase sat on the bench beside him. A folder of papers was opened on the table while he worked a pocket calculator and made notes on a yellow tablet.

"Aren't you coming to bed?" She paused in the opening to the galley, a bare foot resting on the raised threshold.

He didn't even look up at her question. "No. I have to go over these papers before tomorrow."

"In that case, I'll put on some coffee and sit up with you." Dawn started to enter the galley.

"No. Go on to bed." He refused her offer with disinterest. "You know I can concentrate better when you're not around."

She should have felt complimented by that, but he hadn't even looked at her once. He was trying to claim she was a distraction, yet his concentration hadn't faltered once. His fingers continued to tap out numbers on the calculator.

But there didn't seem to be any point on which she could argue. "Good night," she said.

"Good night." His attention remained on his work, his response absently given.

Alone, she climbed into bed and stared at the ceiling, waiting for him to join her. Her mind went back over the evening, trying to pinpoint just when it had gone wrong. It was just shortly after she had told Slater that she was not the rich widow he thought her to be. She had called his attention to the rising moon; then he had said it was time to leave. It had all gone downhill after that.

Had he sounded upset that she wasn't rich? The minute her mind asked the question, Dawn shook it away. Knowing Slater's pride, he was probably relieved that she didn't have another man's money. Besides, he had just been joking when he'd said he was marrying her for her money. It was absurd to think such a thing—and worse to take it seriously, even for a minute.

It was possible he'd been upset because she'd kept it from him. He could have felt she should have confided in him before. But it was no more than that. Dawn rolled onto her side and glanced at the reflected light from the galley. Her eyelids drifted down as she wondered how late he would work.

When she wakened the next morning, it was to the throb of the engines. She sat up, rubbing the sleep from her eyes and holding on to the edge of the bunk to combat the boat's motion. Although she couldn't remember hearing Slater come to bed, the covers were all rumpled on his side.

Since they were already underway, she couldn't delay their departure by lingering in bed. Dawn pushed aside the covers and climbed out to wash quickly and dress.

The skyline of Key West was an indistinct blur on the horizon when she joined Slater at the bridge. "Why didn't you wake me?" she asked, raising her voice to make herself heard above the engines.

"No point." He shrugged, dragging his gaze from the water long enough to aim it in her general direction.

A swirling wind whipped her hair across her face. She turned into it so it would blow it back. The idyllic days seemed to be gone and they were rushing back into the world where it wasn't all love and tranquility.

"I guess the honeymoon's over," Dawn said, but she didn't think it had been loud enough for Slater to hear. She was wrong.

"Nothing lasts forever," he stated.

Maybe that was it, she decided as buildings began to take shape on the horizon. Maybe things had been too perfect, and she had been foolishly expecting them to stay that way. Maybe, last night, both of them had been resenting it couldn't always be as sublime as it had been in that tropical cove.

An hour later they had docked and loaded their suitcases in the trunk of the Corvette. Slater helped her into the passenger seat, then walked around to slide behind the wheel. He still seemed preoccupied and withdrawn, even when he looked at her.

"Where do you want me to drop you off?" He inserted the key in the ignition and started the motor. "At home or your parents'?"

For a stunned second, Dawn couldn't answer. "Aren't you coming home?"

"No." His patience seemed worn. "I told you I had business to handle. I'm going to drop you wherever you want to go and head straight for the office."

"I know that's what you said." There was a hint of sharpness in her answer.

"Well?" Slater prodded. "Which is it?"

"Take me home." It was amazing how he could whip an answer out of her when she wanted to burn him with her silence.

The Corvette seemed to speed through the

streets, not slackening its pace until it swung in the driveway of the "Conch-style" house. While Dawn dug the key out of her purse, Slater lifted the suitcases out of the trunk and set them by the sidewalk. When he slid behind the wheel and shut the door, Dawn stared at him in a kind of angry shock.

"Aren't you even coming in?" she demanded.

"No." He glanced at the suitcases sitting by the walk. "They aren't heavy. You should be able to manage them."

It wasn't the suitcases she had been thinking about. This was their new home. She thought he might carry her over the threshold, but she wasn't about to mention it and possibly have him laugh at her for being so foolishly romantic.

The honeymoon was over in spades.

# Chapter Ten

Opening the oven door, Dawn pulled out the rack and lifted the lid of the roasting pan. The rump roast was more than done; the meat was separating in chunks. She added a glass of water to try to keep it moist, turned the oven thermostat to warm, and slid it back into the oven.

"Boy, that smells good," Randy groaned in a complaining tone. "When are we going to eat? Do we have to wait until Dad comes home?"

In private, he'd taken to calling Slater "Dad," although it was done rather self-consciously when he was in his presence. Dawn felt Slater had been gone so much that his absence had contributed a lot to Randy's occasional unease with him.

"Don't you think we should wait?" she asked, appealing to his sense of right.

"It depends on how late he's going to be," Randy grumbled.

Breathing in deeply, Dawn had to concede that it wasn't an unfair condition. If they waited much longer, the meal would be ruined. She moved to the wall telephone.

"I'll call him and find out how soon he expects to be home. If he's going to be too late, we'll eat without him." She picked up the receiver and dialed the number.

It rang three times before it was answered. "MacBride." His curt voice sounded in her ear, its sharp, clipped tone becoming all too familiar to her.

"Are you still at the office?" she said, trying to sound light and amusing.

A heavy sigh came over the line, weary with exasperation. "I'm busy, Dawn. Why are you calling? If it's just to check up on me and make sure I'm not with someone else, then why don't you drive by my office and spare me these interruptions?"

She gritted her teeth and didn't respond to his biting sarcasm and irritation. "Randy's hungry. He wants to know what time you'll be home for dinner."

Instantly she was angry with herself for putting the onus of the call on their son. She was more interested in the answer than Randy was—and more deserving of an explanation for why they saw so little of him.

"It'll be late. Don't wait dinner for me. I'll send out for something to eat," Slater informed her that she needn't keep anything warm for him. "Tell Randy good night for me."

Which meant he wouldn't be home before eleven o'clock. "I'm beginning to feel like an abandoned bride," she laughed brittlely, because it seemed the best way to keep the tears at bay.

"Don't tell me Simpson never had to work late at the office," he chided unkindly.

"Not night after night," she shot back, her hand trembling from its tight grip of the receiver. Not caring how rude it was, she hung up the phone with a sharp click. She took a couple of seconds to regather her poise before turning to Randy. "He said not to wait dinner, so we can go ahead and eat."

"When's he coming home?" Without being told, Randy went to the cupboard to take down the plates and set the table.

"Not until very late. He said to tell you good night." There was an underlying threat of tautness in her otherwise light-sounding voice.

"Gosh," Randy sighed. "I thought it'd be different after you two got married and we all lived in the same house. But I'll bet I saw him more before you got married."

"He's been busy," she defended Slater's absence to Randy even if she had her own doubts about the necessity of it. "It won't always be like this."

"I hope not." His mouth twisted grimly as if he didn't have much hope things would change.

When they had first returned from their honeymoon, Dawn had been willing to concede that Slater had a lot of work that he needed to catch up on, so she had accepted his late nights without complaint. Sometimes she woke in the middle of the night and found him asleep in bed with her, but half the time she never heard him come home—or leave with morning's first light.

His attitude remained preoccupied, sometimes —like tonight—his lack of patience turned him sarcastic. Naturally with Randy, he was friendly and warm. Dawn was the one bearing the brunt of whatever was bothering him. She doubted that she could take much more.

On Sunday morning, Dawn could hardly believe it when she wakened at seven and discovered Slater had already risen. She hurried to the window and saw the Corvette in the driveway below. It seemed a rarity to discover he hadn't already left the house. She dressed hurriedly in a pair of white jeans and a red-checked blouse, applied a sparing amount of makeup, ran a comb through her hair, and ran down the stairs.

She found him in the living room, sprawled in an armchair with the sections of the Sunday newspaper strewn around him. His shuttered gaze flicked to her, then back to the article he was reading. A cup was sitting on the lampstand.

"Coffee?" She presumed it was made since the evidence seemed to indicate he'd already had at least one cup.

"I've had plenty. Thank you," he refused.

"I think I'll get myself a cup," Dawn announced unnecessarily and turned to leave the room.

The clumping thud of Randy running down the steps checked her as she waited for him to come down. When he was around, things didn't seem as tense.

"Good morning." He was always bright and

chipper in the mornings. "What's for breakfast?" And hungry.

"What would you like?" Dawn gave him his choice.

"Pancakes and sausage." Randy didn't have to think about it.

"Slater?" She turned to him. "The same for you?"

"No, I'm not hungry," he refused again. "I've already had some toast and juice."

"Say, Dad—" Randy sauntered over to the armchair where Slater was seated, "—can we go out on the boat today? You've been saying we would —one of these weekends."

"Not today." He folded the section of paper he'd been reading, laid it aside and reached for the next. "I have to go over to the resort later on. I'll be tied up most of the afternoon."

"Ah, not today, too," Randy complained.

"Surely you can take one day off," Dawn argued.

"If I didn't feel it was necessary, I wouldn't be spending my Sunday working," Slater countered. "The subject is closed."

The paper crackled as he snapped it open. Aware of Randy's crestfallen expression, Dawn curved a protective hand around his shoulder and turned him toward the kitchen.

"Let's fix some breakfast," she said.

Neither of them spoke as they walked to the kitchen. While Dawn put sausage links in the skillet to fry, Randy set the table. She took down the pancake flour to whip up a batch.

"Would you bring me the milk from the refrigerator—and an egg?" she asked.

The door opened and shut behind her while she measured out the mix. Randy appeared at her elbow, holding an egg. "There's no milk."

"I used the last of it last night," she remembered with a disgruntled sigh. "Bring me my purse. It's on the counter over there. You can ride your bike to the corner store and buy a quart." Randy started over to the side counter. "Wait," Dawn called him back. "I used the last of my cash to pay the paperboy. I'll get it from your father. Watch the sausage for me."

Wiping the pancake dust from her hands with a towel, Dawn walked swiftly into the front room. Slater was still engrossed in the paper.

"We're out of milk. I need to send Randy to the store to get some," she explained. "Will you give me some money? I'm broke."

There was a long, cool look from his gray eyes. Something like contempt touched his mouth as he reached into his pocket and pulled out a handful of bills. When she started toward his chair, he tossed them to her. They separated and drifted to the floor like green leaves settling to the ground.

"That's what you wanted, isn't it?" Slater challenged.

When she finally ripped her gaze away from the money at her feet, she glared at him. She made no move to touch it or pick it up.

"Hey, Mom! Should I—" Randy came running in from the kitchen.

"Go outside and play, Randy," she ordered.

"But—what about the milk?" He saw the bills scattered on the floor. "What's all that money doing there?"

"I said go outside and play!" Dawn repeated herself more sharply.

Randy backed up a step, looking from his mother to his father, finally sensing the explosive tension in the room. Then he wheeled, and headed for the front door. It slammed shut behind him. Dawn had a glimpse of him out the window, his arm hooked around a veranda pillar, his head hanging low as if his world had come to an end.

Her temper was trembling on the edge of fury as she knelt down and began picking up the money with false calm. "Would you mind explaining to me what *this* is all about?" She held up a wad of bills to indicate what she meant.

The newspaper was shoved aside, all pretense of reading it abandoned as Slater pushed to his feet. The hard angles of his features were whitened at the edges with barely controlled rage.

"No more games, Dawn," he snapped. "Don't pretend that isn't what you wanted when you know very well it is! Now you've got it."

"What are you talking about?" she demanded.

"I'm talking about you. You're probably going to turn out to be the most expensive lay in the country," he charged viciously. "Well, there's your money. Payment in full for your services. And enjoyable they were, too."

She straightened to stand erect, her head high

and hot tears stinging her eyes. "Just exactly what do you think I've done?" Her voice was strained with the effort to keep it level.

"I can't keep up this farce any longer," he sighed heavily. He was angry, but it was a tired kind of anger. Dawn could see the haggard and worn lines etched in his features from too many nights with too little sleep, but she couldn't feel sorry for him. "You married me for money. Well, now you've got it." Slater flung a gesturing hand in the direction of the money she held. "Sorry it isn't more than that, but I don't carry a lot of cash on me."

"Is that really what you believe?" Dawn asked with a hurt and incredulous frown. She breathed out a short laugh as she looked down at the money, her eyes blinking aside the tears. Events were becoming clear to her. "All this started that last night on the beach when I told you Simpson hadn't left me any money. I knew you had changed toward me, but I didn't know why."

"It was clever of you to wait until *after* we were married to mention that *little* detail," Slater said with dry sarcasm that seemed to mask his pain.

"The irony of this is that I was beginning to wonder if you were upset because you had married me for the money," she admitted her brief suspicion. "And you were angry because you hadn't allied yourself with wealth. I kept telling myself it was absurd, but I never dreamed you would come to this ridiculous conclusion."

"Is it so ridiculous?" he challenged. "Don't forget I know how much you wanted money. You threw *us* away to get your hands on it. When I think what a fool I've been, believing all that garbage about marrying again for love." He swung at right angles from her, running a hand over his hair and gripping the back of his neck. "I'm the one who's been saying it, then letting myself believe that it came from you."

"Love is the reason I married you," Dawn insisted.

"Love for me or love for money?" countered Slater.

"How can you even ask that question?" she demanded with the wad of money crumpled in her rigidly clenched fist. "We honeymooned together. Every minute of it was wonderful. Surely you could tell how much I love you."

"You've had so much practice faking your feelings that you probably wouldn't know a real emotion when it came your way." He shook his head in disgust, unimpressed by her show of evidence. "You played the loving wife for so long with Simpson, you probably don't know how to act any other way. He may have preferred the pretense, but I don't."

"Slater, don't you know that I never stopped loving you?" Dawn was at a loss as to how to convince him. There was a part of her that rebelled at the idea she had to try.

"Maybe I have trouble believing you ever loved me in the beginning," he replied with weary flatness. "If you loved me, how could you marry someone else?"

"What I did was wrong. I learned that very

quickly, but the damage had already been done." She struggled with the unpleasant memories. "I suppose it was wrong to stay married to Simpson after I realized what a mistake I'd made. But I'd made my bed and I thought I had to stay in it."

"It must have been a low blow when he didn't leave you anything," Slater taunted.

"I didn't want anything!" Dawn flared.

"Contesting the will would have meant a long, legal court fight, not to mention a very expensive one. How much easier it was just to find yourself a new sucker—me." His laughing breath was loaded with self-derision. "I swore I wouldn't let myself be fooled by you again. But you had me all set up just right, didn't you? You had a hook waiting for me no matter which way I went."

"No—"

But he didn't allow her to finish. "When Simpson died and you found out you were broke again, you must have looked around for the most likely candidate. And there was good ole MacBride. You knew he had been crazy about you—and there just might be some smouldering coals left in him. He had become something of a success— not filthy rich but on his way up. And the *coup de grâce*, you had borne him a son, a little secret you'd kept all this time."

"I should have told you. I've already admitted that," she reminded him angrily. "I came back here so the two of you could get to know one another. And that's the only reason I came back! It wasn't to trick you into marrying me so I could get my hands on your money."

"You made me believe that once, but I won't be persuaded again," Slater declared with a long, heavy look. "If it means anything, I have finally come to terms with who and what you are. A leopard can't change her spots—and you are a cat of the first order." His gaze flicked to her flaming hair.

"How do you know she can't?" Dawn challenged. "Did you ever ask a leopard?"

"It's no use, Dawn." There was a hard finality in his voice. "You were right when you said a couple couldn't stay together because of a child. And I can't live your lie anymore."

"It isn't a lie," she insisted with cold anger. "But if you don't believe that, then you can't love me."

"It seems we've reached a fork in the road." He sounded calm, painfully so as far as Dawn was concerned.

"It seems we have." She tried to match him and strained for a cool nonchalance that kept wavering on bitterness. "You claimed to have urgent business to attend to, so why don't you go take care of it. I'll pack your things and have them sent to the boat this afternoon."

"Fine." There was a rigidness to his jaw.

"And I shan't be asking for any financial settlement from you," Dawn asserted. "If you feel you should contribute something to Randy's support, then follow your conscience and pay whatever you feel is fair."

"You're fighting right down to the last second, aren't you?" Slater accused tightly, a glint of reluctant admiration in his gray eyes. "It's a great gesture to subtly make me wonder whether I've been wrong about you all along."

That was too much for Dawn. She was shaking with rage. "Do you want another gesture?" she hurled. "Try this!" She pointed a rigid finger in the direction of the front door while she glared at him. "Get out!"

His long strides carried him past her and out the door. The glass rattled in the window panes from the force behind the slamming of the door. Dawn glared after him, hating him at that moment as passionately as she had ever loved him.

The roar of the sportscar reversing out of the drive finally broke her anger-stiffened stance. She turned away from the door and started to lift a hand to her forehead in angry despair. Her glance fell on the paper money of various denominations in her hand. Her fingers tightened on it, crushing it more.

"You think it's your money I want," she caustically informed an absent Slater. "I'll show you what I think of your money!"

Driven by an anger that cloaked a pain too excruciating to be exposed, Dawn swept across the room to the cypress-topped coffee table. She dumped the bills into the large glass ashtray sitting on it. She grabbed a matchbook and ripped out a cardboard match, striking it and holding the flame to the money.

It licked greedily at a corner, then jumped quickly from one paper bill to another. Soon the whole crumpled mass of wadded bills was consumed by fire. Dawn sank onto the edge of the couch to watch it burn with bitter satisfaction.

"That, Slater MacBride, is the grandest gesture of them all," she murmured with a twisted slant to her mouth.

As quickly as the fire had taken hold, it burned itself out. All that remained of the money were black strips of brittle ash. Yet a distinctly smoky smell continued to taint the air she breathed—like something scorched.

"The sausage!" She bolted for the kitchen.

She waved a hand at the smoke-filled air as she entered the room and hurried to the stove, coughing and choking from the smoke invading her lungs. Her eyes smarted. She had to keep blinking as she turned the burner off and slapped a lid on the smoking skillet. After switching on the overhead exhaust fan, Dawn ran around opening all the windows and fanning the air to hurry the smoke's departure.

With disjointed logic, she blamed it all on Slater. Of all times to start an argument, he had chosen when she was fixing Randy's breakfast. She would never have burned the sausages if it weren't for him. She went back to the stove to survey the damage.

"Gee, Mom." Randy came in the back door and stopped, wrinkling his nose at the burnt smell and wispy bits of smoke in the air. "What are you trying to do? Burn the place down?"

Dawn was too upset and angry to answer, but it was a question that didn't need an answer. When she lifted the lid of the skillet, there were four charred-black sticks encrusted in a sticky black mess of burned grease and sausage juice. She poked at the hard stuff with a spatula as Randy came over to take a look.

"Where'd Dad go in such a hurry?" Uncertainly, he peered sideways at her.

"He had business." The words were clipped short as she moved away from him to carry the skillet to the sink. Out of the corner of her eye, she noticed he'd left the back door standing open. "You forgot to close the door." It was an absent reprimand, too preoccupied with her own private turmoil.

"Did you and Dad have an argument?" Randy trailed after her to the sink, pausing just a little bit behind her.

"We disagreed on certain matters," Dawn replied stiffly, preferring to keep from her son how bitter the quarrel had been.

"You had a fight," he concluded with a sinking look. "Are you going to make up?"

"I don't know." She ran water in the skillet and stabbed viciously at the black crust.

"Is he coming back?"

"I don't know." Her voice became more clipped and more emphatic as she repeated the same answer.

"Are you going to get a divorce?"

"I don't know!" The word scraped over her strained nerves.

Dawn swung around to face him, angry with his hurting questions until she saw the frightened and lost expression on his young face.

Something crumpled inside her, letting all the pain and remorse through. The skillet and spatula were dropped in the sink as she reached for him.

"Randy, I'm sorry. I'm upset, but not with you," she assured him. "You aren't to blame for what's happened. You had nothing to do with it."

His head drooped, and she knew he was trying to hide his tears. "I wish I could help. I wish—" His emotionally taut voice didn't finish the sentence as he compressed his lips together to hold back a sob.

"Oh, Randy, you do help." Dawn cupped his cheek in her hand and turned his face up so she could see it. The loving stroke of her thumb wiped away the tear that had been squeezed out of his lashes. "You don't know how much I need you just to be with me. I hate to think what kind of selfish and self-centered person I might have become if you hadn't come into my life so I could finally learn the responsibilities that go along with loving someone," she explained. "You've been more help to me than you'll ever know. And even if you can't help solve the problems your father and I are having, just having you here makes it a little easier. Okay?" Her voice wavered on an emotional note as she forced an encouraging smile on her lips. Randy nodded a hesitant understanding and scrubbed a tear from his other cheek. "Then go close the door before you let in all the flies," she urged in an attempt to instill some reassuring normality to the scene.

Her hand slid off his cheek as Randy turned to

obey. Her gaze started to follow him, then leaped to the opened door where Slater was standing. There was a gentleness in his expression, a light in his gray eyes that seemed to be studying her for the first time.

"I heard what you told Randy," he said. "You weren't faking."

"That's big of you." Hurt, she swung away and gripped the edge of the sink an instant, then reached for the skillet to begin jabbing at the crust again. She shut her eyes briefly when she heard his footsteps approaching her.

"Will you listen to me?" Slater requested and started to turn her chin toward him with his hand. "I'm trying to tell you I was wrong."

Dawn jerked away from his touch and walked swiftly to the wall calendar by the phone to elude him. "I'd better mark that down." She picked up a pen and began writing on the date. " 'Today Slater MacBride said he was wrong.' There!" She flashed him a challenging look.

"I'm sorry," he insisted with persuasive sincerity. "What more do you want me to say? I misjudged you—your reasons—everything."

"I tried to tell you that but you twisted my words up and used them against me." Her anger was weakening but the deep hurt from his accusations wouldn't allow her to easily forgive him.

"I was wrong," Slater admitted again. "I realize that I was more willing to believe the worst than to trust you. I was scared of being hurt. It all seemed too good to be true so I tried to find something wrong with it. I let my suspicion feed on itself and never came to you with it. That was my biggest mistake."

"And I should have told you about being left out of Simpson's will from the start," she sighed, because the omission had eventually compounded the problem. "But I knew you'd take such delight in it," Dawn accused with a brief flash of her old fire.

"I probably would have," he agreed with a hint of a smile.

Randy watched them both cautiously. "Does this mean you aren't mad at each other anymore? You won't be getting a divorce?"

"Does it?" Slater quirked an eyebrow and silently appealed for her answer.

To be forgiven, one also had to be able to forgive. That was one of the responsibilities of loving. And she loved him. A smile slowly lifted the corners of her mouth as she held his gaze.

"Yes, that's what it means," she said softly.

As Slater started toward her, she came to meet him. Randy discreetly wandered to the window while they embraced, arms tightly holding each other. It was a rawly sweet kiss that healed the hurt they had inflicted on one another and gave birth to a stronger love. It shone in their eyes when the kiss ended and they gazed at each other.

Slater enfolded her more lovingly in his arms and nestled her head on his shoulder. They swayed slightly to the tempo of their fast-beating hearts. His hand rubbed over her hair in a caressing fashion.

"What I said about a leopard not changing her spots?" he murmured, tipping his chin down so he could have a glimpse of her face.

"Yes?" She glanced up, now able to wait for his explanation without jumping to a conclusion out of self-protection.

"They're born without spots and acquire them as they mature," he said.

He was blaming her youth for her actions all those years ago. She felt like crying out of sheer happiness because that tragic episode seemed finally behind them.

"Dad?" Randy had heard their murmuring voices and thought it safe to intrude on their conversation. "Where's your car? It isn't in the driveway."

Still holding Dawn, Slater turned his head to look at their son. "It's parked a couple of blocks away. I ran out of gas," he admitted with a wryly chagrined expression. "I meant to fill it last night and forgot."

"Why didn't you walk to the gas station and have the empty gas can in the trunk filled?" Randy frowned.

"There was a slight problem." He glanced down at Dawn, amusement glittering in his eyes. "I didn't have any money on me to pay for it. And the only station open on Sunday that's close by doesn't accept credit cards. So I had to come back to see if I couldn't persuade my wife to part with some of the money I'd given her. Do you suppose that could be arranged?"

"Oh, dear," she murmured. "I burned it all."

"You did what?" He drew his head back, eyeing her skeptically.

"I was mad so I put it in the ashtray and set fire to it," Dawn admitted.

There was a stunned moment of silence before Slater tipped his head back and laughed heartily. "What kind of woman did I marry?" he declared with a shake of his head. "She has to have money to burn."

"I'm sorry." It seemed so childish now.

"Living with you isn't going to be easy," he said.

"We'll make it," Dawn asserted confidently.

"Of course," Slater agreed. "You know what they say—the third time's a charm."